'So what do you have to do?' Susan asked me as she reclined facedown on the ottoman.

'Just write some sexy books,' I replied. 'But first of all I have to put in some extensive field-work.' I eyed her halter neck with meaning.

'Oh you!' she said and reached back to undo it, her breasts spilling out of the loosened material onto the ottoman. 'On a point of semantics,' she added, 'can field-work properly be said to take place indoors?'

'Turn over,' I said, 'and I'll show you . . .'

Hard At It

Anthony Adams

**HEADLINE
DELTA**

First published in 1996
by HEADLINE BOOK PUBLISHING

A HEADLINE DELTA paperback

10 9 8 7 6 5 4 3 2 1

ISBN 0 7472 4952 0

Typeset by CBS, Felixstowe, Suffolk

Printed and bound in Great Britain by
Cox & Wyman Ltd, Reading, Berks

HEADLINE BOOK PUBLISHING
A division of Hodder Headline PLC
338 Euston Road
London NW1 3BH

Hard At It

PROLOGUE

Sex for Sale!

Chapter One

I had never imagined myself as part of the commercial sex industry, but thriller writers living in the South of France in the early seventies, when British publishers sometimes offered as little as £250 as an advance on a new novel, could not afford to pass up any opportunity, however bizarre. And this actually happened to me; this is a true story. The name is Adams, Tony Adams. You may even have seen my books among the paperbacks at airport newsstands.

The opportunity drifted my way one day when I was having a drink in a bar in Antibes, hoping to hell that the manuscript I'd expressed would land in London in time for me to get paid before the next postal strike. A yacht skipper I knew sidled up to me with an empty glass in his hand. 'There's this Yank in St Tropez,' he said, 'looking for people to turn out hard-core porn. You being a writer and that, I reckoned you might be interested.'

'I might,' I said. 'But how come?'

'Well, you know Lafayette Briggs?'

I did. A large, indolent and extremely genial black man who had something to do with the chartering of boats to tourists. I nodded, adding the customary local password admitting the speaker to intimacy. 'What'll you have?' I asked.

3

'Lafayette,' the skipper said when the drinks had been served, 'has a girlfriend works as a secretary for this Yankee character. It was she who put out the call. So Lafayette tips off his author friend, Ronald—'

'Ronald Stokes-Alberry?' I interrupted. Another writer. Women's romances. English – very English, in fact. Lived in Cannes.

'That's him. Lafayette tips him off there's work to be had, and Ron trips off to St Trop – but he makes the mistake of trying to lay the secretary, Lafayette's bird . . . and suddenly they're still looking for a writer. You read me?'

'It sounds complicated,' I said.

'Oh, it is,' the skipper assured me.

'Why not have a go yourself?' I said. 'You have the experience!' And then: 'Is the money good?'

'Not bad,' he said. 'But *you* know. Hardly my line, is it?'

I wasn't sure that it was mine. But I thought I might as well give it a whirl: there were too many buff envelopes already littering my desk. So I made the necessary guarded telephone call and duly drove down past St Raphael and the Massif des Maures and Ste Maxime to present myself at the address I'd been given.

It turned out to be an unexpectedly splendid apartment block, a condo with class, standing in its own grounds a couple of miles out of town. The place was bright with oleanders and bougainvillaea, equipped with an air-conditioned underground car park and two swimming pools – one indoors, for when it got too hot around the other.

I don't quite know what I expected Edward to be like. Blue-jowled, perhaps, with a furtive hand about to plunge between his lapels in search of dirty postcards? Or drape-suited, with a glib tongue and too sharp a crease to the trouser? I was totally unprepared, in any case, for the tanned, forty-year-old college man with the mid-Atlantic accent who came, smiling, to open the door. He was wearing a Harris tweed hacking jacket with a button-down Ivy League shirt, and his blond hair was cut like a London guardee's.

Mrs Edward was blonde too, maybe a couple of years younger than her husband, though the trouser suit packaging her agreeably curved person was anything but buttoned down. Her Christian name was Velvet – it went well with the genuine Deep South drawl. She led us through a simply – and extremely expensively – furnished living room and settled us on the sun deck with two of the largest and driest Martinis I ever drank. Then she undulated away 'to leave you two boys to talk business.'

Among other activities, my host – who had once been an arson investigating expert working with the Boston police – controlled a number of 'regular' publishing outlets in the United States, so for a time we discussed the possibility of placing various ideas for thrillers that I had dreamed up. In any case I had been warned not to bring up the subject of sex books before he did. Halfway through the second Martini, however, he glanced sideways at me and said carefully, 'There is one other thing, old boy. We market a range of . . . No, I won't call it pornography. If the United States Supreme Court says it's not pornographic, that's good enough for me. We produce a range of low-grade adult fiction. But I guess that wouldn't interest you?'

Equally carefully, I said that it might. It just might.

What could he tell me about it? And how low-grade was
it?

'Low,' Edward said. 'We put out sixteen books a month.
They're sold only in the US of A. Mainly on college
campuses and in supermarkets – along with the gum and
candies as folks stand in line for the check-out desks.'

'What kind of folk?' I asked.

'We had one of the largest East Coast market research
organizations do us a survey in depth,' Edward said. 'It
seems that thirty-seven percent of our readers are
unmarried female secretaries over thirty years of age –
most of them virgins for whom these books will be the
only sexual experience they ever have.'

'And the other sixty-three percent?'

'Oh . . . typical one-handed readers. Truck drivers,
gas-station attendants, janitors, college students. You
know.'

'What kind of writers are you looking for?'

'Professionals,' Edward said crisply. 'We don't buy
hippies, flower people plugging love-ins, radical thinkers,
men in raincoats, those kind of guys. With our output, we
have to have reliability. You write for us, you write a book
a month.'

'A book a *month*?' I echoed.

'Sure. Forty thousand words. But we reckon only
around eight thousand of that has to be original material
– that's the part where you explain how they make it
into the sack. The rest, the sex scenes themselves, the
publisher lets you pick up from previous books in the
series. In fact he prefers it. Feel free to copy them word
for word, except for changing the names of course . . . or
maybe switch around an adjective or an adverb here and
there. You know: instead of "lewdly, he eyed her

lasciviously splayed body" you write "lasciviously, he eyed her lewdly splayed body". That kind of thing.'

That was a hell of a lot different from the scene today, when a writer has to think up forty different ways of saying fuck before a publisher will even look at his stuff – even a publisher of hard-core erotica! At the time, I simply said: 'But doesn't this make for an enormous amount of repetition? I mean to say—?'

'This is a pretty basic readership,' Edward explained. 'It's kind of like a dog. It's not the actual words that register; it's the tone of voice. You know what I mean? They've gotten used to a certain rhythm we've established. You'll find it's not even good English, but it's what they want. It guarantees success. See, they feel at home when they reach the climax at the end of the chapter, holding the book in one hand and . . . well, you know.' He drained his Martini and rose to his feet. 'Anyway, I'll give you half a dozen to take home. Read them, and call me again if you think you'd be interested.'

The books were sober enough from the outside: paperbacks with a uniform jacket featuring a blue surround framing a white cutout in which there was a not-too-explicit line drawing. Inside each was a list detailing 300 other titles available, from *The Bride-Ravishers* to *School For Teeny-Swappers*, from *Hungry Young Widows* to *Rampant Studs*. None of them included the word Sex.

The books, Edward told me, retailed at the regular paperback price, and their sales ranged from several hundred thousand to an astronomical seven and a half *million* for their all-time wife-swapping best seller – generating ample revenue to justify Edward's generous salary and the ritzy apartment, especially as they paid no royalty to authors.

What they did offer was continuity of income, an unusual luxury for a freelance.

'So what do you have to do to qualify for this manna from heaven?' Susan asked me when I returned from this first encounter with Edward. Susan was my current girlfriend, big-hipped and busty, with green eyes, dark auburn hair and white skin smooth as silk. She shacked up with me at weekends or when she wasn't crewing and cooking for the owner of a luxury cruiser who ferried high-priced customers around the Riviera coast in the tourist season.

'What do I have to do?' I repeated. 'Just write some books. But first of all, Edward insists, I have to put in some pretty intensive field-work, broaden my experience, as they say.' Meaningfully, I eyed her halter neck.

'Oh, you!' Susan said. She reached back to untie the tapes.

She was lying face-down along an ottoman in the window of my fifth-floor pad in Golfe-Juan. I say pad because flat or apartment would be a shade too grand. The place was converted from four attic rooms beneath the slanting tiles of an old house off the main street. It's hot in summer, cold in winter, without a lift, and there's a lot of traffic noise. But there's a wooden balcony looking south across ancient roofs to the quays of the little port, I can type all night and there's no one to complain about the noise, and the entrance is through an archway which leads to a courtyard where I can keep my car.

Beyond the curve of Susan's back, the late afternoon sun bathed masts and rigging in an amber glow and the sea was a deep and satisfying blue. Light reflected from the open window silvered the line of tiny hairs following the course of her spine.

The tapes of the halter-neck top were undone. Her breasts spilled out of the loosened material onto the padded top of the ottoman. I had inherited this oriental antique from my much-travelled father. It wasn't enormously elegant but we liked it because, having no back and no arms at either end, it offered limitless possibilities for lovemaking of the more acrobatic kind.

Susan planted her elbows on either side of her breasts and propped her chin on her fists. 'On a point of semantics,' she said, 'can field-work properly be said to take place indoors?'

'Turn over,' I said, 'and I'll show you. As for properly, that's something else.' I drew the discarded top out from beneath her.

I should perhaps devote a little more space to Susan's breasts. They merited it – and devotion is not too strong a word. They were the first thing one noticed about her. They were full, those breasts, but *firm*: there was not the remotest chance of their ever, even in the far distant future, becoming floppy. The skin was taut and full of meat. If she ran on the beach when she was topless, at the nudist camp on the Île de Levant, they scarcely bounced.

Turning over swiftly now, she lay on her back on the ottoman with her hands linked behind her bronze head and the familiar, mischievous glint in her green eyes. 'Well, Professor,' she said, 'the student is ready for class.'

Her breasts remained marvellously erect on her chest. Some women with big tits suffer, when lying down, from what I call the poached egg syndrome. Not Susan. Those splendidly swelling mounds stayed upthrust like the twin towers of the World Trade Center in New York.

The blue jeans I was wearing had already lost a little colour along the upper part of the left thigh, where they had been worn by the constant pressure of the hard-ons induced in me by the sight of Susan. Now, once again, I felt the tingling thrill of lust as the pale denim tightened over my rapidly hardening cock.

It wasn't only her breasts, of course, which excited me when I looked at Susan. Below her rib-cage, the waist sculpted from her body was small and trim, blossoming – billowing, almost – into generously padded hips and a belly that was deliciously soft and loose, and yet at the same time tautly pliant and muscular. However hot the rest of her became, that belly always seemed to me to stay cool.

At the base of it, between sturdy but finely tapered thighs, the russet triangle of pubic hair grew thick and lush.

Shifting slightly on the ottoman – her belly slung easily between the satined prominences of her hip-bones – Susan parted her thighs enough to reveal a sliver of creased, pinkish inner flesh at the top of which a tiny pearl of moisture glistened. It was moisture too which suddenly darkened the paler patch of denim covering my crotch.

I licked my lips, eyeing the springy hair thatching Susan's loins; that curving slit of flesh with its attendant, shining bead . . . the crescent and star, I thought, on the flag of the Ottoman Empire!

The slit gaped abruptly red as she spread her thighs with a lascivious gyration of belly and hips, and I forgot about flags. The ache in my rigid and restricted cock was becoming unbearable. I unbuckled the belt of my jeans, tore open the zip, and pushed them down to my knees. My cock sprang free, jutting lewdly towards the auburn-haired beauty spread-eagled before me.

'Thank the Lord for free education,' Susan said.

I ripped off my shirt and flung it away. I leaped onto
the ottoman, kneed her thighs still wider apart, and lowered
myself between them. I was in like Flynn. It was always
like this with us, the first time – the sudden scalding clasp
of hot, wet flesh on my bursting staff, the sucking grasp of
that inner throat as we settled at once into the easy,
rocking rhythm that has no beginning and sees no end.

Buoyed up on the pneumatic bliss of Susan's
upperworks, I thrust and withdrew, thrust and withdrew,
allowing the thrills exciting every nerve in my body to
concentrate on my plunging cock as her sun-warmed hips
arched fiercely up against me.

When the twin partners of what a poet once termed the
two-backed beast are as physically in tune as Susan and I
were that day, the well-oiled reciprocating parts induce a
mounting surge of delight that accelerates relentlessly
towards its pre-destined climax, yet seems at the same
time strangely timeless.

Bars of sunlight striped my back where Susan's hot
hands clenched and clawed; her scissored legs wrapped
my hips; the need for words had vanished in that
monosyllabic duologue of exhaled grunts and groans, the
moaned intimacies of shared pleasure that communicate
joy more intensely than the syntax of all the languages in
the world.

And then . . . suddenly . . . it was there. The wild cry
into the welcoming dark. Her trembling belly's slippery
heave. The shuddering spasms and the thunder of the
breaking wave. I was a fountain spurting into a furnace, a
rocket bursting in the sky to fill my head with golden
stars.

After that, silence, peace, joy . . . and the slow return to
earth.

That was the first time.

Some time later – the sunbeams had withdrawn from the ottoman to sweep across one wall – Susan said lazily, 'Well, are you going to do it?'

'Do it?'

'Write obscene literature for the expensive gentleman at St Trop.'

'Oh, yes,' I said. 'I think I'll have a go. I mean one can hardly lose: they offer a three-month trial run; you write three books and get paid for them, even if they're not used. Edward told me, quote, it takes an author that time to get the hang of the style and familiarize himself with the lingo.'

'And then?'

'If they like what you've done, or it seems promising, you get a contract.'

'Do you think you can do it? What are the books like?'

'I've only had a glance,' I said. 'As the man said, they're low-grade. Low-grade descriptions,' I patted her wet cunt, 'of high-grade activities.'

'And you really think there's enough variety, in what after all is going to be no more than a series of fucks, to fill sixteen books a *month?*'

'That's what he said. From what I saw, the organization's not exactly short of money.'

'But you, darling – you're a *thriller* writer. Do you honestly think you could think up a whole new book every single month?' Susan was still lying on her back. She turned her head to gaze quizzically at me with wrinkled brows. 'Enough crude porn to fill a book?'

I shrugged. 'It's a professional problem, no more. A question of technique: find out what they want, then supply it. And I did say activi*ties*,' I added. 'In the plural.'

I realized my jeans were still tangled around my ankles. I kicked them off.

Susan said: 'Okay, they don't all have to be missionaries. But, field-work and all, are there really enough variations . . .?'

'Turn over,' I said, 'and I'll show you.'

PART ONE

A Drop of the Hard Stuff?

Chapter Two

The first of Edward's books that I picked up, *Violated By Her Cousin*, fell open at page 23. I read:

> Mervyn was panting hotly. His breath played over her nakedly exposed breasts. 'Jane, baby,' he moaned frantically, 'I want you. My God, I want you! I gotta screw you, kid. I must!'
>
> 'No!' gasped the lustfully aroused young co-ed. 'No, Merv, please. You . . . you'd hate me afterwards, really you would. We mustn't!' Drawing up one bare knee, she clamped shut her lewdly spread thighs, craving his taut athlete's body with every fiber of her ripely sensual being while her brain struggled to maintain control of her inflamed senses, crying No! No! No!
>
> 'C'mon, honey,' the boy groaned desperately. 'I got to; you know I have!' And he clenched shaking fingers more tightly over the pliant, silk-sheathed globes of her trembling buttocks, thrusting with his lean hips in a savage attempt to squirm the wildly pulsating staff of his maleness between those thighs, forcing the bulbous, blood-engorged head into the upper part of the girl's wetly hair-lined slit, fighting to force apart the fleshy folds she denied him.
>
> 'Ooooooohhh!' she groaned. 'No, Merv darling, don't – Aaaaaaggghhh!'

Hmm. This book, and the two others I had been given, adverbially over-written, crude and ungrammatical though they were, certainly qualified as obscene within the British legal definition of the term. But pornographic? In the sense that they turned you on? That they were inclined 'to deprave and corrupt'? Not really. Not for me anyway.

They did however afford a revealing insight into the *mores* of late twentieth-century America – or so I told Susan in my prissiest, most chauvinistic and priggish manner.

All the females of course were nubile and bedworthy; all breasts were big; all of the males were massively endowed – and each one of them (a case maybe for the Race Relations Board?) was uncircumcized.

The formula, as invariably as the male organs so minutely described, was rigid. Jane and her like, the good girls, wore white undies; the bad girls who helped the studs seduce them wore black, frequently with lace trimming. Homosexuality was non-existent: a girl might be servicing five men at the same time, yet none of them so much as brushed against another. Lesbian activity was permitted only as a means to a heterosexual end. And no hints of sadism, masochism, flagellation or fetishist turn-ons were allowed to sully the lurid and immensely detailed descriptions of swaps and orgies.

Curiously, the stories, the plot lines, were marked by a naivety, a primness almost, which required the heroines – from whose unfulfilled point of view the action was often seen – never actually to *enjoy* sex: they were all innocents 'persuaded' through unhappiness, drugs, liquor or moral blackmail to suffer the frightful indignities heaped upon them by the rude and rednecked males. Only towards the end of each book did they experience the first faint thrills of response, and even then they regretted it afterwards.

Editorial imperatives extended to the order of events. 'We like to have oral sex by page 18,' Edward told me the second time I met him, 'detailed coitus before page 32, one rape per book, and always a climax scene involving a boy-girl-boy sandwich. But the rape must be because of mental, not physical coercion. Likewise anal penetration – a must at least once per book – has to remain strictly hetero. After that, old boy, you're on your own.'

We were meeting this time in the office. Edward and Velvet lived in the penthouse apartment; this was on the ground floor. It was a spacious suite overlooking one of the pools, with balconies and striped sunblinds front and back. The oxydized plate on the door announced: *Export Advisers Incorporated (cable address: Expadink)*.

Inside – modernistic steel furniture, high-backed leather tilting chairs, photocopying machines but no computers yet – there was a staff of five: two very proper girl secretaries named Miriam and Sonia, and three editors. This trio was perhaps the most unexpected thing about the entire enterprise: a tall, thin brunette called Mabel with a PhD from Vassar; her boyfriend Edgar, a naturalized Pole who had trained as an astro-physicist; and Randall van Eyck, a bearded medievalist who specialized in thirteenth-century minstrelsy. Randall had brought twelve Siamese cats with him from California when he was hired. He was faced each month with a bill of between fifty and a hundred dollars to repair the damage to carpets, curtains and upholstery in his furnished apartment.

I had already handed in my first attempt before this meeting. 'Fine,' Edward told me. 'I guess this is just the kind of thing He wants.'

The capitalized initial was just discernible, as it was

19

each time Edward referred to the subject as the Publisher. It was this man, I discovered later, whose money funded the project. His name was Frank Maddox. He was one of a group of Danish-American businessmen with investments in the sex industry. He was rich enough to own a whole house in Paris's snob Avenue Kléber, and to have bribed the chef from the Tour d'Argent to hand in his notice and supervise the kitchens of this mansion.

Maddox's brother in Boston, who owned a printing works, manufactured the books, which were promoted and marketed by a cousin in the advertizing business.

Edward was down on the headed paper as the President of the French company, but in fact, apart from providing the raw material, he had little to do with the finished product. All decisions on style and content, which were based on market research data, were made either by Maddox himself or the cousin in Massachusetts. Astonishingly, Edward was given no sales figures and remained ignorant of which books sold well and which died the death. His job was simply to keep the wheels turning.

Most of his writers – there must have been at least thirty, recruited like the secretaries through discreet small-ads in the *International Herald Tribune* – were scattered through France, Italy, Germany and Holland, sending in their monthly manuscripts by mail. Because I lived nearby and delivered mine by hand, I was invited to attend editorial conferences each week.

These were held at four o'clock in the afternoon because this was the time in Boston at which the executives there were sufficiently awake to teleprint their sales directives to the South of France.

Like Edward and his wife, each of the three editors –

and indeed the girls who took notes at these meetings – was eminently respectable, conservatively dressed, and highly intelligent. The conferences at which they solemnly discussed the subtler aspects of their arcane trade were a delight to anyone with an ear for irony.

The first time I was there, Edward tore the initial teletype strip from the clicking machine, settled gold-rimmed spectacles on his nose, read the briefing and announced: 'Okay. As of today, folks, the word prick is out.'

'Even in dialogue?' Randall van Eyck queried. 'People do, you know, say—'

'Right. Except in dialogue. Instead, we can say—'

'Cock,' Mrs Edward supplied.

'Shaft,' one of the pretty secretaries put in. 'Rod. Penis. Weapon.'

The PhD from Vassar was plucking at her lower lip. 'Staff,' she said slowly, savouring the broad A. 'Cudgel.'

'Yeah,' Edward agreed, looking at the ceiling and rolling the phrases around his tongue to see how they fitted the formula. 'His . . . lustfully pulsating shaft . . . His thickly gleaming rod . . . The lewd spear of his inflamed weapon . . . His stiffly upstanding – uh – cudgel. Fine.'

The medievalist had answered the phone. He was talking to a writer. 'You want to kill that corset and boots scene, Ed,' he said. 'It's too way-out, too sophisticated for our readers. Have the boy take his mother anally instead.'

The story I had submitted was based on an anecdote related by Susan, about a frigid spinster so overwhelmed by the sight of a stallion and a mare coupling, witnessed during a holiday in Corsica, that she had thrown herself with dire results at every male in a mountain village. Approved by Edward – and of course the Publisher – this

21

was paid for but not in fact used. I fancy there was a lack of adverbs in the text. It did however bring me the promised contract. 'But don't for God's sake regard the money as a *salary*,' Edward warned. 'We figure we can help guys like yourself, British and American writers who wouldn't otherwise be able to afford to stay on the Continent. But you have to treat it, you know, just as a means of paying the rent while you do your own thing, a way of buying time to write the things you really want to write.'

'Would I have any time left?' I had asked dubiously. 'I mean, hell, a book every *month* . . .?'

'God, yes. Sure you would. Even if you only wrote two thousand a day, and most authors can make that, you'd still have ten days a month free. After the first few, you should be able to make one in a week anyway. One of our writers, a Dutchman who lives in Paris, France, he reckons to knock one out over a weekend. He writes three in a week and a half, then takes two months off. And there's an old woman in Milan can do one in thirty-six hours!' He paused, shaking his head. 'Dirtiest books I ever read in my life,' he said.

An 'Editor's Report' was mailed to authors after each manuscript had been received, copy-edited, weighed against an outline Edward would have approved, and made to conform where necessary to the house style. These solemn critiques were in two parts: General and Specific. The former gave the editor's overall view ('Good, fast-moving story line with believable characterization and our imperatives on the whole respected. But too much space wasted on foreplay in summerhouse scene – our readers want to be in there, pitching – and heroine's reaction to the third aggressor underplayed'). The second section lived up to its name. I was told after my first submission: 'In the scene with her sister, Sandra says the dirty words too easily: even with words she must be forced; she should never say them willingly until the final chapter. The oral sex with the lumberjack comes too rapidly: you need more of a cliffhanger here. Avoid such terms as vulva, vagina (use pussy, lips, folds, etc); tits (make them orbs, globes, swelling mounds of flesh); and organ (be specific).'

Further guidance was given in Editorial Directives circulated to all writers from time to time. These came not from Edward's office but from the Publisher, never named but always accorded his capital P. The directives were tense. 'Do not,' one of them warned, 'employ words like filthy/sickening/vile when describing the heroine's reaction to the sex act. Preferred terms include: fear/horror/shame/humiliation/lewdness/lust.'

So much for the joys of sex.

'British writers,' another directive said sternly, 'must remember their readership. A recent manuscript contained the sentence: *The battered husband hauled himself painfully up to the rocky ledge where his young wife had been so obscenely abused.* For Americans, hauling is something locomotives do – or members of the Teamsters Union driving Mack trucks.'

The shortest communication from the Publisher's office – a suite in the PanAm building on the Champs Elysées – was also the least didactic, possibly because it related to real life rather than fantasy. 'Please,' it requested simply, 'make it a *middle* finger whenever practical.'

The organization's extraordinarily impersonal attitude to what I had been accustomed to call lovemaking, plus the fact that the product, the dirty books, were discussed by 'respectable' executives as objectively as if they had been cornflakes or floor polish, and above all because the descriptions of sex came not from oneself but from previously written material . . . such factors resulted in a situation where the romps about which I wrote bore no relation whatsoever to the real sex I enjoyed when I could find time to leave the typewriter.

Strangely enough it was through the organization itself that this oddly anomalous situation was reversed.

One of the 'extras' available to authors on the payroll was a furnished apartment in a modern block near the Arc de Triomphe in Paris. This guest flat, which was owned by Maddox, could be used, without charge, a week at a time, by any writer wishing to finish a book in a hurry, do research, or simply enjoy a few days in the capital. Edward had talked me into using it because he knew an American publisher I wanted to meet was passing through Paris and he reckoned it would be good for my morale if I met him. He even gave me a written introduction to the publisher.

He was a good guy, Edward. He knew about freelancers.

There was a small favour I was to do in return. Edward had a niece who was also passing through Paris. And who wanted to meet the publisher as much as I did, because she had a collection of short stories she hoped might be suitable for one of his magazines. Would I be a sport and take the kid along with me when I went to see the man?

Well, natch.

The 'kid' was in fact twenty-five years old, a short, tight-breasted brunette who couldn't have been more than five feet one or two. Her name was Frances.

The meeting was promising for both of us. But afterwards it turned into one of those drinking jags like a ball rolling downhill: once the impetus has taken over, there's no getting out of the way.

The publisher had a friend in tow, an elderly pepper-and-salt Armenian journalist who acted as stringer for a number of London publications. This man prided himself on being the doyen of foreign newsmen in Paris . . . and as the only reliable guide who really *knew* Montmartre. We had an apéritif at the Moulin Rouge (where else?); we had another in rather sweaty premises which had once been Aristide Bruant's turn-of-the-century Chat Noir; we ate in a large, bare, wooden-floored restaurant where Renoir had painted his famous *Moulin de la Galette*. After that we started on the Pigalle clubs.

The publisher cried off at midnight. He was a man of experience.

Frances and I were left with the Armenian in a pink-lit B-girl joint off the Rue Notre Dame de Lorette – the kind of place where champagne, so-called, is the only drink, at ten dollars a glass.

Five girls wearing tall boots and sequins sat on high stools along the bar. A sixth had installed herself on the lap of a drunken Scot – which was just as well as the *boîte* wasn't much more than twice the size of a telephone kiosk. We were the only other guests.

The madam, laced into a high-necked black dress and perched like an elderly raven over the till, was enthusiastic. 'Ah, Monsieur Henri!' she crowed. 'What happened? We were afraid you were ill. This is the first time we have see you this week!'

I learned later that the Armenian, who had no living relatives, spent every single evening like this, always ending up in one of the sleazier clubs, inevitably 'going upstairs' with one of the girls, in an attempt to get rid of a lifetime's savings before the man with the scythe struck him down and the tax man seized what remained of the loot. A sad –

if industrious – way to end a busy life.

But at least he was enjoying the ending. He preened under the blandishments of the raven. He accepted with modest diffidence the outrageous compliments paid him by a girl with pink hair who brought the bottle of champagne he had ordered to our table. It was rather pathetic really: he was showing off – had been showing off all evening – his man-of-the-worldliness.

We stuck it out, Frances and I. After all, he had insisted on picking up every tab since we started out. The strawberry blonde sat on his knee and ruffled the tufts of hair bordering his bald patch. Above a shiny red strapless top she was displaying an enormous amount of what Edward would have called swelling mounds of flesh.

Monsieur Henri ordered up a second bottle. Madam, smiling her vulpine smile, brought it to the table herself. She sprung the cork and refilled our glasses.

When our host leaned forward to bury his face in the deep cleft between the B-girl's breasts, Frances looked at me over his back and whispered, 'Do you think you could possibly get me out of here and escort me back to my hotel?'

I nodded. We got to our feet, said our thanks, paid our respects, left. The girls were glad to see us go. Madam was saving her smile for future punters. Mentally, Monsieur Henri was already 'upstairs'.

'I'm sorry about that,' I said as we settled into a late-night taxi.

'There wasn't much you could do about it, was there?' Frances said. Her voice was surprisingly deep, with a mellow undertone. 'God, how that artificial, commercial, nightclub sex turns one off!'

I murmured something suitable. She launched into an

impassioned criticism of the introverted, neurotic, *dishonest* northern attitude to sex; in the south it was freer, more natural. One could be *spontaneous*. The tirade ended with a description of a frightfully rewarding affair she had had with a fisherman she met one night when she was sleeping on a beach in Elba.

I hadn't really paid her much attention until then. But the honeyed voice, the gleaming eyes occasionally visible as the cab passed beneath a street lamp, were clearly telling me, now, that it was available if I wanted it.

Suddenly, after that dispirited evening, I decided I did want it.

I got it.

'If you're one of Uncle Edward's writers,' she said, 'I guess you're shacked up in the Maddox guest flat. Is it comfortable?'

'Maybe you should come and see for yourself?' I suggested.

'The cab fare would be less,' Frances said. 'My hotel's in Montparnasse.'

The flat was in fact comfortable, if impersonal. It comprised a double bedroom, a living room with a balcony overlooking the Avenue de la Grande Armée, a shower room and toilet, and a miniscule kitchen with tea, coffee, canned food and vacuum-packed croissants in the freezer. There was a round, glass-topped table with tubular steel chairs in the living room, along with a leather settee and a Scandinavian teak sideboard. Two Bernard Buffet lithographs, blue and spidery black, graced the white walls.

Frances walked straight through into the bedroom and made an experimental pass at the mattress. 'Dunlopillo,' she approved. 'And quite new. That should do nicely.'

She unbuttoned the waisted jacket of her neat black suit.

I realized then that the fisherman story, together with certain sexual allusions dropped here and there throughout the evening, were not as I had assumed boastful ploys designed to suggest a non-existent sophistication but plain statements of fact. This girl was an enthusiast, and she didn't care who knew it!

She stripped off her jacket and hung it over the back of a chair. She was wearing nothing beneath it. When she turned back towards me, I saw that the large nipples tipping her small, tight breasts were already swollen and erect. 'I don't have too much in the way of liquor,' I said awkwardly, a little taken aback by her boldness, 'but I could offer you an Armagnac. How does that grab you?'

'Why not?' she said.

I had the impression that Frances was likely to make the same reply whatever was suggested, however extreme it might be. 'Coffee?' I added.

'Why waste time?' she said.

By the time I came back from the kitchen with the bottle and glasses, she had pushed the skirt down over her narrow hips and was stepping out of it. She peeled off darkly shadowed pantyhose and stood naked by the bed with a thick bush of black hair centred on the creamy paleness of her body. 'Pour it out,' she said. 'I'll be back with you in a minute.' She went into the shower room and closed the door. I heard water running.

By now, confronted with such a display of bravura and self-confidence, I was feeling a trifle unsophisticated and gauche myself. If I wasn't going to look like a clodhopping yokel, there was only one thing to do. I took off my own clothes and stood hesitantly by the bed. I couldn't be taking too much for granted, could I? I'd look pretty silly

28

if this was nothing more than another show of bravado, some kind of feminist gesture designed – *without* any sexual overtones – to demonstrate that, clothed or unclothed, we were all good chaps together.

Don't be bloody silly: even in the second half of the twentieth century, no personable young woman is going to strip naked in front of a virtual stranger, late at night, in the stranger's apartment, just to prove that she's a libertarian!

Frances was back in the bedroom. 'The water's not very hot,' she complained.

'You have to pull out the control fairly hard,' I said.

'Show me.'

I followed her into the shower room. She stood in front of the cubicle with her back to me. I reached around her with both arms and took hold of the faucet. It was one of those newfangled ones with a single tap operating all the mixture controls: pull towards you for hotter, push for cooler; turn right for a heavier flow, left for less. As I leaned in to pull harder, the tip of my cock touched the smooth, cool curve of flesh immediately above one of her buttocks.

At once, Frances shifted her position, slightly gyrating her hips so that my limp stem nestled at the top of the cleft between those pliant cheeks. And at once the shaft too moved, lengthening, stiffening, swelling with excitement at the contact with her skin.

In her turn she leaned back, grinding against my hardness, rolling the rigid cock between the fleshy globes of her arse.

I'd let go of the tap – the water was at the right temperature anyway – and dropped my hands to cup her taut little breasts, moist now with the fine spray drifting from the shower. She allowed herself one final writhe of the hips, then reached back to slide a hand between us and seize my aching staff.

Her damp head was resting against my chest. She tilted up her face, eyes gleaming wickedly, and showed me the wet, pink tip of her tongue. A moment later, still grasping my cock, she separated herself and dragged me into the shower with her.

I slid shut the frosted glass door of the cubicle. The water, soft as a caress, fell warmly around us.

Frances reached up and wound her wet arms around my neck. I reached down to cup the muscular mounds of her buttocks, taking the weight of them on my palms as I lifted her up until the hairy cleft between her legs was poised above my spearing shaft. She scissored her legs across the small of my back and I lowered her, gently, gently, until the swollen tip nudged the liquid lips of her cunt. And suddenly I was in, as tight and hot as I'd ever been, with her nipples sliding over my streaming chest.

'Oh,' she moaned against my mouth, 'my *God* but that's so goooood!'

In that torrid, steamy cascade, we had started a wonderful fuck. I sensed it; I knew it; I felt it in every fibre, in each dilated throbbing vein of my monstrously swollen cock. The aching, distended shaft was as tall as the Eiffel Tower, spearing far up into the scalding centre of this diminutive girl as she rode up and down my staff as easily as a monkey on a stick.

Her arms had tightened around my neck. Her legs clamped my back in a scissor grip. Her tight little bottom clenched against my palms each time I raised her up, sliding her against me until that sucking lower mouth withdrew to the very tip of my cock . . . and then allowing gravity to do the work, plunging her body down against my grasp until my whole hard length was engulfed again and my pelvis instinctively flexed to drive me even higher up into her welcoming heat.

I don't know how long I stood under that shower with Frances twined around me and the splash of falling water rivalled by the suck and squelch of pistoning cock and cunt. I know that we exhausted all the hot water in the apartment's electric immersion heater and the shower finally ran cold. I know that by the time we were each shaken by the ultimate, infinitely thrilling climax, I was sitting on the wet tile floor with my back to the wall and Frances straddling my hips as I spurted the proof of my lustful desire into her quaking belly. I remember particularly the groaned and shuddering litany she mouthed against my face as we fucked, the words choked out between each slobbering thrust of her tongue between my teeth, into the hollows of my cheeks, around my gums. 'Oh, *yes*, lover . . . Give it to me; shaft me; *drive* it in! Push that great cock up into my hot, wet belly . . . Aaaah, shit, that's all I want, and *God*, I love it so! Oh, Christ, how I need that lovely, steaming prick . . .!'

Well . . . she wanted it, needed it; I gave it to her; she got it.

It was only later that I found *myself* needing it even more. If that was possible.

It seemed to be. Towelling down that compact body with its tight little breasts and its muscular, practised bottom, I felt as she writhed under my ministrations a sudden urge – and a sudden hard-on – that eclipsed, but totally, even the lustful excesses spurring me on during that steamy session in the shower.

Frances was into it at once, of course. 'Maybe,' she said in a small voice, leaning provocatively back against me as my hands roved her terry-towel covered breasts, 'it would be an idea if we went back to the bed now?'

I said – a little hoarsely – that it might. So we went.

And it was then, as I mentioned earlier, that the romps I wrote about for Edward and the real life I lived became for the first time excitingly entangled. But that's another story.

Don't think for a moment that I'm not going to tell it to you.

Chapter Three

There was a story going the rounds that year, when it was still considered humorous to make jokes about the forty-nine different positions available for coitus. It concerned a worried man who consulted his doctor because his sex life with his wife was unsatisfactory. Eventually, the medic asks: 'Well, what position do you usually adopt when you are – er – making love? How, actually, do you do it?'

'Do it?' the man repeats. 'Like everyone else, I guess. The doggie way.'

'The what?'

'*You* know. The wife's on her hands and knees and I come in from behind. Kind of lying along her back, like.'

'I see.' The doctor clears his throat. 'There are alternatives, you know. Perhaps you should try what is known as the missionary position.'

'The missionary . . .?'

'Yes. Your wife lies on her back with her legs spread; you lie on top of her, face down, and enter between her thighs.'

'*What?*' screams the husband. '*And miss the television?*'

It was the inventiveness of Frances that reminded me of this fable – in more ways than one.

I think I said that there was a round, glass-topped table in the apartment's living room. She looked at this

33

reflectively for a moment, allowing the towel to slide from her nubile body. 'There's an oval mirror in the hallway,' she mused. 'If you were to take it down and lay it on the floor in here, do you think the four legs of this table are wide enough apart to stand on either side of the frame?'

'Possibly,' I said. 'I could easily check. What were you—?'

'I was thinking: if the mirror was immediately below the table, whatever was happening on the transparent glass top would naturally be reflected in the mirror glass underneath. If you sat on the table and leaned forward, I mean, you'd see your *own* underneath.' Frances giggled. 'It would be like lying on the floor and staring up at your own bottom, only the other way round. You see what I'm getting at?'

And of course I saw. 'What a *clever* lady we have here!' I approved. I was already in the hall. I unhooked the mirror and took it down. It was about eighteen inches wide and almost twice as deep.

The frame, which was of polished wood, was heavy. As I staggered back into the living room with it, I could see in the lower part of the glass the image of my stiff and upthrust cock wagging as I walked.

I laid the mirror on the floor. I picked up the table and planted it down on top. The legs fitted on either side of the oval with half an inch to spare. On its longer axis, the elliptical mirror projected a few inches beyond the curved edge of the round table at each end.

'Wonderful!' Frances enthused. 'Marvellous!' She climbed up onto the table and squatted there, staring down through the glass at the mirror. The whole hairy furrow of her genital cleft, including the tight, puckered ring of the anus and the pink, still slightly gaping lips of her cunt, were reflected· back up at her between the spread cheeks of her buttocks and the upper part of her thighs.

She was breathing rather fast. A thin thread of saliva linked her lower lip to the inside of one thigh.

I was staring too. It was a splendid sight. She reached out a hand and wrapped hot fingers around my aching staff. 'That looks so good,' she murmured, 'I think you should put it somewhere safe!'

I seized her ankles and pulled her feet out from under her, so that she fell forwards onto her hands and knees on the table top. Now the reflection was completely different. I saw pointed tits hanging, the darkened nipples swollen and huge; I saw an outward curve of belly, a thatch of hair already damp between parted and slightly trembling thighs. And from immediately behind her I saw what had previously been only a reflection but was now in 3-D, as it were: that bushy cleft between taut round cheeks with its slice of pink flesh showing. 'I know just where to put it,' I said.

I climbed up and knelt behind her. There wasn't a lot of room, but a man with good muscles at the back of the thighs and a knack of flexing the hips should be able to manage.

Steadying myself with one hand on her back, I grasped my thick, still hardening prick and played the swollen, distended head up and down between the folds of that glistening slit.

Frances caught her breath . . . and it was then that I flexed my hips and rammed it into her, the whole hot length tunnelling up into the wet clasp of her belly as she smothered a small scream and backed fiercely up against me.

I began ploughing in and out of her with powerful strokes, each one deeper than the last, peering over her shoulder with lascivious glee as I gazed down through the glass at the salacious coupling reflected below.

It was fascinating: a completely different viewpoint on something that was, after all, a fairly routine activity . . . well, if not exactly routine, let's at least say familiar.

The belly, for instance, free of the normal compression, the *tonus* which kept it taut and trim, now had a tendency – only a tendency – to sag: the loose flesh trembling, quaking almost, with each stroke I pumped into her. The breasts too, as I said, shuddered and swung every time my pistoning hips thudded against her thrusting backside.

Lower down her arched body, the moving image in the mirror below showed me the hairy silhouette of my own balls squashed against her pubic mound . . . and then, slowly emerging, the glistening rod of my cock each time I withdrew. As the shaft wetly retreated, the lips of her cunt came into view, sucked outwards, pouting, as if reluctant to let the joystick go – only to be flattened back into the dark thatch, greedily swallowing as I lunged again.

Above all this, with eyes glazed and mouths hung open, the reflections of our lewd and lustful faces leered knowingly out at us.

'We . . . don't need to consult . . . any doctor . . . to enjoy . . . this kind . . . of sex!' I panted as I plunged and withdrew, plunged and withdrew.

'What? . . . *Ooh, that's so gooood!* What did you say?' Frances gasped, pausing for an instant and then ferociously thrusting back once more.

'Nothing. Just a story. I'll . . . tell you . . . later.'

We didn't need to worry about the television either, I

thought as I changed into top again. Not when we had our own live show to watch!

Soon, however, the exertion began to take its toll of us both – especially since it was less than half an hour since we left that shower.

Eventually, Frances collapsed face down across the table, bringing me – still blissfully trapped inside – down with her. 'It's no good,' she said weakly. 'The spirit is only too willing. But the flesh . . .'

'The flesh is splendid,' I said.

And I started again, but in a totally different way.

Now that we were both pressed against the glass top, the two bodies in tension, as it were, any energetic movement on my part – in particular any abrupt hint of withdrawal – risked altering a whole lot of angles so that my cock would drop out of its nest. And it might then be difficult, without raising ourselves again, to replace it. And that, I thought, wouldn't be cool.

I continued to fuck, but in a different, in a sense more subtle, way. With my hands caressing her shoulders, I lay with my hips resting on the exhausted girl's buttocks, almost – but not quite – immobile.

Very gently, instead of pounding away as I had before, very gently I began an almost imperceptible gyration of the centre part of my body, tensing first the muscles of one hip and then of the other, varying this with an occasional tiny flex, followed by a relaxation of the pelvis as a whole. The effect of this was to caress the inside of her vagina with infinitesimal movements of my cock, rolling the hardened shaft first one way and then another, easing it back for a fractional withdrawal, then slowly, oh so slowly advancing the distended head to part the hot, wet walls at the neck of the womb. At the same time, Frances rhythmically contracted and then relaxed the inner muscles gripping me, moving her own flattened hips just enough to rub the juiced outer lips of her cunt against my streaming balls.

Beneath us, the scene had changed again. Distorted in the mirror, breasts and belly were now squashed against the glass under our double weight, the glass itself misted with moisture. The sound of our quickened breathing was suddenly very loud in the quiet room. Frances groaned. An early morning workers' bus splashed down the street outside. Had it been raining when we came in?

Gradually, between us, hardly moving, we built up – we constructed, one with the other – an almost unbearable intensity, an inexorably mounting, shared excitement resembling in its advance an ocean wave rearing up, curling, curling over, about to break with a thunderous explosion of roaring foam.

It was Frances herself who triggered the blast. A sudden, unexpected quickening of the contractions massaging my throbbing cock, a tightening of the buttocks around my balls, a sudden, demonic heave of the pelvis . . .

The wave broke.

I was whirled away into the stars; the tumbling of that crest into a maelstrom of threshing foam and the squirting fury of my sated lust were one and the same as I spurted my load up into her scalding little belly.

I had cried aloud in my ecstasy, but my voice was drowned at once in the tempest of shuddering sobs that shook her own frame into release.

Daylight was filtering through the shuttered windows when at last the four arms and four legs falling limply from the round table stirred. We tottered into the bedroom, this time to sleep.

It was almost eleven o'clock when I dragged on some clothes and rode down to the entrance to call Frances a taxi. I was handing her into it when she turned towards me, smiled, and said: 'That was . . . brilliant. Fantastic! I really can't . . . I don't know what to say.'

'The protocol in these matters is simple,' I told her. 'You say, "Thanks for the memory". I say, "Thank you for having me". And then we both say, "See you again *soon*".' I closed the door and waved the taxi away.

Back upstairs, I downed a mug of instant and hurried to the typewriter.

I already said – twice, I think – that the stuff I wrote for Edward and my real life sex experiences did finally get tangled together. This was the turning point.

I rolled in a sheet of paper, carbons, and began to type. I made the girl big, blonde and busty. Otherwise I described both scenes, the shower and the table top, exactly as they happened, omitting no detail, however slight. That took care of Chapter Three for a start.

'I was knocked out by that new sex scene of yours,' Edward said when the manuscript was handed in three weeks later. 'The shower and the glass table. Terrific. It beats me how you guys think up these ideas.'

'There's a song,' I said. 'The first line goes, "Imagination . . . is funny".'

I had another meeting with the American publisher later that day – this time without Monsieur Henri. It was even better. It was encouraging, in fact.

I had a couple of drinks at the Café de la Paix, and I was feeling pretty good by the time I returned to the apartment.

There were two suitcases in red leather with matched

white hide corners, standing by the glass-topped table (the glass was still slightly opaque in the centre).

I frowned. A tooth-brush that wasn't mine projected with a tube of raspberry-flavoured dentifrice from one of the bathroom tumblers.

What the hell? Surely Edward couldn't have over-booked? Let some other writer move in while I was still officially here? In any case there was stuff of mine all over the place.

The problem was solved before I could waste any more time on it. A ring at the apartment door. I went into the hall and opened it.

Frances.

Frances, this time in a little flowered number with a deep vee-neck and a tiny waist, artfully cut to maximise the small breasts, and a flared skirt at just the right length to minimise her lack of height. Printed cotton, I think, but it looked great.

'Oh, you're back already,' she said. 'I'd hoped maybe I'd get here first.'

'Are those your suitcases in there?' I said as the penny dropped with a resounding clang. There was, I liked to believe, a certain edge to my voice.

'Why, yes,' she said cheerfully. 'I bribed the concierge to let me in and unlock the door so I could dump them while I did some shopping.' She glanced down at the bulging carrier-bag from Fauchon, the most expensive provisions shop in Paris. 'There aren't many doors in this city that can't be opened with a fifty-franc note.'

'Very civil of you,' I said, still standing in the doorway so that she couldn't actually come in. 'But it happens that I'm here to work.'

'Of course. I thought I could save you time if I prepared

40

the meals. And of course it would give *us* more time . . . later.'

I swallowed. When a friend asks you, as a favour, to squire the little niece around the big city for one evening . . . well, you don't necessarily expect a voracious sex-pot with an insatiable appetite – and the kind of dominating personality that results, well, in this kind of situation.

It was awkward, just the same. I mean, it wasn't my flat; I wasn't renting it and she was related to the owner in a sense. Did she think that just because the place belonged to her uncle's employer, that gave her the right to move in whenever she wanted? Did she saddle herself on *every* writer who was given the run of the apartment?

On the other side of the balance, it had to be admitted that it was I who made the first move, who talked her into coming here in the first place. And of course it was flattering. Plus, to be brutally honest, it was no bad thing having a free fuck available all the time I was in Paris.

But not tonight. At all costs, not tonight.

'Frances,' I began.

'Some of this stuff needs to be stowed in the freezer,' she said, pushing past me into the apartment.

Well, what could I do but move aside?

'Frances,' I called after her, 'it's great to see you. Really lovely. But it just so happens that tonight it's, well, not convenient.'

'What did you say?' she called over the noise of unwrapping paper in the kitchenette.

'It's not convenient,' I repeated. 'Not tonight.'

The fridge door closed. 'What do you mean, not convenient?' She appeared in the doorway. 'There are two rooms. I won't be in the way while you tap at your

41

machine, if that's what you mean. What time do you like to eat?'

'It's not that,' I said wretchedly. Chapter Four wasn't working out at all in the way I'd planned it. I was seized by an unreasoning fear. Not only would I be saddled with her during the whole of my Paris visit – saddled was a good word, I reflected, thinking of the shower – but she would follow me down to the coast; she would get pregnant; I'd have to marry her. Christ!

Forget that. Concentrate just on tonight.

There was, you see, this leggy blonde I'd met that afternoon. I'd picked her up in the Deux Magots after my talk with the American publisher, and I was hoping great things of her. She breathed out that I've-got-it-and-you-want-it-but-don't-you-dare-touch-it attitude that unfailingly acts as a challenge and a come-on to almost any man. And she'd agreed at once when I'd suggested dinner – preceded by an apéritif (oh, you *artful* seducer!) at the apartment.

She could read the signs as well as I could.

And she was due in less than an hour.

'Frances,' I said desperately. 'Look, honey, it's super seeing you, honestly, sincerely, but the fact is . . . well, it's just that – it happened before we met, you see – the fact is, I have a date.'

She was looking at me. Her face was quite expressionless.

'And the . . . lady . . . is due to call for me here,' I finished lamely. 'Soon.'

Frances smiled. 'Oh, that's all right,' she said. 'No problem. We'll make it a threesome.'

Chapter Four

The blonde's name was Peggy. She was American, a professional golfer. She was spending a few days in Paris on her way down to – guess where! – the Riviera coast, where she was to play in an invitation-only tournament inaugurating a new course reserved for the richer of the rich denizens.

As Susan would be away on a cruise at the time, it had seemed to me that there might well be material here for Chapter Four – mine, not Edward's – since Peggy would be staying at a hotel in Juan-les-Pins, less than a mile from my own eyrie in Golfe Juan.

Provided that, like Dickens's Barkis, she was willing.

And provided that Frances-the-leech was not going to foul up the whole thing.

'Look,' I told her, 'this is all very well, but I hardly know this girl. I haven't even . . . that is to say it's a first date. I've no idea what her reaction would be if you suggested—'

'Don't worry. I give great suggestions.'

'I mean, she might very well refuse even to consider such a thing; she could get the dead needle and flounce straight out, offended or outraged.'

'Very few people will refuse,' Frances said easily, 'provided the . . . suggestion . . . is made at the right time, in the right way and above all in the right *atmosphere*. And I don't mean by this that one has to make them drunk first.' She grinned. 'Although sometimes it does help.'

'Well, I hope you're right,' I said. 'Okay, it's a super thought, and if it came off it would certainly be a wonderful—'

I paused. The interphone was buzzing.

I went to the door, lifted the handset off the hook, said: 'Yes?'

'Peggy Metford,' the receiver told me. 'You *were* expecting me?'

'Most certainly. Come right on up. Scotch, brandy or vodka?'

I heard a small spurt of laughter. 'Scotch on the rocks would be fine.'

I pressed the button. By the time the lift arrived, I was standing by the open door with an outstretched hand. 'Welcome,' I said. 'So glad you could make it.'

Peggy was wearing skin-tight brown leather jeans with a fringed, off-white Mexican shirt and ivory calf ankle boots. A lightweight poplin raincoat with a shawl collar was slung over her shoulders. Very transatlantic.

I said that Peggy was a leggy blonde. The hair, which was soft and glossy with plenty of body, was shoulder-length. And the legs, long, slender and well tapered, were certainly impressive. But this doesn't give anything like a picture of the person as a whole. She was not, you see, a pretty woman. This was no hourglass figure: the measurements between slim hips, waist and bust cannot have been different by more than a few inches; her features were well-shaped and strong, but the result was . . . well, almost handsome rather than beautiful. Apart from the hair, the most striking attribute Miss Metford had was her eyes, which were very large, very wide, and a particularly luminous grey.

And yet she distilled this essence of sexuality, this female, almost feline aura that many beauties strive vainly to acquire, that would leave the pneumatic Grishkin a wallflower in her own drawing room.

Peggy in fact was a living, breathing, highly successful example illustrating the lesson that so few men learn before middle-age and some not at all: that, of all the things which draw a man to a woman, whether or not she is 'pretty' – beautiful, if you like – is by far the least important.

Between the ages of, say, eighteen and twenty-five, we have this maniac drive to be dating the prettiest girl in our group, if possible the prettiest girl in town. But if only we were honest with ourselves, or sufficiently intelligent, we would admit that our real motivation was simply *to be seen with* this object of desire: it's the proprietary bit, the appearance of the top-dog, this-is-*mine*, pecking-order syndrome. Of course, the physical thing is all-important at that age; it's only later that we learn the prettiest girl is not necessarily the best lay, that it's more rewarding to go to bed with a person than a pin-up or a magazine cover. By then, nevertheless, it's often too late. Thus the failure of so many early marriages.

I was fortunate enough myself to be 'initiated' into the subtleties of sex by a woman in her forties when I was still in my teens, and once the idea had taken hold that 'women' could be more adventurous, inventive and physically exciting than 'girls', the world was my oyster, the sky the limit. Even today, I recall that the most thrilling, sexy and electrifying bedmate I ever had in my life was a fifty-five-year-old Portuguese chambermaid with slightly sagging breasts who worked at a small hotel in Marseilles.

It's a simple enough maxim, but until it has been accepted, I do not believe that a man can truly be described as 'grown-up'.

The visual, my masters, is not all.

As anyone who ever had anything to do with leggy Peggy, the grey-eyed golfer, will happily confirm.

I'm talking now with hindsight, of course. At the time, so far as she was concerned, I was only instinctively aware of her . . . qualities. But I didn't have long to wait.

Frances already had the Scotch-on-the-rocks prepared. Peggy draped her raincoat over the back of a chair and dropped herself into another as I made the introductions. If she was surprised to find a second female person there, apart from one swift glance at me and a tiny, quizzical twist of the lips, she didn't show it.

We talked of this and that. My work, the jobs that Frances did, the new golf club. We discussed the differences in France since the general strike and student revolt in 1968. We had a second round of drinks.

Since it was clear that there was no chance whatever of Frances leaving, I suggested that maybe it was time we went out to eat. There was a little bistro in a back street only a couple of hundred yards away, where the owner, who came from the south-west, made a very fair *cassoulet*.

'Oh, let's have one more first,' Frances said. 'One for the road, even though it's only a short one.'

'Well, we're knocking back short ones anyway,' Peggy said, draining her glass. 'I'm all in favour.' She glanced at the glass-topped table, where the smears testifying to the previous night's excesses were still shamefully visible. Then, very deliberately, she looked first at Frances, then at me. 'I always agree with the French,' she said, 'that three's an improvement on two.' Very carefully, she set the empty tumbler down in the centre of those telltale smears.

I knew then that, Frances or no Frances, the evening was going to be all right.

The *cassoulet* was good. We had a bottle of Bordeaux with it, and then champagne to accompany the baked Alaska. 'Why don't we go back to our place for coffee?' Frances asked. 'Uncle Edward always leaves a bottle of cognac around somewhere. He knows his writers.'

'Why not,' Peggy agreed.

I made a mental note, chalking up a black mark for the proprietary 'our' place – and the crafty mention of the uncle to underline that the apartment was no more mine than hers.

Little bitch.

But there was no point in arguing or splitting hairs at that point: the flat was where I wanted to go anyway. And the kind of hair-splitting I had in mind was a sight more carnal than a shout-up in a 16th-Arondissement bar, however good the *cassoulet*.

We went back to the apartment.

I had turned on the heating before we left, so the place was only slightly cooler than a Turkish bath. 'My Gard,' Peggy said at once, 'you'll have me thinking I'm back on Malibu Beach! You guys mind if I remove an article of my attire?' She peeled the Mexican number over her head and shook the blonde hair loose.

'Go ahead,' Frances had said before I could even leer. 'Make yourself at home. As a matter of fact, I think I'll lose something myself.' She climbed out of a lightweight lambswool bolero she'd put on before we went out and tossed it onto a settee.

'Hey!' Peggy said, eyeing the deep cleft below the throat of the printed summer dress Frances wore. 'Those are great little tits you have there, honey. So smooth, so firm, so taut . . . Shit, I sound like an underwear commercial! So what kind of brazzeer do you wear?'

Frances named a make famous for its outline and uplift.

'Gee, I wish *I* could,' Peggy sighed. 'They give great shape. But I don't have enough here.' She grinned, touching herself halfway between the waist and shoulder. 'Not enough body; I do not, you could say, fill their cups to overflowing!'

'But you have a super shape,' Frances said. 'Trim, and firm, and . . . athletic. Super.'

Peggy, in fact, certainly looked athletic. And indeed trim. But beneath the buttoned, sheer silk tee-shirt she wore under the fringed garment, there was little more than a soft roundness at the bust.

She was, however, undoing the buttons.

'Look,' she said. 'Shall we quit horsing around? I mean, it's, you know, obvious that we're going to have sex. Right? So why don't we strip off at once and save time, cut out all the fancy dancing around the subject when we all know damned well the question had been posed – and answered – before we even went out to dinner?'

The last button slid through the buttonhole. She allowed the tee-shirt to glide down her arms and drop to the floor, then she reached behind her to unsnap her bra and leaned forward to shrug out of that.

Well, I thought – Frances had already unfastened the front of the flowered dress and was stepping out of it – that was certainly one way to kick off Chapter Four. My personal one anyway. For his, Edward would require at least three pages of titillating lead-up to the first hint of sexual contact.

There was in fact nothing wrong with Peggy's breasts. Okay, they were not very large, a little loose and slightly pear-shaped, but the nipples and dark-fleshed areolas surrounding them were big, they moved easily on her rib-cage – and somehow the contrast between those soft breasts and the smooth and firm curve of her waist, although that was hardly smaller than her hips, seemed to me one of the sexiest sights I'd ever seen in my life. I was filled with an insane desire to bite into that pliant wall of muscle.

You see what I mean? This was one of the least voluptuous females I'd seen undressed, yet she was at the same time one of the most physically compelling.

Frances was naked. Peggy still wore her tight leather pants. I had taken off my jacket when we came in, but otherwise I was fully dressed.

The American unbuttoned a flap at the waist and then slowly lowered the zipper fastening her fly front.

The brown leather clung to her muscular thighs like a second skin. She began peeling down the pants.

'Here, let me help you,' Frances offered. She moved across the room, spring-heeled, tits bouncing, and inserted her hands between leather and flesh, easing the pants legs down past Peggy's knees.

Finally Peggy sat down on the settee and raised her feet to let Frances pull the jeans off altogether. And it was then that I saw – after the eyes – her second most splendid attribute: a truly marvellous honey-blonde bush, a thick triangle of springy, tufted hair that stretched from the labia almost to the hip bones, covering all the lower part of her belly.

Nestling at the lowest point of this elegant thatch was her cunt, the wide lips slightly parted in a vertical smile.

There are three main species of cunt in my personal classification – the pouting, the sliced and the concealed-compressed, which can of course be sub-divided into three hundred and seventeen local variations. Peggy was the owner of an example in the first, my favourite, category – welcoming, seductive, fully visible from the start. It was the kind of cunt that made me feel I'd like to dive in head-first, and then swim upstream like a trout.

Right now, however, it had disappeared from my view. Peggy stood behind me with her arms around my waist and her hands flattened against my belly just below the navel. Through the stuff of my shirt I could feel the stiff buttons of her nipples centred on the warm soft weight of her breasts against my back. 'Well, we've displayed the contents of our own treasure chests,' she breathed in my ear – we were about the same height – 'so why don't we take a look and see what he has to offer?'

'Why not?' Frances trotted out her well-used reply.

Peggy's hands slid down beneath the waistband of my pants, the fingertips easing themselves under the elastic top of my jockey shorts.

Frances planted herself in front of me and unbuckled my leather belt. She seized the tag of my zip and drew it down.

Then, carefully, she pushed up my shirttail, drew aside the Y-fronts, and inserted a hot hand to grasp my prick.

Lengthened and hardening since Peggy had got rid of the Mexican shirt, the shaft now jerked to full rigidity. By the time Frances had plunged in the other hand to take hold of my balls, dragging the full set out through the gap in my trousers, I had a massive hard-on and the throbbing cock-head was distended ·to bursting point.

Peggy peered over my shoulder. 'Not *bad*,' she approved. 'I guess I could use that if pushed.'

'Baby, you're going to be pushed all right,' I said huskily. But the macho line was a sham. Because already the pattern was established; the cards had been dealt, and there was nothing we could do but play out the hand.

There is always, you see, in any social 'transaction' as the shrinks call it, the leader and the led, the prophet and the disciple, the boss and the yes-man. It's not a conscious decision imposed on one party by the other. The follower in one situation can be the boss, with a different companion, in another. But there's never a total equality. With Edward, for instance, I was the led – because he was my employer, he was older, he had more experience. Broadly speaking, when we were together, whatever it was we were doing, we did it his way. With the yacht skipper who put me on to Edward in the first place, however, I was the leader. This was because I was A Writer, someone a little outside his maritime ken.

This is true of the relationship between any two people at any given time. It's just the way things work out. End of story.

When it comes to a trio, the same principle applies – only now, mathematically, it has to work as a pair on one side, a single on the other. Two 'against' one – with the one naturally always losing out. The decision can be conscious or unconscious, overt or covert, and 'against' doesn't necessarily imply hostility (although sometimes, below the surface, it's there). But from suburban hen parties to three men in a boat, from group sex to girls on a day out, that's the way it has to be.

With the three of us on that night in Paris, it could

have gone anyway, since one of the trio was a newcomer: it could have been Frances and me against Peggy, Peggy and myself against Frances, or the two girls on one side and me on the other. As it happened, that last one was the way it was. It had been implicitly decided from the moment Peggy said, *'we've* displayed the contents of *our* treasure chests . . . let *us* see what he has.' The alliance was cemented then.

That was okay by me. I mean no problem. Especially because of another maxim I hold dear. In my experience of women – which is not of course all-embracing, though I'm working on that – the female of the species is generally not only more dangerous but also a great deal hornier than the male.

It used to be said that, once a man has come, he at once begins multiplying numbers, or wondering whether sheep shit or horse shit would be better for the roses, or was it really time to splash out on a new convertible. A woman, on the other hand, regards that first orgasm – if they have been lucky or skilful enough to have one together – as no more than a rite of passage to the next. And the next. So, when she's still screaming, *what's for afters?* he's already paid the bill and left the restaurant.

Nothing that I'd seen so far of Frances appeared to contradict this observation – and from the little, the very little I knew or guessed about our guest, that should be par for her course also. I mean I already told you about this aura of lasciviousness that was almost tangible.

What was tangible at that moment was my cock. Peggy was holding it now. She held the base firmly between the forefinger and thumb of one hand, using the other to milk the shaft with feather-light caresses, expertly skimming what loose skin she could find up and down the iron-hard core. Frances, for her part, was now cradling my balls, gently scratching the wrinkled pouch with her nails as she squeezed.

It seemed to me that I had begun to breathe rather fast.

Peggy rested her chin on my shoulder so that she could peer down at the reddened and quivering object of her manipulations. 'Well, that looks serviceable enough,' she said. 'What say we strip him and take it into the bedroom with us? There *is* a bedroom here?'

'Oh, yes,' Frances told her. 'There's a bedroom all right.'

Once the three of us were in there in the altogether, I waited to be told what to do. 'Tell you what,' Peggy said to Frances. 'I give great head, or so they tell me. Why don't you just lie back and relax and let me? He can hang in back there and pleasure me while I suck, okay?'

Nobody had to tell me the response of my unexpected flatmate. I could have written the script while we were still at dinner. 'Why not?' Frances said.

Nothing loth, as they used to say in nineteenth-century novels, I kneeled up behind our golfing guest. The blonde head was already buried between Frances' drawn-up thighs. From behind, the cleft dividing the sportswoman's narrow hips seemed entirely to be filled by those inviting folds of secret flesh I had so much admired, and which now, pinkly gaping, already glistened with anticipation.

My cock wasn't going to get any harder; for minutes now it had been aching like a broken leg. I leaned my hands on Peggy's hips and slowly drew the cheeks of her bottom apart. Beneath the tight, puckered ring of the anus, an oval of close-packed blonde hairs could now be seen framing that dreamy cunt. I flexed my own hips and drove the shaft in, right up to the hilt in a single lunge.

'Hole in one, by Gard!' Peggy gasped, raising her head for an instant. 'Let's see what you score when I turn over and you have the whole fairway to shoot across.'

'Come back here, bitch!' Frances cried, seizing Peggy's head with both hands. 'Oh, Jesus, that's so good! Yes, do it to me there . . . and again *there!* God, when you draw it up between your teeth . . .'

I had settled at once into a powerful, slow, almost monotonous rhythm, moving in and out of Peggy with long, deliberate strokes, nothing forced or jerky, only the slightest impact as my hips nudged her at the end of each deep penetration. Her cunt was a delight, with a personality all its own. Instead of the clenched and clasping welcome I received from the ridged vaginal muscles of Frances, or even Susan, here at the other extremity of the sensual scale there was nothing but a gliding caress, an oiled and sucking friction which drew the quivering nerves almost to the agonizingly ecstatic point of no return. Almost but not quite. There was always room, always time, for just one more stroke. And another. And another . . . and perhaps just one more . . .

It was whipped cream contrasted with butter, silk with tweed. Each bliss in its way, but completely different.

Whichever, tonight it was the way I wanted it. I continued gently plunging away there in a dreamlike trance.

Until Frances came.

In terms of real time, that didn't in fact take long. Her legs were already scissored around Peggy's neck when the first convulsions shook her small frame. Her head threshed wildly from side to side on the pillow. Her belly spasmed and she began choking out her release in a series of shuddering sobs.

It was at that moment that I froze.

So strong were the movements arching her body repeatedly up from the bed that Frances, bouncing the sprung mattress in time with her thrusts, was carrying Peggy up and down with her.

And if, still embedded within the American, I remained perfectly still, instead of pumping myself in and out of her, she would automatically ride up and down the throbbing length of my staff.

Same blissful effect; very much less effort. It was gorgeous.

In fact I was within a millisecond of coming myself – almost past the point where you cannot stop yourself – when Peggy rolled off Frances to cradle the dark head between her soft breasts.

Separated just in time, I went to the kitchenette for brandy and glasses.

Edward said to me once, 'Even with readers like ours, old boy, guys and dames who want nothing better than to press on to the next sex bit, there has to be an occasional dip into the think-tank, a short shot of a lead-in to take care of the how and why. I'm not saying we have to get very heavily into the psychology of sexual compulsions, but it's good to know sometimes just what led them into the sack. Between each bout, I mean. Otherwise, if we're serving up nothing more than a continuous succession of whip-it-in-whip-it-out-and-wipe-it sessions . . . well, shit, we don't have a novel; we have a fucking catalogue.'

'In every sense of the term,' I said.

Certainly there was little time spent on philosophical discussion during my night with Frances and Peggy.

There was still brandy in my glass when I found myself lying on my back on the bed with Frances impaled on my prick and Leggy Peggy squatting over my face with my tongue up her cunt. The two girls were kissing voraciously as they leaned together over my prone body and fondled each other's breasts.

Soon the bedroom was loud with our wordless grunts and squeals as Frances rode up and down my rigid cock in her invisible stirrups and Peggy's athletic pelvis squirmed avidly above my exploring tongue.

That young woman's cunt was a treasure-house, a voyage into the wet-walled velvet dark with the muscled tip of my tongue seeking out ever-more-secret folds of sliding flesh as my mouth gobbled the nutty interior and my lips sucked out her throbbing clitoris bud until it swelled like a miniature penis.

This time, the two of them came together and I was lucky not to suffer a broken nose.

I don't remember what lead-up there was to Position Three, and if there was one I couldn't write it. We were all twined together this time, flat out on the bed. My hands were smothered in breasts, hot nipples hard against my palms. My cock was in Peggy's mouth, the base and balls manoeuvred by her practised hands. She herself was being alternately sucked and finger-fucked by Frances. There was a heated thigh against my cheek and I think – though I wouldn't swear to it – that I felt pubic hair and at least one vaginal lip against my teeth.

The next thing I remember, I was lying on my back on the mattress with a girl on either side of me. My cock, marbled with the distended veins, rose vertically from the base of my belly, stiff as a flagstaff, and they were licking it, both together, as if it was an ice-cream cone. At the same time, Peggy kneaded and fondled the bunched scrotum below and Frances, whose turn it was to grasp the dribbling shaft, was milking the lower part with slow, increasingly powerful, hypnotic strokes.

Well, of course . . . to be sucked and caressed and tossed-off by two naked, sexy women at the same time . . . there could only be one end to that cadenza! And this time there could be no turning aside at the last minute.

I could feel it building, building, every nerve in my body draining its most exquisite sensation down to concentrate at the inflammatory point between my thighs; I was aware of the tension inexorably mounting until the pressure was all and I was the pressure.

Peggy's large lips closed over the bulbous cock-head; her thumb rotated the most sensitive area of skin immediately below it. Frances, still licking, increased the speed of her milking hand.

And then suddenly both girls withdrew their heads and there was nothing but the tight-wrapped hand clenched on my throbbing shaft, pistoning me forcefully, inevitably, cruelly . . .

My cock was the world; it was going to burst into a thousand stars – and it was as though a giant fist inside me had punched violently upwards and outwards, forcing the gathered sperm out in great spurting gouts, a vertical fountain of hot white drops spattering my belly, the bed and the bodies of both girls in its forceful shower.

'My, *my!*' Frances enthused when the spasms had dwindled to an occasional exhausted squirt and the hammering of my heart had quietened a little.

'Impressive,' Peggy added. 'It was like watching a scratch player blast his way out of a sand-pit with a mashie-niblick! How old did you say you were?'

I hadn't, but what the hell. 'Thirty-four,' I said. 'Why do you ask?'

'Question of stamina, guy,' she said. 'If that's what you

57

have to give, it's going to be a long night. And there's two mouths and two cunts here for you to fill.'

'Maybe this time *you'd* better go fetch the brandy,' I said.

Chapter Five

The books produced by Edward's team slotted into several distinct categories. The most popular at that time, affording a glimpse into the stability of the American marriage as an institution, was the '*Neighbourhood*' series, which was based on wife-swapping. This swingers' charter was followed by the teacher-and-pupil syndrome (strictly no paedophilia, though); nurses and patients; summer camp frolics and sexual excess in an office environment. The subject matters dealt with in others could be more esoteric.

'Old boy,' Edward said to me apologetically at the first conference I went to after my return from Paris, 'I'm afraid I'm going to have to ask you to do one of the dog books.'

'Dog books?'

'Yeah. You know. The lovely lady in an isolated country cottage . . . hubby away on a business trip . . . she's horny, sitting in her negligée, wishing . . . and outside, on the edge of the forest, peering in through the lighted window, there's this randy German Shepherd . . .'

'Good God!' I said. 'You don't mean . . .? You're not telling me the *dog* . . .?'

'Why sure,' he said. 'Very popular line, especially in Tennessee and the Dakotas. The Caesar series is into its third book; Rajah Two comes up in August.'

'But isn't that . . .? I mean that's bestiality. Isn't it illegal?'

'You have a guy making it with a lady dog – *that's* bestiality. And, yeah, it would be illegal in the US of A to publish text describing it.'

'Presumably,' said Edgar, the Polish astro-physicist, 'because there would be no way to establish whether or not the bitch was a consenting partner?'

Edward ignored the interruption. Low-grade erotic fiction was a serious business and there was no place for humour in it. 'A woman stimulating herself with the help of a dog, however,' he said, 'that's *not* bestiality; not in the criminal sense anyway. According to the Supreme Court, that is.'

I must still have been looking worried, because he added: 'No sweat, though. We'll give you models.' He turned to one of the secretaries. 'Sonia, honey – fetch Mr Adams a copy of *Rover's Happy Christmas*, would you?'

Even with the crib, I remained nervous. It showed too, because another writer who happened to be there – an American poet with a large black beard – caught my eye when Edward had left the room. 'You should worry,' he said gloomily. 'I have to do one from the point of view of the dog.'

Crib or no crib, nervous or confident, there could nevertheless, as I found out, be problems with the dog books.

I finished mine, later in the year, on a trip to London, and was obliged to dash out to Heathrow at two in the morning and put the manuscript on a plane in the freight section to make my deadline. Within hours – I was still toying with a late breakfast – there was a frantic telephone call from my editor, Mabel, the Vassar graduate.

'Honey,' she said breathlessly (I am not inventing this), 'you fixed the jealousy motive, the way Edward wanted. Fine. But he meant all *three* of the dogs to be German Shepherds. Having one of them an Airedale and one a Dalmatian, the way you have . . . God, that's a bit too far out for our readers!'

Until then, my acquaintance with dogs as characters in a story had been limited to one of those black comedies popular in the sixties.

This particular one concerned a man taking part in the Paris-Dakar or some similar trans-Sahara motor rally.

Anyway, one or two days out, the guy misses a marker and loses his way. He circles around, hoping to hit the right trail, but he doesn't make it and his Land Rover runs out of petrol. He's alone in the blazing desert with nothing but a can of Coca-Cola, a box of matches and his faithful dog.

Panicking, he breaks the golden rule: when lost in the desert, stay by your vehicle and wait until rescuers locate you. He starts to walk in what he hopes is the right direction. It isn't. He's going around in circles. The dog's too exhausted by the heat to use his homing instinct.

Finally the man collapses. He's drunk the Coca-Cola, he's dying from thirst, he's starving, and he's been hit by the scorching sun and the cold desert night. It's terrible, but there's only one thing to do if he's not to perish in the wilderness. He picks up a large, flat, heavy stone and he kills the dog. He scrabbles together a pile of dry desert scrub and he uses the matches to start a fire. He cooks himself a meal.

Replete in the cool air of dusk, sucking the last shred of flesh from a rib, he looks sorrowfully at the small pile of picked-clean bones by his feet and he shakes his head.

'What a shame,' he said. 'Rover would have loved those.'

Well, if you don't like it, you can read another erotic book. Or buy your own can of Coca-Cola.

Long before my dog book, however, my life had been complicated in a less anthropomorphic way . . . this time in the person of Sonia, the secretary who had been dispatched during the conference to fetch my copy of *Rover's Happy Christmas.*

Sonia was Scottish, a slight girl with large, very round blue eyes and long, pale hair which she wore in a ponytail. Visually, she was perfect casting for what she did: help with the production of pornographic literature. She had big breasts, a tiny waist, and splendid legs. Her mouth was wide, with one of those extra-full lower lips that always seem to glisten, whatever the climate. She wore dark glasses and extremely tight sweaters over uplift bras that gave her that thrusting, almost conical silhouette typical of the glamour girls of the fifties. With these she wore black jeans, often made of leather, and knee-high boots which even then were still considered a little daring. To complete the picture, Sonia rode a ritzy Italian motor scooter loaded like a Christmas tree with bright chromed lamps, mirrors, horns, badges and anything else that could be found in an auto-accessory boutique.

I said to complete the *picture*. Okay. I meant exactly that: what we saw. But the gear and bravado did less than nothing to explain the person; they were no more than a palisade, a rampart behind which she could hide.

For, to tell you the truth, although she would die rather than admit it, Sonia was in fact both shy and inexperienced.

I didn't catch on at first, of course. Nobody did. That

was what the act was for, and it was a good act too. It was not until she called at my place in Golfe Juan one day with some copy that needed revising that I began to tumble.

Until then I had only seen her in Edward's office, and had always treated her with the sort of flip sophistication the image seemed to demand. But here, in my own flat, the casual, sardonic approach appeared somehow out of place. I was facing a young kid who'd had a long, hard ride on a hot and dusty day, a girl who needed a long, cool drink a great deal more than any sophisticated badinage – and probably a drink of fruit juice at that!

As soon as we'd skimmed rapidly through the changes Edward wanted in the middle of Chapter Nine, I suggested just that. 'Oh, that would be dreamy,' Sonia said, the soft Edinburgh burr most agreeable to hear. 'You wouldn't happen to have fresh grapefruit, would you?'

'Certainly,' I said. 'With ice?'

'That would be just lovely.'

I plugged in the electric juicer, fixed her a long one in a tall green glass, poured myself a Campari and soda and took the drinks into the living room. It was hot up there under the roof. The ice tinkled pleasingly against the glass. Sonia was already perched on the ottoman.

I handed her the grapefruit juice and sank into one of those beanbag chairs covered in artificial leather that were popular that year. 'Tell me, Sonia,' I said. 'How come you got into this job?'

'Och,' she said, 'I was in Paris anyway. A dull job in a British library, and there was this ad in the English-language papers: just a wee three-liner in the classifieds. "Bilingual secretary-typists required for permanent work on French Riviera". Well, of course, it sounded fab. I applied and I was interviewed by Edward.' Sonia laughed.

Then she said, in a very fair imitation of Edward's mid-Atlantic delivery: '"I have to tell you that the texts you will be asked to re-type may contain words and phrases some folks would consider coarse, rude, outrageous or even disgusting. Is that understood?"'

I grinned. 'Good old Edward! Covering every available track. And did you?'

'What? Find the copy all those things? Not really, not after a week or so. After all, I've yet to come across a word I've no' heard before.'

'Exactly,' I said. 'They're words you hear all around you, every time you walk down the street or have a drink in a pub, every day. You hear them in mixed company, socially. Women feel free to use many of them – some liberated women anyway. And yet until recently there was this extraordinary taboo that you weren't allowed to write them down or use them in a book – words as common today as nose or lip or foot, actions as common as blowing your nose or coughing. Forbidden, censored, punished. Crazy, isn't it?'

'I guess it is. Or was,' Sonia said. 'Tell me though. The words don't worry me, but the things people do, the things you all describe in the books; do people really behave like that and do all those things?'

'Well,' I said carefully, 'perhaps not *all* of them. The books are fantasy, remember – things the readers would like to do. Or think they'd like to do. You don't have to take them one hundred percent literally. Most of the plot lines, just the same, have some basis in reality. Maybe not everyday reality for every person, but reality for some people, somewhere. That's where the fantasy comes in: it's like the grass on the other side of the fence always seeming greener.'

'Thank you. I don't like to ask these things in the office,' Sonia said awkwardly. 'Folks will think I'm daft or simple. But you're different: being on the outside, as it were, I feel I can talk to you.'

'I'm flattered,' I said. 'Truly. Can I get you some more grapefruit juice?'

That little talk, and one or two other snatched confidences that followed it in St Tropez, put me on my guard a little. I'm no cradle-snatcher, but at times it seemed suspiciously as though I was being metamorphosed from confidant to something dangerously like a substitute father. The trouble, you see, was that I did find the girl attractive. I would have loved, for a start, to find out what lay beneath – or rather what filled out – the pyramid cups of that fifties uplift brassière. But prudence forbade. Initiating someone that young into the mysteries of sex could too easily result in a dependence – a dependence that came ready wrapped with strings. And clinging ivy was my least favourite indoor plant. So I never dated Sonia; I kept the confidences at bay as far as possible; I made sure I was only ever alone with her when this happened naturally in a business way – a third person called out of the office, for instance.

There was no doubt however that she would have welcomed a closer contact. I don't mean in any way that she was making a play for me. Sonia was much too 'nice' a girl for that. Too shy also. But she had a certain openness, an honesty if you like, that could be disconcerting.

'I'm no' a vairgin, you know,' she confided once (the Scots accent always became more pronounced when she was embarrassed or unsure of herself).

'Oh?' I said, somewhat nonplussed. 'But I thought . . .

didn't you tell me once that you were, well, completely inexperienced?'

'Oh, aye. When it comes to sex, that is. Real sex, I mean. With men.'

'You don't mean . . . with women?'

'Aye. At school. All girls, you know, together. You begin to find out about yourself. You want to know more. It's exciting too. In the South we heard they called it wanking – an ugly word for sure. For us in the dormie it was doing-yourself-up. And once one of us looked old enough, or was brave enough, to walk into one of those sex shops . . . well, you know how many different gadgets you can buy there.' Sonia laughed a little self-consciously. 'I lost my vairginity, you might say, by my own hand!'

I was not, in fact, quite sure what I might say in reply to this intimate confidence. But Miriam, the other secretary, came back into the office at that moment, so I didn't have to make any comment at all.

Miriam was something else. She was a wiry, red-haired Canadian, with a compact, athletic figure, who spent most of her free time playing tennis. Her image couldn't have been more different than Sonia's. Verging on the hippie, it combined the blue-jean syndrome with loose, shapeless, often secondhand tops in dun colours, a total absence of chic, and a shaggy, self-cut hairstyle worn close to the skull. Miriam, who spoke in clipped monosyllables whenever possible, appeared in fact to be something of a hardboiled number, even formidable at times. Yet she was, I happened to know, extremely kind – almost maternally protective – towards Sonia.

Appearances of course can be deceptive.

One day – I think I'd just finished my fourth book for Edward, *The Ravished Babysitter* as I recall – Export

Advisers Incorporated (Cable address Expadink) threw a party for as many of their writers as could make it to St Tropez.

I forget the excuse. Mrs Edward's birthday or their three hundred and fiftieth published volume perhaps. Whatever, it was a rather grand gathering, held in the penthouse apartment, with good, proper vintage champagne and delicacies served by white-coated waiters from the Hostellerie Beaumanoir at Les Arcs de Provence. Very high class stuff.

Maddox Himself was playing host, and among the dozen or so writers who turned up there was also the local mayor, the chief of police, a member of the Departmental Council with his bejewelled wife, and a couple of high-powered Paris lawyers on holiday – none of whom, naturally, was remotely aware of what it was that Expadink exported or the kind of advice the company gave.

The writers were a motley crew: a handful of grey middle-agers with spectacles, who could have been dentists or bank clerks; a vociferous couple from Copenhagen; the bearded poet; a raucous old woman with a raddled, over-painted face; a university lecturer who taught English at the Sorbonne.

There were only two – both professionals – I felt I could be bothered to meet again. Most of the others I took for amateurs, folks either with repressed sex lives or, like myself, with too many bills to pay. I wondered if it was the old woman who wrote what Edward had described as 'the dirtiest books I ever read in my life'. Certainly his wife and Miriam and the three editors had their work cut out trying to stop her shrilling out confidences about the semantics of her trade in front of the local dignitaries. Fortunately her French was even worse than her Italian.

The fellow hacks who interested me were Helen Chalmers, a lean, jokey brunette of about forty, who was Paris correspondent for a London photographic agency, and a young blond American named Jeff Adlam who looked as though he was a football half-back.

Helen, who seemed a very forthright woman, told me: 'Whatever you do, don't forget to look me up whenever you're in Paris, and we can sink a jar together.' Maybe she fancied my careworn face as photographic material.

Jeff was married to a very beautiful young Norwegian girl named Inge. They lived in a rented apartment in Monte Carlo – and at first it was this geographical proximity more than anything else that made me agree to his very warm suggestion that we should meet again and keep in touch. Anyway, how could anyone resist cultivating a man whose home address Stateside was Apple Tree Hollow, Broken Cedar Loop, Oregon?

We exchanged addresses and telephone numbers.

Around ten o'clock, when a great deal of champagne had been drunk and everyone was reasonably juiced and the honeys and darlings and *chers amis* were flying thick as the leaves in Vallambrosa, I reckoned it was time to leave. I had quite a buzz on myself, and the road across the hills to the autoroute is snaky.

Well, it happened that Miriam lived some way beyond Ste Maxime, on the other side of the bay, and the battery of her car, an old Renault, was flat. As it was more or less on my way, old boy, would I mind awfully taking the coast road instead of crossing the Montagne de Roquebrune to the autoroute? Then, if I would be so kind, I could drop Miriam off on the way.

Thus Edward at his most persuasive.

Well, what could I do but accept with as wide a smile

as I could manage? It would take me a good half hour longer and the twisty coast road is a bore at night with all the lights (they're always coming in the *other* direction, have you noticed?). Still, always the gentleman . . .

We started off carefully: it's hell at St Trop between ten and midnight, with hordes of rich drunks haring about in Ferraris and the larger BMWs. But once we were clear of the port, with the windows open and a warm breeze blowing, I opened up a bit and began to enjoy myself. We were on the long straight bit just after Port Grimaud when Miriam said: 'This is an Alfa-Romeo, isn't it?'

'Yes,' I said. 'A 1300 GT Junior.' The car was in fact the pride of my life. It was thanks to Edward that I'd been able to afford it, secondhand, from a gallery owner in Toulon who was investing in a Maserati. It was a super car, fast, with marvellous acceleration and a gearbox that was a dream. Behind the wheel, it was like driving a pot of cream. Not too expensive to run, either.

'Nice,' Miriam said.

'I could never find out why they called this model "Junior",' I said. 'Especially as the 1750 and the 2000 have exactly the same bodywork.'

'Lucky you, anyway,' Miriam said. And then, a few moments later: 'I've never been screwed in an Alfa.'

'There has to be a first time for everything,' I said. Just joking, I thought.

But she said: 'Well, find a convenient lay-by, excuse the word, and pull in.'

You couldn't, to be honest, actually have knocked me down with a feather. Not really. Especially as I was jammed into the driving seat of a sports saloon. But it would be fair to say that I was surprised by my companion's remark.

In the millisecond it took me to master this reaction and determine what my rejoinder should be, Miriam said: 'There! A hundred yards past the white gates. On the right. The bushes will hide us from the road.'

It was in fact a loop off the old road, a sharpish right-hand turn above a rocky inlet, which had been bypassed by a gentler curve of the new coastal highway blasted from the hillside. And indeed the quarter-circle of pitted macadam, screened by a line of bushes, could still be driven into across the grass verge.

Considering that the lay-by must have been at least two hundred yards ahead when Miriam spoke, and the gates at half that distance were not obviously white, I had the distinct impression that my passenger was experiencing one of those I-have-been-here-before phenomena. Either that or she had infra-red eyes.

I braked, bumped across the grass, and parked behind the bushes. Sited immediately above the sea, the place must have been a popular picnic spot in daylight. Before I switched off the headlights I saw the familiar litter of beer cans, orange peel, crumpled cartons, the ashes of a fire.

In the Alfa GT Junior – mine was the 1968 version – there is not a great deal of space between the lowest part of the steering wheel rim and the driver's knees. There was enough for Miriam's right hand. She had ripped down my zipper and was scrabbling aside underclothes in search of my cock before the cooling engine had begun to tick.

I was already ticking myself, though. As I leaned awkwardly across to grab her shoulder, she literally projected herself towards me, wet-mouthed, the hot tongue probing the inner surfaces of lips, teeth and cheeks. I had been going to lift the loose top she was wearing, a Fair-Isle design but in the softest of Shetland wools. But once more she was there before me: my hand was seized and thrust up beneath the garment.

I felt soft flesh, heated skin, a curve of belly. She was wearing no bra. And she had – although you could never guess it from the clothes she wore – surprisingly good breasts, firm and full. I had cupped one and was thumbing the hard nipple when her fingers wrapped around my cock, by now as stiff as a plank, and pulled it out into the open.

'Ah!' she breathed.

Just that. But the monosyllable was as expressive, as sensual as ten pages of Edward's lead-up-to-the-sack narrative.

I don't remember exactly how I extricated myself from behind the wheel without opening the door and walking around to the other side – the buzz was still buzzing, remember – but I do recall kneeling on the floor with my cock out in front of Miriam's seat, with my tongue buried in her cunt and her feet pressed to the low roof with the jeans still around her ankles.

I was hoisting myself up in an attempt to remove the tongue and replace it with my throbbing staff when she twisted suddenly away. 'No, not like that: you can do that in any car,' she said. 'Even a Triumph Spitfire.'

'You must draw me a plan,' I said. 'What do you suggest?'

'Do these seats recline?'

'Of course.'

'Let's put them down, then. So we can be a little more adventurous.'

The seats in the Alfa sports saloons are very deep and very soft. Comfortable, but without a great deal of purchase for gymnastics.

71

Miriam, nevertheless, was clearly a girl who would try anything once. Twice if the situation demanded it or there was a minor point of technique to perfect. Soon, the windows were misted up, and the interior of the car was redolent of hot leather, winey breath, a little sweat and excited woman.

She positioned herself on hands and knees, facing the rear of the car, with her hands gripping the lowered seat back while I shafted her from behind – the scorching clasp of her athletic cunt at last affording my distended cock the warm welcome it craved.

We tried the same thing on the driving seat, which seemed to recline further still and left Miriam bent forward with her head almost into the rear footwell. But the wheel itself imposed a very hunched stance, especially on me, although she pronounced herself satisfied with the deeper penetration this involved. But after only a few strokes, withdrawing perhaps a shade too far, my arse thudded against the horn button and the shrill blare of sound that resulted left us both collapsed across the seat with helpless laughter.

It was time to move further back. I'm not a world authority on back-seat snogging, but it seems to me that Miriam and myself must have run the gamut in that lay-by – well-named as she had implied – after the Expadink party.

We lay along that rear seat with her feet in the air; with my feet against the streamlined back window; with the two of us facedown, each with one knee in the footwell. We un-reclined the passenger seat and folded the seat-back forward, so that she could cling to it froglike, and then lower herself gently down onto my lighthouse prick, jutting lewdly from my loins as I sat on the rear seat.

After a while we changed positions automatically, exchanging scarcely a word, much as she might, playing doubles in a tournament with a new partner, say perfunctorily: 'Left after service, right?'

Perhaps the most adventurous pose we struck involved Miriam lying on the back seat with her legs draped over the rear shelf and her head tilted into the footwell, while I squatted on the inclined passenger seat-back with my cock in her mouth and sucked her off. The Alfa rocked on its independent springs.

I suppose it must have been well after one o'clock when at last we called it a day – or rather a night. Miriam had come three times. I had made it twice. There hadn't been much traffic on the road; just an occasional headlight beam sweeping past and then the crackle of an exhaust as the driver accelerated away from the corner. Once a big car cruised into the lay-by and left the headlamps on and we froze, fearing a police prowl, Peeping Toms or even motorized muggers. But it was only a long-distance traveller, taking the opportunity to have a leak.

I lit two cigarettes and handed one to Miriam. She was struggling back into her jeans – they had been flung off, along with my trousers, a long time ago. In the suffused glow of the dashboard cigar lighter, I had seen that she was smiling. A curious, half-secretive, very *personal* smile.

'It's the cars, isn't it?' I said, blowing out smoke. 'I mean like it's a thing with you. That's the kick, right?'

She nodded. 'I guess so.'

'I suppose it's like any other fetish,' I said. 'Except you can't exactly stuff it out of sight at the back of a dressing-table drawer!'

She made no reply to that.

'You collect them, is that it?' I asked. 'Like when we

were kids we used to collect the number of railway engines of a certain type that we'd seen. Or the registration letters of planes or pop stars' autographs. You collect the makes of car you've been fucked in.'

'It's not a crime,' she said a little defiantly.

'Of course not. It's a pleasure,' I said. 'And at least its original.'

I drew on my cigarette. 'Tell me: does it make any difference to you who your . . . partner . . . is?'

'Not really,' Miriam said candidly. 'Of course it has to be someone I like.'

'It doesn't have to be someone different every time?'

'Not necessarily.'

'So you wouldn't mind having the same guy twice – especially if he had switched to a new model.'

'It's the cars I collect, not the people,' she said, as if explaining to a backward child.

'It must be pretty difficult in some cases,' I said. 'Actually to get screwed, I mean. Which was the toughest you remember?'

'Oh, the little Fiat 850 Sports Coupé,' she said at once. 'My back gave me hell for almost a week!'

'And the easiest?'

'An old car belonging to a young doctor I knew. It was a 1927 Sunbeam 16 saloon. It was enormous! There were silk curtains on all the windows, a tiny skylight in the roof, and so much room between the front and back seats that, if you lay just a bit diagonally, you could do a missionary without any part of you touching the bodywork!' Miriam laughed. 'It was lovely.'

'Have you ever scored in a Roller?'

'No,' she said. 'Not yet.'

When we had finished the cigarettes, I asked her: 'How

much further on is it? Where you live, I mean.'

'Only about half a mile. It's a big house, lying back from the road. With iron gates and cypress trees.'

'Lucky you.'

'Oh, it's not mine,' she said. 'I live with my parents.'

It was Sonia who told me, some time later, that Miriam had once had a long affair with a tennis pro who promised to divorce his wife and marry her, had reneged on both promises, and had left her with an autistic child and not a penny of maintenance. That explained why she lived with her parents. Perhaps it explained also why it didn't really matter to her who drove the cars she chose to have her sex life in. It certainly explained her knowledge of the lay-by!

'Do your parents know the kind of work you do?' I asked her. 'For Edward, I mean.'

'*My parents!*' she echoed. 'Do me a favour! It's as much as I can do to let my Dad see me in tennis shorts.'

Three minutes later, I coasted the Alfa to a stop outside the iron gates. There was still a light burning in the porch. I opened the passenger door and kissed Miriam on the cheek. 'Thanks for the ride,' I said.

Chapter Six

Susan's boat was back in port at the end of the week, but only until the Monday, when they were setting off again on a new charter – a round trip taking in Genoa, Elba, Corsica and the southern part of Sardinia.

'We'd better make hay,' I said. 'How long will you be away?'

'Ten days at least,' Susan said. 'They've booked the boat for a fortnight, but there's some talk of returning early and doing a few days trip along the coast.'

'It's about time I did a few more day trips around you,' I said, allowing my gaze to sculpt out for me the breasts and waist and hips I knew to be hidden beneath the loose smock thing she wore that day with her jeans.

'The haymaking will have to be brief,' she said. 'I've got to get in supplies and the whole of the galley has to be done over. You know how long that takes.'

'We already had lunch,' I said. 'It's a good day to stay in.'

It was, too. The Mistral was blowing great guns. The pegged-back shutters rattled and shook with every powerful gust. Through the open window, beneath the iron-hard blue of a swept clean sky, I could see whitecaps surging in to rock the boats moored along the quays. The wind roared in the attics overhead and tinkled the wire stays of the sailing ships against their aluminium masts.

Susan was already untying the three tapes that held together the edges of the deep cleavage slitting the front of her smock. Our relationship – the stage of intimacy at which we had arrived – was such that we no longer needed the mental stimulation, the anticipatory thrill of the ritual seduction, the undressing bit, the dance where the cock bird flaunts his finery. We knew we were mad about each other, so the quicker we got naked the better.

This is not to say that we didn't enjoy the odd verbal exchange, the sly, meaningful remark before we knew we were going to fuck. But anyway, on this particular day, this particular cock had been stiff as a board ever since the coffee was finished, just *thinking* about the lady.

I whipped off my jeans and tee-shirt to prove it.

Susan pulled the smock over her auburn head, and those gorgeous full, firm breasts bounced into view. I'd been hoping she was bra-less, and the fulfilment of that simple wish made my afternoon. Anything that came later would be a bonus!

She pushed the jeans down over her hips; the springy triangle of her pubic mound, and then the discreet pink slit of her cunt rose into view between the zippered margins of the gaping fly. Naked, she sprang onto the old ottoman and kneeled up with a smile on her face. A marble goddess suddenly flesh.

Preceded by the speared bowsprit of my prick, I advanced towards her.

'Come and sit beside me,' she said.

'I beg your pardon?'

'I know we always slam into a quick one, to get the lust out of the way before we start the interesting stuff,' Susan said. 'Nothing wrong with that. But we mustn't make it a

78

routine. Today we are going to do something different. Okay?'

'Be my guest,' I said. 'Feel free to indulge whatever libidinous fancy drives you insane with desire.'

'Feel me,' Susan said.

I felt her. All over. Breasts and waist and buttocks and the moist kiss of her stroked pussy. And what a joy it was!

'Now lie down beside me,' she said.

Obediently, I lay.

Upright beside me, with her knees snuggled into the curve of my waist, she reached for my cock. It was already rising like a flagstaff towards the ceiling. At the touch of her cool fingers the ache in my loins increased to a point where it was scarcely endurable. Spontaneously, my hips arched up to meet her firm grasp. They're inclined to make up their own mind at such moments.

'Put your hands behind your head, darling,' Susan said. 'Lace the fingers together. Just relax and let me play, all right?'

'I wouldn't dream of trying to stop you,' I said, my breath already accelerating a bit. 'Although – God, that's so good! – I do frequently dream of trying to start you!'

She was stroking me lazily, sliding the loose skin up and down the rock-hard core of my shaft in a slow, magical rhythm that made my pulse feel as if it would jump out of my wrist.

For a moment there, I was afraid that I was going to come right away. But then she changed position and hovered above me on all fours with her face only inches from the moist and bursting head of my cock. She held it tightly now in both hands, caressing the head between her palms in a sliding, rotary motion that was sending me up among the stars.

I caught my breath, exclaiming aloud. She had lowered her head and flicked out her tongue, boring the tip excruciatingly into the wetness of the tiny opening in the distended head. Chills rippled along my spine. She lowered her face further still, enclosing the entire head in a moist, warm clasp. Her lips tightened around my shaft like an elastic band, trapping it within the pressured cavern of her mouth.

I was going out of my mind. Susan stroked the base of my cock between the thumb and forefinger of one hand as she began to suck rhythmically, easily up and down. With her other hand she lifted and gently massaged the hairy sac of my balls.

I could feel the resilient softness of her tongue twirl around the ridged cock-head at the limit of her withdrawal, the tip flicking maddeningly across the distended glans. I flexed my buttocks, raising my head in fascination to gaze at that auburn hair flying up and down above my tortured loins.

Sensing my hotly throbbing reaction to her labours, Susan sucked harder, digging the tips of her small teeth gently into the hard, resistant cock flesh to leave tiny white trails on the skin where they had scraped the sensitive surface. She was shifting her position again, on all fours between my legs now without ever disengaging her mouth from that pulsating shaft. Pulling my loins up tighter still to her face, she ran her practised tongue around the growing head until I was convinced it would explode my full load into her gargling throat then and there. She had almost the entire shaft deep in the sucking clasp of her rubber lips.

Great swirls of lust built up deep within me as I watched her contorted face working furiously over my loins, slaving to provoke the final bursting of the dam whether I wanted it or not.

Rivulets of sweat rolled from beneath her generous breasts and down her sides as she sucked and slavered. My belly tightened, arching up off the ottoman to penetrate even further between those prehensile, gobbling lips. Thin pink ridges of flesh pulled out from her mouth on every out-stroke, clinging to the hot, thrusting staff. I had been groaning out my delight, an incoherent muttering spilled through clenched teeth. But now suddenly I gasped. I shivered. This was it. 'Yes, *now!*' I screamed. 'Take it, bitch . . . and swallow it all!'

Somewhere way inside me, I felt a convulsive spasm start, racing to the outlet of my quaking loins to spew the first hot jet of sperm forcefully into Susan's sucking mouth.

Her cheeks expanded and hollowed as she swallowed the warm, flooding gushes, sucking on wildly while I emptied the white-hot evidence of my desire into the wetness of her mouth. Involuntarily, my hands tangled in her hair, forcing her down on me as I thrust my squirting instrument all the way to the back of her throat. Even as I groaned out the last of my titanic release, she continued – more gently now – the sucking of my deflating cock until the last hot drop of sperm had been extracted from my loins.

I collapsed, arms flung wide, across the ottoman. Susan nibbled gently at me for a short eternity, the auburn head resting softly on my thigh, then crawled up beside me to cradle my own head against her still heaving breasts. She leaned across to kiss me on the lips.

My reaction was as fervent as if we were meeting after a seven-month separation. When our interlaced tongues at last disengaged, Susan gazed tenderly into my eyes and murmured: 'Oh, my! What a splendid engine you have there, darling! I don't suppose . . . I mean, you *would* like to try placing it – elsewhere – wouldn't you?'

'Try me,' I groaned. 'In eight and a half minutes.'

'Why eight and a *half*?' she asked, one hand reaching for my cock.

'It was enough for Fellini,' I explained breathlessly.

'I'll give you eight,' Susan said.

We made it, with her expert help, in seven. After that, it was the full, languorous, entwined, afternoon-length communion – the long, gentle, scarcely moving embrace with the hot cock deeply buried, the heels hooked over my thighs and the bellies heaving as our wet mouths sang together. And if that wasn't the most marvellous fuck I ever had in my life, my memory refuses to supply the one that was.

Chapter Seven

After Susan's healthy, bouncy, joyful celebration of sex –
and even allowing for Miriam's rather more . . . shall we
say *personal* view of the subject, I felt justified in the
assurance I'd given young Sonia that people didn't
necessarily indulge in *all* of the frolics described with so
many adjectives and adverbs in Edward's books.

It was not long afterwards that I discovered, although I
was well aware that there were different *kinds* of sex,
alternative approaches to the final, shuddering thrill, that
I might have to revise my opinion. It does indeed, as they
say, take all sorts.

The day this was brought home to me was the day I
delivered the completed manuscript that Sonia had brought
to me for revision.

The office was quiet. Edward and Velvet were in Paris.
Edgar was quietly copy-editing someone else's manuscript.
Mabel was in town shopping. 'Welcome to the office
Romeo!' Miriam said as I came in.

'An Alpha-plus to you, Miss, for accurate observation,'
I riposted, playing the other card in our shared and secret
hand.

'I know what you mean by that,' Sonia said, raising
her head from her typewriter. 'It's because you have
an Alfa-Romeo, isn't it? Miriam's mad about cars, did

you know that? She's a car buff.'

And *in* the buff too! I thought to myself. But I just said: 'Well, I had an idea.' And then, *sotto-voce* to Miriam: 'Wait until you get a boyfriend with a pre-war racing Bugatti. There isn't even enough room for the *driver* in those!'

She grinned. 'That'll be the day,' she said. 'But it'll have to be a fine one – I mean like with the top down!'

'Amongst other things,' I said. Once you've started this double-meaning caper, it's hard to stop (there I go again. Sorry).

'What *are* you two talking about?' Sonia demanded.

'Nothing,' I said, waving an airy hand. 'Just a joke.'

'That's right,' Miriam said. 'Just a joke.' She handed me an envelope. 'On a more serious note, Edward left this for you.'

'Manna from Heaven,' I said. 'Thanks.'

The envelope would contain my cheque. The company paid instantly on delivery. The only trouble was, they banked with an American concern in Monte Carlo, and the cheques had to be cashed over the counter there. What the hell – there were enough bills on my desk to make it, as the guide books say, worth a detour.

La Grande Chaleur – the Big Heat – had arrived on the coast early that year. The sky was cloudless, half veiled in a sulphurous haze, and the impact of the sun was like a whip across the shoulders. There was plenty of time, however, so I thought I'd break the discomfort of a blistering sixty-six mile drive with a cooling dip in the sea at Cannes, roughly halfway there.

But it was so hot on the Croisette that I couldn't put my bare foot on the sand of the Martinez beach, and the brown girls prancing down to the water's edge lifted their oiled legs as if they were pulled on wires, feeding the maximum amount of air to their scorched soles between each step.

I left my sandals between two breasty goddesses pretending they hadn't come there to be worshipped and trod the coarse, thistle-sharp grains to the sea, hoping to escape the prickly heat beneath the surface.

But the water was tepid, sickly with the scent of sun-tan lotion filming the glassy swell, so exhausted by the heat itself that it could scarcely summon the force to flop over into an occasional wavelet. I waded past screeching, splashing children, rubber canoes, pedalos and lobster-tinted middle-aged ladies spread-eagled on lilos, and then I gave it up. The battering of the sun against my skin above the surface was so intense that the shrieks of the bathers and the steady roar of traffic along the Croisette above faded in my ears, absorbed by the asbestos sky.

I brought an ice-cream cone from a kiosk but it melted and ran down my wrist before I could eat it. There wasn't an inch of shade on the whole beach and the hard glitter of the sea had begun to hurt my eyes, so I dodged into the *vestiaire*, washed away the sweat with a lukewarm shower, and hurried to retrieve my jeans and tee-shirt from my locker.

Although there are cubicles if you want them, the Martinez beach changing room is unisex. Since it was late lunchtime, and most of the hotel guests were either applying a second layer of Ambre Solaire, were unconscious, or were fucking in their rooms, the place was empty. Except for the girl standing by an open locker a few feet away from mine.

She was tall and slender, with a close cap of dark hair and very straight black brows above wide grey eyes. As the *vestiaire* leads directly off the private beach, it was no surprise to see that she was topless, or that the lower half of her bikini was so brief that the rear part plunged between sandy cheeks to expose the entire fleshy complex of her bottom. What was unexpected was the approach.

First the smile, a grin really, as she turned to face me. The breasts were firm, separated by a deep hollow traversed by a tiny trickle of sweat. The nipples and areolae were very dark against her suntanned skin, and there were dark hairs curling crisply out at each side of the jade green triangle sheathing her pubic mound. 'Are you staying at the hotel?' she asked before I could speak.

I shook my head. 'I live down here. Over at Golfe Juan.'

'Pity,' she said, the voice deep and a little husky.

I took her at first for a hustler. The entire fourth floor of the Martinez, at that time, was occupied all summer by business girls. This was because a high proportion of the clientele was family based, and a thoughtful management had laid on this service to occupy unattached sons while their rich parents gambled at one of the town casinos. The girls, who were very beautiful, came each year from all over Europe, and there was a brisk, if discreet, trade in the hotel lobby during the apéritif hour and immediately after dinner. The hotel, of course, had a piece of the action. The fourth floor rooms were free; the girls, if they were still unattached, were given a one-course dinner; and if they hadn't clicked by 10 pm, they were permitted to go out and troll the bars and discothèques and nightclubs nearby.

The beach beauty near my locker wasn't one of them however.

But she certainly knew the score, and she must have

86

read my thoughts because the smile grew wider, and she said, with emphasis: 'I'm on the *fifth* floor. Room five-seventeen. The name is Zita; I'm here with my parents, but they spend all their time at the tables and I'm bored to sobs because everyone at the hotel is a hundred years old. Except the kids who go upstairs with the tarts, of course, but who's interested in *them*!'

I don't know what I said in reply. She was standing very close to me, it was airless and stuffy in there beneath the low roof, and I was all at once agonizingly aware of her near-nudity. Small beads of perspiration glistened among the roots of her eyebrows.

'Funny, isn't it,' she said suddenly, 'how we have to cover up the sexy bits, the parts that attract attention and really turn us on' – fingering one of her breasts – 'and expose all the dull areas nobody wants to see.'

I heard a sharply indrawn breath as she spoke. It was mine . . . for she had reached out her free hand on the phrase 'sexy bits' and cradled the testicles swelling out the crotch of my swimming trunks.

'Very funny,' I said hoarsely. 'Hilarious in fact. I often laugh at this.'

She was staring at my trunks. She had only held me for an instant, but the lemon yellow stretch material was beginning to stretch into an unmistakable elongated shape. 'Well,' she observed, holding my gaze now, 'at least there's *someone* around who isn't a hundred years old. Perhaps Monsieur would care to escort me back to the hotel?'

'Oh, Christ,' I said wretchedly, 'there's nothing I'd like better – but I can't: I have to go to my bank . . . and it's in bloody Monte Carlo, and it closes at four. I should be back by six, though. Could we . . . could we perhaps have dinner together?'

'Seven o'clock in the entrance lobby,' she said. 'I'll be waiting.'

She whisked a beach robe from her locker, shrugged into it, and walked away along the underground passage that passed beneath the Croisette to the hotel.

There was still an uncomfortable – if agreeable – tightness against the denim of my jeans as I climbed the steps to the scorching sidewalk and hurried to my car. What a girl! It wasn't only the fierce heat of the sun that kept the blood hammering behind my eyes as I slid beneath the wheel. The rim was hot enough to hurt the sticky fingers of my hand, and the whole interior was searing as the inside of a spit-grill, heavy with the smell of baked leather (shades of Miriam!) and the thin, aromatic stink of evaporated petrol. But the legend *seven o'clock* blazed even brighter at the back of my mind, and I was heedless of the diesel fumes laced with the odour of melting tar pumped into my lungs by the blower as I drove towards Nice.

There was a gap between the parasol pines beyond Golfe Juan, and I could see an arrow of white carved into the aching blue of the sea by a speedboat towing a water-skier. Everything else on the journey was eclipsed by the memory of the challenging look in Zita's grey eyes. The heat that was sticking my shirt to my back and sucking the sweat from my thighs where they pressed against the burning seat served only to conjure up for me the stifling, sexy closeness of a shared and shuttered room in the Hotel Martinez. Hadn't there been a pop song, generations ago, called *Room Five Hundred and Four*? Well, after tonight, even if I couldn't find a rhyme for it, there was going to be a better one.

Room Five Hundred and Seventeen. (What about 'The

Sexiest Place I've Ever Been'?)

The cicadas were jubilantly waving their football rattles
among the trees as I left the tourists jamming the
Promenade des Anglais in Nice and climbed to the Grande
Corniche. I double-parked in front of the Hotel de Paris
in Monte Carlo, handed the car keys to the bemedalled
doorman with a lordly air, and strutted up the steps as if I
was hosting a meeting of company heads in the Conference
Suite. Inside the lobby, I bought a newspaper and sneaked
out of the rear entrance. I walked the two hundred yards
to my bank.

Although the sun was angling down towards the foothills
of the Maritime Alps in the West, the concrete tower
blocks above the port still trembled in the heat haze as I
returned to the hotel to buy back my car from the doorman.
I was thinking of Zita's legs. Was it true that they hadn't
quite matched the slenderness of the rest of her? Were
they really just a little bit . . . well, sturdy? It had all
happened so fast that I couldn't be sure, I hadn't had time
to take everything in. My pulses raced, imagining the legs
locked over my back.

I was approaching the hotel when I remembered I had
promised to buy a birthday present for the young daughter
of one of Susan's married friends. It would be simpler to
do that here in the Principality than find a parking place
in Nice on the way back. I glanced at my watch. Yes –
plenty of time. There was a funny little gift shop I'd
noticed once or twice a little way up the hill in the
Beausoleil quarter: I should be able to find what I wanted
there. Sweating, I turned back and began to climb the
slope. If the traffic wasn't too bad, I should have time to
drop back home for a long, cold shower before I went to
the Martinez. Did she in fact have tufts of black hair

under her arms in the French manner? or was that just my imagination, fired perhaps by the memory of those pubic curls escaping from her bikini?

I grinned, remembering for some reason that old schoolboy joke about the sixteen-year-old in bed for the first time in his life with a naked woman. When it's all over, the lady leans back on the pillows, yawns, and stretches her arms above her head . . . and the initiate exclaims: 'Oh, goody-goody: two more!'

The shop was in a narrow street leading up to a flight of steps. Above the stairway, paths zigzagged up the slope between hanging clumps of geranium and bougainvillaea. I looked into the tiny window, but the display was obscured by a sheet of amber plastic hung there to protect the stock from the rays of the setting sun. An old fashioned bell clanged as I pushed open the door and went in.

I had a momentary impression of folksy tea-cosies and rows of small dolls in national costume, and then: '*Qu'est-ce qu'il vous fallait, Monsieur?*' An old, grey-haired woman in a shapeless cardigan was peering at me over the top of her spectacles from behind the counter.

What did I want? 'An apron,' I said. 'One of those Provençal ones with red and white stripes and a black lace edge. For a child. A little girl of about eight.'

'Ah. An apron. For a little girl.' She put down a bundle of black knitting and rose to her feet. She was quite tall. 'I will see what I can find.' She went to the rear of the shop, opened a door, and disappeared into a back room.

As I waited, I became aware for the first time of the noise. The whole place was alive with a sibilant whirring, ticking, shuffling sound that seemed to come from every corner at once. And as I swung around to stare at the packed shelves and narrow window, I saw that most of the stock appeared to be alive and moving.

In the centre of the display, a three-inch figurine in the shape of a ballerina tirelessly pirouetted at the command of a magnet mounted on an eccentric revolving beneath the mirrored floor on which she danced. She was flanked by trays of jumping beans and tiny model ladybirds tumbling and jerking in their compartments. Beyond these, ranks of plastic penguins, seals and nodding dogs bobbed their heads in idiot unison as some clockwork mechanism jolted the platform on which they stood. A chromed hoop twirled relentlessly behind a band of furry pussy cats stiffly scraping at their soundless instruments. And a gnome with a coiled wire neck shook his painted grin at a toy locomotive endlessly circling a loop of model railway below.

Over the buzz and tick of the stock, I heard a murmur of voices, and I turned towards the inner door. A cuckoo clock hung from the wall on either side of it. Instead of a pendulum, each clock was activated by carved wooden children bouncing at the foot of a hairspring. A lettered card beneath one clock announced: *Ladies' frocks and suits made to measure. Garments for gentlemen made up to your own design.* Through the open doorway I could see in the gloom of a shuttered back room the grey-haired woman whispering to an elderly companion seated behind a table by a tailor's dummy. You know the kind of thing – in England they used to be called 'busts' – a headless, armless stuffed torso on a stand, usually fussed over by dressmakers with mouths full of pins, arranging the panels of a cut-out pattern. This dummy too was armless – the table was covered with a floor-length green baize cloth, so I couldn't see the stand – but there was a featureless head above the padded shoulders. Perhaps the old ladies made hats as well as frocks? At the moment, though, the one in the back room appeared to be re-covering the bust itself rather than sewing together any garment fashioned over it. She was finishing off a seam running up the centre of the pouter-pigeon chest . . . only instead of the usual dun-coloured rep, this dummy was covered with soft black leather. I could see highlights sliding off the wrinkles in the material as the woman smoothed it flat and pulled the thread up tight. The one with glasses had disappeared for a moment. Now she came back holding a small red and white striped apron with black lace edges. Closing the door carefully behind her, she spread it on the worn counter for my approval. 'Seventy-three francs ninety,' she said briskly.

The handstitching was beautifully done. The lace was delicate. The apron was exactly what I had in mind. But I had to find an excuse to make her go back: I had to see inside that room again.

It was probably a delusion prompted by the suffocating closeness inside the shop, an aberration provoked by the hypnotic effect of all those mechanical novelties jerking and ticking away on the shelves, but I could have sworn, just before the door closed, that I saw the head of that dummy move!

I picked up the apron. 'It's very nice,' I said. 'Er – don't you have something a little more decorative, though? Perhaps with flowers embroidered in the middle?'

She compressed her lips – I could almost see the pins bristling between them – and turned towards the door. 'I will go and see,' she said coldly.

This time she half closed the door and I couldn't see into the room. The cuckoo clocks creaked and whirred. A painted bird bobbed out of each one and called. It was five o'clock.

Outside, the sun was low over the roofs and the narrow street was tiger-striped with bars of shadow. Inside the stuffy shop the stealthy susurrus of all those rustling, twitching toys seemed suddenly sinister, tinged with menace. Just because you're a bloody thriller writer, I told myself, you don't have to imagine everything you see is part of some deadly plot; you don't have to cast everyday shopkeepers as characters in a police series. Don't be such a dope!

Nevertheless, I skirted a shelf of fluffy poodles equipped with rubber bulbs to make them jump and pushed the inner door open. 'Look,' I began, 'it doesn't really matter if you haven't got—'

But the woman forestalled me. She was already on her way back. Before I could cross the threshold, she blocked the way, holding a different, more ornate apron. Pulling the door shut behind her, she placed a hand on my arm and guided me back to the counter. Between the edges of the unbuttoned cardigan I could make out loose breasts moving under the thin, grey woollen jersey. 'Perhaps Monsieur will find this more to his taste,' she said, smiling. It was the first time I had seen her teeth. The whole set were in shining, stainless steel. 'One hundred francs, *tout rond.*'

While I was pretending to examine the second apron, which in fact I liked less than the first, the woman turned to press a switch protruding from the plinth of a tall glass dome on a shelf behind her. Inside the dome, a near-life-size doll child, dressed in Victorian nursery clothes, began moving its arms and legs, miming the action of walking. At the same time a musical box concealed in the base trilled out the notes of the nineteenth century song *It's Time To Say Goodbye*. Looking at this jerking clockwork marionette, I was uneasily reminded of the death struggles of an insect pinned to an entomologist's display board.

'That will do nicely,' I said over the churr of ancient machinery. Avoiding the glassy, knowing stare of the doll, I pulled out my wallet and counted five twenty-franc notes into the woman's wrinkled hand. She cranked the handle of an antique cash till. The jangle of its bell cut through the whispering symphony produced by the machinations of her stock.

I took the small parcel I was handed and went out past the rows of heaving, clicking animals and birds, past the endlessly twirling ballerina and the nodding dogs, out into the evening sun. But I had seen enough to confirm my suspicions: in the brief moment between my shoving open the door and the woman pulling it shut, I had seen what I hoped not to see.

At the sound of my voice – there could be no doubt whatever about it – the anonymous, leather-encased head of the dummy had jerked and then twisted blindly towards the door.

Unless the two old women were manufacturing the biggest working model yet for their stock, there was a human being sewn up in that leather shroud . . .

The sun was out of sight behind the flounced Edwardian façade of the Hotel de Paris. A band of pale green separated the sun from the darkening sky. But there were still long shadows of palm trees outside the café in front of the Casino. I sat among them sipping a pastis while I wondered what the *hell* to do. The heat had lost its ferocity but it was still uncomfortably close.

I didn't want to get entangled in something that read like the plot of one of my own thrillers; I was in a hurry to entangle myself with Zita in something more like the plot of a book that Edward could sell.

But whatever devilry was going on in the back room of that extraordinary shop with its packed shelves of buzzing, twitching miniatures, I couldn't pretend I hadn't seen it. Who in God's name could be held captive by the steel-toothed woman and her companion? And why should they be imprisoned in such a bizarre manner?

My mind raced among melodramatic images. I recalled the Israeli spy who had been drugged and then roped into a chair fixed inside a steamer trunk some years ago. Customs investigations officers had discovered him at Fiumicino airport, Rome, on a plane bound for Egypt. Had I stumbled on some similar conspiracy?

The plots of a dozen books concerning kidnapping, espionage and torture – some of them my own – came back to me. Was it conceivable that I could unwittingly have become mixed up in a real-life drama of that kind?

The more I thought about it, the less likely it seemed. Yet I knew I wasn't mistaken: there *had* been somebody sewn into that black sheath. Why would the woman suddenly have switched on that noisy musical doll if it wasn't to mask the sound of any muffled cry for help that might have come from the closed back room once the victim realized there were strangers present? On the other hand, if there was indeed something sinister going on, why hadn't those innocent-seeming females simply shut up the shop and gone to work undisturbed? The loss of trade that would imply could scarcely be worth the risk of discovery!

My mind was brimming with questions and I didn't have the answer to any of them. Plus it was already almost five-thirty: if I didn't leave Monaco within the next half hour, I'd be late for my date with Zita, let alone have time for a shower and a change of clothes. The situation was impossible.

Should I make a dash for the nearest police station? I cringed at the thought. I could imagine the official reaction when I offered my 'evidence'. Another crazy foreigner! This one *thinks* he saw a kidnap victim in the back room of a novelty shop run by two harmless old ladies in Beausoleil! Folks who are not used to the heat should remain indoors . . . and of course I'd read, and written, enough thrillers to know that, even if I did persuade a cop to go and check, there would of course be no body there.

One thing was clear: I couldn't turn my back on the mystery; but I had to find out more before I called in outside help. But how? Return to the shop, push my way into the back room and demand to *feel* the dummy? They would be the ones calling the police if I did!

But, Christ, I had to do something. There was a real victim, who might be – who almost certainly was – in real and deadly danger. He or she might already be in the boot of a car on the way to . . . what? A mountain retreat? An abandoned farm where kidnappers would be undisturbed until a ransom was paid? The hold of a small craft at any one of half a dozen ports along the coast?

The whirr and click of fruit machines in a one-arm-bandit hall behind the café reminded me more acutely still of the yellow cellophaned window and what lay behind it; the grey eyes of the pretty waitress who brought me my bill reminded me of Zita. My pulse quickened, imaging her challenging gaze. I saw the eyes melt into the slumberous regard of sated desire. But for that to happen, I had to be there, back in Cannes. I hurried to the phone booth outside the washroom and called the Hotel Martinez.

There was no reply from room five-seventeen.

It was dark outside now. In an agony of indecision, I found myself pacing the streets under the hot black sky. So far as Zita's eyes were concerned, challenging was the operative word. I knew instinctively that if I stood her up there would be no forgiveness: even a later arrival, even if it was preceded by a phone call, a telephoned excuse, could be a problem with that kind of girl.

The bright rectangle of a public phone kiosk stood out against the night further up the hill. I called the hotel again. 'Five-seventeen is still not replying,' the switchboard girl told me. Would I like the party paged? In which case she would put me through to the hall porter's office.

'Fine,' I said. 'The only thing is . . . well, er, in fact I only have a Christian name: if Reception could tell me the surname of the guest in room five—'

'It is not the practice of the hotel to give out the names of guests,' the girl said, suddenly cool. She cut the connection.

It was a quarter past six. I kissed the candle-lit dinner goodbye. Forget those promising lips, the fleshy breasts, the legs – even if they were a trifle sturdy – scissored over the hips. There was nothing I could do to regain the lost time now.

I sighed. Some you win . . .

There was however something I could do here, right here in Monte Carlo. The shop with the dummy was less than a block away.

The street leading to the flight of steps was empty. No parked cars, no light behind the cellophaned window, an overflowing dustbin on the sidewalk in front of the barred door. Very domestic.

I walked past the shop. Five doors away, an alley split

97

the block in two. And from the alley, I discovered when I ventured cautiously into it, a narrow lane ran between the houses' small backyards and those of the block behind. Without consciously taking the decision, I submerged myself in the river of darkness between the high walls and forged upstream.

Wooden doors were set in the wall behind each house. I felt my way to the sixth, stopped outside, and listened. Traffic noises floated up the hill from the waterfront. Someone in the next block was having a party and the sounds of voices and canned music flooded out into the sultry air. Nearer at hand, televisions blared behind closed shutters. I stared up through the dark at the top of the wall. It seemed very high, and the dustbins were out front, so there was nothing I could climb onto. But there was no sound from the far side. My fingers scraped along the peeling paint of the door and found a latch. I pressed it down and the door squeaked open.

The yard was small and apparently overgrown. Chinks of light showed through the shutters of the houses on either side, but the façade in front of me was black against the night sky. I stumbled towards it through knee-high grass and weeds.

Stone steps led to the back door, which was locked. Beside them, a lean-to shed was built against the house. And above the sloping corrugated-iron roof of this was a narrow window. I took a deep breath and looked around me again. An amber glow suffused the sky over the backyard wall, where the buildings fell away towards the port. Overhead, a puff of warm wind rattled the leaves of a eucalyptus tree in the next yard. I could feel the sweat trickling between my shoulderblades. If anyone had seen or heard me come in, they weren't making a song and dance about it. I was committed now: there was nothing for it but to go ahead. Flashing a farewell glance at the image of Zita – perhaps even now squirting deodorant over those tufts before she went down to the lobby – I reached for the edge of the roof and hoisted myself clumsily up.

It seemed to me that there was a hell of a clatter as I fell forward against the slant of ridged metal and crawled to the window. I lay panting on top of the shack while my watch ticked away the seconds in my ear. But no shutters were thrown open; no flashlight lanced the dark; and no angry voices demanded to know what the devil I was doing there. I rose warily upright to explore the window.

The shutters were folded back against the wall and, astonishingly, one of the casements was open a crack. I stretched in an arm to unhook the catch and opened the window wide. A moment later I was standing in the stuffy darkness of the house.

It was then that the enormity of what I was doing really hit me. Zita, certainly in room five-seventeen now, would be stuffing her breasts into a bra, maybe even taking a last look at herself in a mirror. And I was here in Monaco, having feloniously entered someone's premises. In the eyes of the law, I was a burglar. If I should be discovered here, nothing I could say would be remotely believable . . . unless of course I could produce the evidence I had come to find. I had better get on with it and hope I could do just that!

Moving blindly forward into the blackness with hands outstretched, I jarred my hip painfully against something hard, staggered sideways, tripped over a chair and lost my balance. For an instant I was falling . . . and then my palms brought me up against the far wall with a shock that jolted my shoulders . . . and light blazed dazzlingly into my eyes.

I couldn't stop myself crying out in alarm.

It took me some time to realize that I had not been caught red-handed. My out-thrust fingers had simply struck against a flush-fitting wall switch as I pitched forward, and one of them had turned on the ceiling light.

I leaped to the window and leaned out to pull the shutters closed. It would look less suspicious from outside if I left the light on, rather than kill it immediately. Besides, how else was I going to see? Apart from my wallet, a clasp knife and a cigarette lighter that needed filling, my pockets were empty. A big-deal kit for a would-be private eye!

I could see now that, because of the hill slope, the lane and the backyard must be at a lower level than the street, for I was in fact in the back room behind the shop. Two chairs were drawn up to the baize-covered table, on which tailor's scissors, scraps of material, wool skeins, leather cuttings and a workbasket were neatly laid out. I saw cartons of mechanical toys waiting to be packed on a polished sideboard. Above a glass-fronted cabinet stacked with aprons, Provençal blouses and children's garments in plastic envelopes, a group of theatrical marionettes in costume hung from their strings. But of the tailor's dummy or the victim I supposed to be inside it there was no sign.

Three doors led off the cluttered room. The first I knew: it communicated with the shop in front. I opened it a crack. In the dim light filtering through the amber cellophane window shield I could just make out the counter, the antique till and the shelves of moving models. Some of them were still ticking away in the gloom. I closed the door hastily and opened the next. It led to a small lobby from which stairs climbed steeply to the upper floors. I would leave that until later: first I must check the third door down here. As soon as I turned the handle, my pulse quickened. The door was locked . . . with the key on the outside.

And the moment I unlocked it and pulled the door towards me, I knew I'd hit the jackpot.

The gust of warm air that swept into the room was heavy with the rich, oily perfume of heated leather – and underlying that was the acrid, onion stench of sweat.

Beyond the door was a closet full of topcoats and mackintoshes. There was something else too. On the back wall, suspended from coathooks thrust through two heavy metal rings sewn into the shoulders, hung the dummy: a cocoon of dully gleaming black whose mummified outline clearly revealed the shape of pinioned arms.

The leather-encased feet were six inches from the floor. The old women's prisoner had been parked there for the night as impersonally, as callously – and as efficiently – as the marionettes hanging above the store cabinet. God knew what fate was in store for the captive tomorrow: my planned debauch with Zita was in ruins, but at least I had the reward of knowing that I'd arrived on the scene here in the nick of time!

Or had I? Suppose the victim sewn with such cold efficiency into that constricting sheath were dead already? My mouth went suddenly dry. I could feel the heart thudding in my chest as I walked into the stifling closet. I poked a wary finger at the black skin stretched over the chest.

The dummy jerked and twisted slightly; a muffled grunt came from within the eyeless, mouthless head, and a jet of hot breath blew onto the back of my hand through two tiny holes piercing the leather shaped over the nose.

My sigh of relief was forceful. At least then the prisoner was alive. My fingers trembled as I pulled out my knife and opened the blade. Pricking the seam than ran up the chest, I sliced through two of the stitches, slid the flat of the blade through the gap, and opened up a dozen more. I seized the edges of the rent with both hands and ripped the seam apart as far as the head.

I saw a crisscross of adhesive plaster sealing a mouth and chin beneath tanned cheeks dewed with sweat. I ripped away the plaster. A wadded sponge flopped damply to the floor from the victim's open mouth. 'My God, it looks as though I got here just in time,' I panted. 'What the hell's going on? What kind of a mess have you got yourself into? Why are those two old bitches holding you?'

The man inside the leather sheath – it had never occurred to me that it might be a woman – cleared his throat. 'Frightfully decent of you, old man,' he said in English. 'Most obliging. But the fact is . . .' The cheeks flushed if anything a shade darker. 'Well, you see, the fact is I'm actually here of my own free will.'

'*What* did you say?' I paused, dumbfounded, about to tear apart the final few inches of the seam and expose the upper part of the head.

'I mean I'm into the – er – scene. Bondage is my thing. And since the old girls run a sideline making up the gear, well, I slip them a bit extra from time to time to complete the picture, as it were.'

I tore open what was left of the seam and pushed the leather hood back off the man's head. That was when I got the real surprise.

The eyes staring fixedly at a point just above my right shoulder were those of Edward – *Président-Directeur-Général* of Export Advisers Incorporated and my current employer.

PART TWO

A Penetrating Insight

Chapter Eight

Well, yes – as I'd said to Sonia, it takes all sorts. But I should have added (if you'll excuse the term) a rider: all sorts of sex as well as all sorts of people.

A fellow hack with a war record once said much the same thing in the introduction to an autobiographical account of a commando raid which he had disguised as a novel. 'To the truism that fact is stranger than fiction,' he wrote, 'there is a corollary – that fiction is often "truer" than fact; that the real truth of what actually happens can be conveyed not only more forcefully but also more completely through the medium of a "story" rather than a straightforward, objective report.'

Applied to my own experience on the Coast that year, this turned the confidences exchanged with Sonia arse (pardon me once more) about face: for if the sexual excesses described in Edward's books were indeed larger than life, the discovery I'd made in the old ladies' shop in Monte Carlo – and the idiot fantasies my writer's mind had woven around it – were certainly stranger than anything in the books. To say baldly, on the other hand, that I discovered my boss was into S&M doesn't quite convey the *flavour* of the event. Which is one of the reasons I'm writing this book.

Edward himself was pretty nice about it, especially

when he realized who it was that 'rescued' him.

He wasn't all that embarrassed, for a start, which helped to suppress the awkwardness I felt at my own naive and oafish behaviour. Once I was wise to the fact that he was not in Paris as advertized, and why, there was nothing I wanted more than to get out of there, fast. For the first time, I really *felt* that old cliché about wishing the earth would open and swallow one up.

But – perhaps because he figured it might help to overcome my confusion, perhaps to lessen his own – Edward insisted on a cards-on-the-table, matter of fact approach to the whole thing: we would discuss the mistake coolly, like grown-ups, rather as if I had inadvertently broken an ornament in his home or nudged his car with my bumper in a parking lot. Embarrassing, but no big deal.

Much the same thing had happened once when I was writing for a newspaper. I was working late and I barged into the Editor's office to recover a file I'd left there earlier, to find him crouched in his swivel chair, with his secretary, bare to the waist, squatting in the kneehole of his desk with his cock in her mouth.

Red-faced and stammering an apology, I was about to withdraw when the man said: 'No, no. That's all right. Just so long as it's understood that Eileen is my *personal assistant* as well as being a *private* secretary.'

Message received and understood. I never breathed it to a soul . . . and I kept my job.

Edward didn't make some excuse to fire me either. He was very decent about what must have given him quite a jolt – his secret life discovered by an employee! When I sheepishly and in halting words offered to make up for my stupidity and fix him back in his leather shroud, he chuckled. 'Not to worry, old boy. Hearing you break in and move around, I thought: *Jesus, burglars! What if they find me?* And I dreamed up a scenario as scary as your own. That was quite enough anticipatory dread for one night!' He shook his head and laughed aloud. 'Imagine the old birds' stupefaction when they find out I've flown the coop! They'll think I'm a second bloody Houdini!'

'It's an odd sideline,' I said, desperately trying to make conversation, 'for a couple of old bags running a novelty shop in the Principality.'

'Not if you know the score,' Edward told me. 'A good few years ago they ran a specialized whorehouse in Cannes. Making up fetishist gear for old clients is a way, I guess, of keeping the ancient hands in. Gives them the feeling that life hasn't passed them by, maybe.'

'I thought you were in Paris,' I began. 'I'd *never* have—'

'You were supposed to think that,' he interrupted. Velvet, he said, *was* in Paris, where she had interests of her own. They had a *very* free relationship. 'She knows about my . . . tastes,' Edward said. 'She understands them. If you spend your life publishing books about fucking, anything a little different is welcome. Or maybe it's because I'm having all the time to make decisions, and if you're sexually submissive the decisions are made by someone else. Whatever, she understands – but unfortunately she isn't actually into domination herself. And if you have to tell them what to do, it doesn't work: you're back to giving the orders, making the decisions therefore, yourself. So who's the sadist and who the masochist then?'

Edward sighed, unbuckling a strap that forced his genitals into a spiked leather penis corset. 'She sympathises,' he said, 'but the most I could ever get her to do was hold a whip and dress up in boots and leather while I photographed her in mistress poses!'

When he was back in civilian clothes, we let ourselves out of the shop, swallowed a couple of café-cognacs at the nearest bar, and then walked back to our respective cars.

So it was fact or fiction all the way, that particular day. But there's another truism pairing neatly with that one in the philosophical writer's handbook.

Metaphorically speaking, was the secret I had stumbled upon art imitating life . . . or life imitating art?

You tell me.

I had visited St Tropez for a special conference (should we republish *The Wife-Swappers' Syndicate* with the names of the characters changed?) on the day that it rained.

Bad weather had been forecast on both radio and television, hastening towards the Coast from Corsica, but nobody took much notice: the met man had got it wrong again; it never rained on the Riviera at this time of year, not in the seventies.

When the ten-tenths cloud cover which had blotted out the sea reached the mainland, it unleashed a deluge, a real tempest. Unseasonal hailstorms destroyed more than a hundred glasshouses between Antibes and Vallauris; ninety-miles-per-hour gusts of wind toppled construction cranes and overturned a bus; in Nice, huge waves scattered half a shingle beach across the Promenade des Anglais.

When the downpour became so heavy that the wipers were unable to clear the screen and I could no longer see the road, I pulled off the autoroute and parked under a clump of threshing pines in a lay-by.

We were between St Raphael and Cannes, on the lower slopes of the wooded Esterel massif. Beyond the wire perimeter fence of the rest area, the undulating green

of a golf course rolled away beneath the pelting rain. I
could make out a waterlogged fairway, a couple of flooded
bunkers, and a dispirited group of people sheltering under
striped umbrellas themselves covered by the spreading
branches of parasol pines. They looked pretty wet just the
same. There seemed to be quite a crowd, and I realized
suddenly that this must be the new course that Leggy
Peggy and her professional companions had come south
to inaugurate. Indeed, squinting through the stair-rods of
rain, I thought I could distinguish her blonde head among
the collection of caddies, spectators and other golfers.
Above most of them in fact, for I remembered Peggy was
as tall as I was. The shoulder-length hair was topped, of
all things, by a heavy tweed deerstalker hat!

From what I could see, two separate foursomes and a
handful of officials had joined the members of the public
sheltering beneath these particular pines. There was also
a lady press photographer, still snapping the drenched
refugees from the storm.

God knows what prompted me to quit the haven of the
Alfa's driving seat and join them. Maybe it was the memory
of the animal sexuality distilled from the American
sportswoman's athletic body; perhaps it was just because
it was becoming a spot claustrophobic, sitting there
listening to the rain drumming on the roof and wondering
if the bloody rain would ever stop. At all events, scarcely
realizing I had actually made the decision, I manoeuvred
myself into a plastic raincoat I kept in the car just in case,
crammed an old tugboat skipper's cap on my head, and
abandoned myself to nature in the raw. I squeezed through
a gap where the wire fence had been trodden down and
squelched down a slant of rough towards the parasol
pines.

Before I had gone ten yards, the cap was a sodden wreck, my trouser legs were plastered coldly to my calves, my shoes were awash and water was cascading down inside the plastic to soak my jacket. By the time I reached the trees, my face was stinging under the assault of the rain.

Peggy saw me coming and broke free of the group to run out and offer me a wet cheek to kiss. 'My Gard,' she cried, 'you shoulda stayed in Paris where the weather's fine! What in hell are you doing here, man?'

'Looking for a lady to take home,' I said on the spur of the moment. 'I guess this round's kind of abandoned, yes?'

'I should say.' Tossing her head, she glanced up into the black sky, twitching the peak of the ridiculous tweed hat as she did so. 'Impossible to play another hole until someone yanks out the bloody plug and lets this lot drain away!' She swept out a dismissive arm to indicate the entire sodden countryside. The photographer crouched down to get an upward angle on the gesture, and I saw, within the tightly belted, shiny outline of a black mackintosh that it was Helen Chalmers, the press agency type I'd met at Edward's party.

Peggy herself was once more wearing the brown leather jeans, almost black now with moisture, and a proofed bomber jacket laced up to the throat. 'It's not that I mind the round being scrubbed,' she complained. 'It's only an exhibition match anyway, and we're working for a straight fee. But this is the ninth hole we're on, and it's damned nearly a mile back to the clubhouse.'

She stared up at the steadily dripping branches. Another tweak to the deerstalker; another whirr and click from Helen's Speed Graphic. 'I'm getting kinda cheesed off with this scenic oasis. On the other hand' – a heavy shrug; one more click – 'the thought of an up-and-down mile in *this* . . .' She shook her head.

'That's why I'm here,' I improvised. 'At the top of that slope of rough, beneath those other pines: Madam your carriage awaits. Why not let me take you back to your hotel – stopping off at my place on the way for a dram of something wet and warming?'

'Swell!' Peggy crowed. 'That'd be just dandy. But do you have room for three? Helen here's been hired to cover my whole day.'

'My pleasure,' I said.

I'd poured out the malt and gone into my kitchen to whip up an omelette when I heard the girlish laughter. I leaned back to peer around the door.

The two whisky glasses were empty. My two guests, each stark naked, were entwined on the ottoman, one pair of spread thighs with a dark head between them, the other with a blonde. From somewhere between the softly heaving matrix of two bellies and four breasts, a contented, lapping murmuration emerged.

I coughed. 'With mixed herbs, cheese or plain?' I asked. 'The omelette, I mean.'

Leggy Peggy – she was the one on top – momentarily raised her head. 'You did say warm and wet,' she reminded me. 'And our clothes after all were *cold* and wet. We thought this might do by way of what you might call an entrée.'

'No sweat,' I said. 'I mean like be my guests. It's nice work if you can get it!'

'And you can get it if you try,' Helen completed the song line from somewhere underneath.

'Mixed herbs, I think,' Peggy said. The blonde head burrowed down again.

I went back into the kitchen.

When I returned with plates, knives, forks, a tossed green salad and a large, folded omelette – in an entrée dish, naturally – I was wearing a plastic apron just long enough to cover my genitals . . . and nothing else.

The two young women sat up, each with her pubic hair damp and a little matted.

'If it wasn't essential to eat an omelette while it was piping hot,' Helen observed, 'I'd be inclined to go in for a spot of prospecting.'

I grinned. I'd chosen the apron specially because it was decorated with a picture of the machinery at the head of a mine shaft. 'Experimental bores can be drilled when the factory whistle blows,' I said. 'Unless you insist on afters.'

'I was rather hoping,' Helen said, 'that you would be the afters.'

I was, too. No sooner were the plates cleaned and the third shots of malt sunk than the two of them got up, walked across the room, and perched, one on each of the padded arms of the easy chair in which I sat.

Above my crotch, the thick shiny plastic was already peaking visibly into a discernible mound. 'Interesting,' Peggy said. 'Despite the picture, there's definitely something surfacing here.' She leaned forward and closed a forefinger and thumb tightly over the protuberance.

My breath hissed in sharply. I could feel the blood that stiffened my cock pulsing against her grip. Cool air flowing in under the uprisen apron played on my heated, swollen shaft.

'Perhaps we should investigate?' Helen said. 'I didn't

114

hear a whistle, but the man did say experimental, didn't he?'

'Why not? And he certainly did say that.'

Peggy's grip relaxed. She grasped one of the lower corners of the apron. They exchanged glances as Helen picked up the other. Very slowly, they lifted the plastic away from me and peered beneath.

I couldn't see, of course: the apron, held there, screened my own crotch from my view. But somehow, with a throbbing erection as tall as a tower and the whole staff quivering, the wrinkled flesh of the scrotum tight against my balls below, I felt more *naked* than I'd ever felt before in my life. My breath, hoarse and deep, was coming very fast.

'Ye-es, very in-teresting,' Peggy said again. 'I think we could make use of that, don't you? One way or another.'

'It looks perfectly serviceable to me,' Helen agreed.

She inclined her body inwards to lean against me. One of her breasts, small, tight, with very large nipples, brushed my upper arm. She was one of those hardbitten journalist types with a lean, lived-in face and a lithe, sinewy body that you knew at once would be matching you thrust for thrust in bed, the hard, urgent, no-nonsense reciprocator whose cries when she came would be bitten off as sharply as a stifled sneeze.

Suddenly she was nibbling the lobe of my ear. Small, firm, very even white teeth teasing the flesh . . . and then, with a roaring burst of sensation, the hot, hot tongue wetly invading, the secret channels violated by that muscled and probing intruder as forcefully as a cunt by a cock. There was warm breath fanning my neck; I could hear nothing but the amplified slurping of that lingual assault.

I could feel, though. Beneath the apron, Peggy's hand

was toying with my stiffened shaft, skimming the tightened flesh up and down the solid core with practised ease. Helen's tight breast was crammed against my arm. Huge waterfalls thundered inside my head.

Abruptly the lean brunette separated herself. The tongue withdrew, leaving my ear tingling and damp as the cool air played on the heated skin. Helen was breathing hard and fast, air jetting through flared nostrils as she gasped out: 'God, it's *ears*! What they do to me. I've got a thing about them, honest!'

'No kidding!' Peggy sounded amused. She was kneading the distended flesh crowning my cock-head. 'Just what *do* they do for you, honey?'

'Christ, they're so *sexy*,' Helen panted. 'I don't know – it's the contrast between the tender, fleshy softness of the lobe and the gristly, whorled complications against the tongue when it's in there, pushing.' She shook her head, laughing. 'The thought of it sends shivers right down through me; I feel as if someone smacked me on the mons!'

'Well, yeah, sure,' Peggy said. 'I guess I feel like that about cocks. But ears? Well, maybe I ought to try. I mean just for kicks. There's a spare one this side after all.'

All at once tongues raped my head right and left. I was deafened by the hot, wet, swarming impact of the twin attacks. Two different hands now savaged my genitals, but I was lost to the waves crashing through the middle of my head to drown my brain.

My own hands were tucked meekly down between the arms and the cushion of the chair I was sitting in. I just hung in there and let them get on with it.

Aural sex, eh?

Before long, however, nature took over. Both of the

harpies, after all, were naked; each had been masterfully stimulated by the tongue, teeth and fingertips of the other . . . and we had also sunk a fair amount of the malt.

It was Peggy at first – perhaps finding the male ear less intriguing than her photographer – who called the shots.

'I don't want to miss out on *anything*,' she said briskly. 'I have a press conference at six. The hotel's no more than five minutes away; ten at the most. So between now and five fifty I aim for us to go through the whole book – anything that can be done between three people, two chicks and a guy, we're gonna do it. And I do mean anything. Okay?'

'*Anything?*' The second tongue was withdrawn to form the question.

'Anything at all.'

'Oh boy!' Helen said.

It started off with her kneeling in front of the chair with her upper half along the cushion. Peggy was already sitting in the chair with her legs draped over Helen's back – so guess where the photographer's mouth was, and what it was doing. At the same time, kneeling too, I threaded my bursting cock in and out of the wet and gaping slit visible amongst the dark pubic hair between the clenched cheeks of Helen's backside. If Peggy leaned forward and I stretched up while I thrust away, our mouths could mash together and we could kiss. In this way each of us had two sexual areas attended to: the cock and the mouth for me, mouth and cunt for each of the girls.

Peggy soon changed all that. Just as the warm clasp of Helen's inner flesh was about to milk me to a spurting climax, we were heaved away from the chair and all the positions were reversed – or at least everyone now had a different portion of someone else to stimulate and be excited by. We were still centred on the chair. But this time I was sitting in it again, Peggy was on her hands and knees in front of me, furiously sucking my cock . . . and Helen? Well, she was perched on the padded back of the chair, half kneeling and half squatting, so that my face was buried between her thighs and she could lean forward and down over my chest, supporting herself with one hand on the chair arm. The other hand, at the full stretch of her free arm, was plunged between Peggy's buttocks.

For me this was a doddle. I was comfortably supported. Peggy, as she had told me when we first me, gave great head. Helen's thin-lipped cunt was muscularly active, and my mouth and tongue roved through fascinating explorations of her dark, tight and secret inner canal. I was, as you might say, sitting pretty.

But the position was less easy to maintain for my two partners. Clamped between my jerking thighs as her wet-lipped, bobbing head squelched up and down my rigid staff, Peggy laboured under the inverted weight of Helen along her back as her belly and hips writhed and gyrated under the marauding fingers teasing labia and anus. And the photographer herself, belly quivering as I sucked and probed, was hard put to it to maintain her precarious balance while her wet fingers worked.

After only a few minutes, Peggy disengaged herself, crawling out from under, as it were, and went to refresh our drinks. Helen and I stayed where we were – except that now she was able to use both hands to support herself on the arms of the chair. I kept on gobbling as she bent further over and took my cock in her mouth.

When at last we separated, Peggy had drained her glass. Pushing me back against the cushions as I was about to struggle up, she fed me a slug of whisky and then turned over to lower herself onto my still upstanding prick.

I already explained the extraordinary sensuality distilled by this young woman's not really beautiful body. But I cannot describe the ecstatic quality of the particular thrill that flamed through me the moment the hot weight of that heavy pelvis slid down the greased pole of my own desire. Taut buttocks grounded against my hipbones, the muscles of her athletic waist and belly contracted and relaxed, my throbbing cock was swallowed whole.

Levering herself up with her hands on the arms of the chair, and then allowing her body to subside again, Peggy fucked me with a slow and drawn-out pumping action that rendered me delirious with lust. My hands clenched on her breasts; my tongue speared between her lips as she twisted her head to kiss me, still rising and falling in that trancelike sucking clasp of cunt and cock.

Helen this time, contenting herself at first by gleefully watching, finally adopted a role that was purely active.

On her knees again between my spread thighs, she placed her hands on Peggy's hips and then thumbed apart the creased folds of the sexual lips engulfing my thrusting tool. She bent forward then and jerked me into the deepest penetration yet by taking my balls in her mouth.

In this position the two of us were wide open to her invading mouth. She licked and lapped, sucking and nibbling the underside of my cock each time Peggy raised herself and withdrew, transferring lips and tongue to the inflamed, distended labia, drawing the erect clitoris between her teeth each time the loins with their blonde thatch were lowered and the shaft was swallowed again.

That was when Peggy came for the first time.

And that was it as far as the chair was concerned. It

was on the ottoman (shades of Susan!) that we arranged ourselves next.

My recollection of what happened from then on is a little clouded, but I remember Peggy was still quaking from the force of that shuddering orgasm as we collapsed on the padded top. I was lucky not to have come myself under the galvanized assault of that threshing body, but I was keen to save myself for the next scene – one that I was determined to stage myself.

I lay on my back along the ottoman, positioned Helen over my hips, facing my feet, and then impaled her from behind, forcing her to bend forward sideways so that she could suck Peggy, who was lying on her back beside me, with her pelvis canted Helen's way for easier access. As the scene developed, she swung over a thigh to clamp her photographer's dark head.

The circle was completed as I raised myself on one arm and twisted to join my mouth with Peggy's. Our hands were free to rove, but I couldn't tell you exactly where they were or what each was doing to whom. I only know that one of mine was forced to grasp my own cock, so that it would stay inside Helen's thrusting cunt, holding it there at a down-thrust angle as our coupled bodies writhed and squirmed.

Soon the wordless gasps and groans of mutually expressed desire were climbing to a three-part crescendo. The bucking, quaking contortions straining our linked breasts and bellies became more spasmodic; fingers plunged and tweaked and stroked and grasped; exposed flesh quivered as breaths were sharply caught.

And it was Helen's turn to be triggered to climax. Her stomach tightened and convulsed. Buried deeply somewhere in her jerking loins, an accelerating shudder manifested itself, increasing in power and speed until her whole frame shook furiously under the force of its impact. She choked back a gasping cry, then pounded the sides of the ottoman with clenched fists as she voiced that monumental release with a low, muffled, keening cry.

I was almost over the top myself, but in fact we had changed positions several times again before I came. If I attempted to tell you what those positions were – who did what and with which and to whom, as the old story goes – I would be using such skill as I have as an inventive writer rather than my memory. The rest of that stormy afternoon passed in a blur of twitching limbs as each of us thrilled in agonized ecstasy at the touch of the others. I only know that in the end I was on my back on the floor.

Rain beat on the windows in time with the hammering of my heart. The girls squatted over me, one at each end, all four hands working my pulsing genitals as I arched up with a great shout and shot my load, splashing the breasts and bellies poised above me with the squirted gouts of my white-hot delight.

We made the hotel, at one minute past six. Miss Metford conducted her press conference with total aplomb, the coolest thing since cucumbers. My God, I thought, watching the sports writers scribble and snap, if only they *knew*!

Chapter Nine

Velvet – Mrs Edward, always, to me – was a 1930s Hollywood sex queen restored to life.

She had big, heavy breasts with a pliant waist and billowy hips. A luscious scarlet mouth and a swaying walk that was the perfect foil for that sleepy southern drawl. She was wonderful, straight out of the original mould.

Even in the mornings, Velvet wore dresses with scooped-out necklines of the kind I thought nobody ever wore outside of the movies. The creamy slopes swelling above the low-cut tops she poured herself into in the afternoons were so expansive that I wondered once whether she actually had any nipples: there didn't seem room below the exposed flesh for anything more to hide in.

That was before I saw her at the pool in a swimsuit. She had nipples all right.

Privately, I thought Edward was out of his mind, fooling around with whips and chains and leather gear when he had this sex-bomb waiting at home in bed. But it takes, as I said more than once, all sorts.

Another private thought I had centred on Velvet herself.

Edward had said she 'understood', but didn't share his arcane tastes. Had she, I wondered, anything of her own, in whatever direction that might be, to match her husband's esoteric sex life?

There wasn't the slightest thought, I promise – not the faintest fantasy – of imagining myself in any way connected. Rule One in the game of life: do *not* aspire to lay the wife of the man who writes the cheques. Indeed it was because Edward's original choice, Ronald Stokes-Alberry, had done precisely that, that I was now in the position of receiving the cheques myself. Admittedly Ronald hadn't made a pass actually at Velvet, but he had propositioned the girlfriend of Edward's contact, the genial Lafayette Briggs, which came to much the same thing. I mean like O – U – T . . . *out!*

Another thing I had wondered, on and off, was just who that girlfriend was. My yacht skipper friend had merely identified her as 'the' secretary.

Miriam? Sonia? Or was Lafayette sweet on some girl who had worked for Expadink before?

What did it matter? It was a trap I myself was always careful to avoid.

So far as Velvet was concerned, I restricted myself to wondering. The answer, when it came, was in reply to a question I hadn't really permitted myself to ask.

I was in St Trop again, delivering the final draft of my second dog book, *Major's Lost Weekend*. I had sweated blood over this damned story, and there were a couple of things I wanted to check with my editor Mabel – or if necessary Edward himself – before I started on *Teenage Victims*.

The office was empty. The girls were out to lunch. There was no sign of Mabel, and I could see through the open window that the other two editors, Mabel's astro-physicist boyfriend and Randall Van Eyck, were lying beside the pool with frosted glasses of beer in their hands. It was a windless day, with a hard sun blazing down from a blue sky dark with heat.

I didn't want to hang around until the lunch hour was over – which could be anything up to three o'clock – so I thought I'd whip upstairs and put the question to Edward himself. It was non-specific, purely a matter of principle: even if they were eating, it would only take a minute; all I had to do was excuse the intrusion, frame the problem, and wait for a yes or no. I took the lift up to the penthouse.

Rather to my surprise, the polished teak door with its stainless steel fittings was ajar. Without really thinking – I was a family familiar now anyway – I pushed it open and went into the apartment.

Most villas, flats, workrooms and offices on the Riviera are floored with wood, quarry-tiles or stone, the more expensive ones with marble or terrazzo. Edward and Velvet, clinging perhaps to their origins, had chosen deep-pile wall-to-wall carpet in pearly grey. My footsteps were silent, therefore, as I traversed the hallway and walked down the long corridor, past closed bedroom and bathroom doors, to the wide open-plan living and dining area that fronted the terraced roof garden.

Marble floors, even those strewn with rugs, harden and amplify the acoustics of a room. Fitted carpets tend to swallow the sounds. I didn't hear the voices, therefore, until I was almost there: Mabel's clipped Bostonian, Velvet's drawl, no evidence yet of mid-Atlantic Edward.

I was about to call out and announce my presence when I realized that there was a certain muffled quality to those voices, Mabel's especially, that was not entirely due to the fitted carpets.

I froze in mid-step.

I was perhaps fifteen feet from the door, and this one too was ajar. Through the six-inch gap I could see a pier glass not far from the picture window leading to the roof garden. And reflected in this glass were the images of Velvet and Mabel on a corn-coloured *chaise longue*. The mirror also contributed a supplementary item of information.

Mabel's voice was muffled because her face was buried between Velvet's naked breasts, Velvet's because her mouth was lowered to Mabel's hair.

I turned, about to steal away . . . and halted again when I heard Velvet say, clearly and sharply now: '*It's Tony! Y'all better come right in, honey!*'

I had forgotten that when a mirror image is facing you directly, the subject can at times see you as clearly as you see the subject. I must have made some slight sound as I turned; Velvet had raised her head in the direction of the noise – and glimpsed my hovering shape behind the partly open door.

I swallowed. I was back in the newspaper editor's office. Red-faced and sheepish as hell, I slunk into that room. 'I'm most *terribly* sorry,' I mumbled. 'I didn't know . . . I mean I didn't have the slightest intention—' I choked. 'I wanted to see Edward,' I said lamely. 'The door was open, you see, and I . . .' My voice died helplessly away.

'Open?' Mabel exclaimed. 'God, how careless can one be?'

'Edward's in Paris,' Velvet said briskly. 'Really in Paris this time. Frank Maddox beckoned and gave a tug on the leash. Come in, Tony: there's liquor on the buffet; fix yourself a drink. You can freshen ours while you're about it.'

Dazedly, I crossed the room. There was nothing more I could do.

In those few seconds I had taken in the scene. Bright flowers and polished leaves trembled in the heat outside the wide glass open windows. Beyond the roof garden balustrade, a sliver of sparkling sea separated a wooded rise from a line of hills blue with distance. And inside the room, sunlight streaming from the south caressed the bodies of the two women dramatically exposed among the amber curves of the chaise-longue.

I remained astounded by this splendid, if totally unexpected, sight.

It was almost too like a stage set, you see, or a carefully dressed and posed group in an artist's studio. Mabel, for instance, so neat and prim with her little dark suits in the office, was wearing nothing but underclothes – and sexy, provocative ones at that. Above the waist, her breasts were clasped snugly within the hooped cups of a lacy black *corsetière* known as a 'Merry Widow'. The lower part of this garment was stretched along the top of each thigh into black suspenders tightly drawing black silk stockings up her elegant legs – not tights but real stockings with dark seams scaling the calves. Her feet were thrust into patent leather court shoes with stiletto heels that must have been four inches high. Black, of course. Scarlet ribbons tied into tiny bows decorated the frilled suspender elastics, and her hair was caught back by a wide silk bow of the same colour.

She had been kneeling when I first saw her, but now that she was sitting next to Velvet on the chaise-longue I could see that the curved line linking the two suspenders at the lower end of the belt was not desecrated by panties, above or below: within the arch of stretch material a plane of pale, flat belly was visible, and then again the dark, springy hairs thatching her crotch.

127

The erotic picture so shamelessly suggested by this was so at variance with the businesslike young woman I knew professionally that at first I scarcely had the time to revel in the semi-nudity of the luscious Velvet.

I had picked up two glasses from the floor and now, having found a clean one for myself, I allowed my eyes covertly to linger as I busied myself with vodka, ice, lemon, and whisky for myself.

No bra was needed to support the magnificently swelling mounds of flesh tautly projecting from Velvet's rib-cage: solid but supple, heavy yet weightless in their thrusting outline, these superb tributes to mother nature – dark nipples and areolas included – eclipsed anything the writers of Edward's books, myself included, could throw up on the printed page.

I could well understand why Mabel had buried her face between them.

Beneath the breasts there was a soft, almost slack curve of naked belly. And then a gauzy, diaphanous cloud of material, shadowed only by a darker triangle between the thighs, falling to the ankles. Barefoot, Velvet had clothed her lower half in Turkish harem trousers which suited her heavy body perfectly. She was the only person I ever saw whose toenails were a perfect, symmetrical shape. Both these and her fingernails were painted a shining gold.

'The thing,' she said when I had been persuaded to sit down, 'is . . .' She shook her head. 'How to explain?'

'You don't have to explain,' I said. I was still dreadfully embarrassed. 'It was all a terrible mistake. I mean . . . well, I'm not a voyeur, a Peeping Tom. It was just that I wasn't thinking, I—'

'There you have it,' Velvet interrupted. 'Voyeurs, gays, trannies, fetishists of one kind or another, folks into SM or CP. Everybody wants to do his or her own thing. I allow Edward as much freedom as he wants to indulge his kinky jinks . . . I know you know all about that; he told me.'

'Oh, God,' I said wretchedly. 'Another *awful* mistake. I felt such a fool.'

'On the contrary. Believing what you believed – a natural enough mistake in the circumstances – I think you were very brave. Resourceful too. Edward was impressed.'

I made no reply to that.

'Since you happened upon our . . . lunchtime scene,' Velvet continued, 'I'll tell you that, in the way of specialized tastes, I *am* in fact a voyeur. Not of Edward's scene, unfortunately. Of sex. For me, sex isn't something you do – not if you want to get off on it; it's something you watch other people do. That's what turns me really on, the purely visual aspect. Especially, if I'm to be truthful, if the folks doing it are mainly gays.'

So the gorgeous Velvet was not only a peeper herself, but also basically *une gouine*, a lesbian. Fascinating. I remained silent, eager to know what revelations were coming next.

'Mabel here and I can help each other, you see,' Velvet drawled. 'It thrills *me* to see her dressed like this; *I* can help *her* some because of relationship trouble—'

Mabel was looking me in the face. 'With Edgar,' she interrupted, addressing me directly for the first time, 'my physical relationship is zero. I no longer exist.'

'That's tough,' I said. If you can think of a better line, let me know.

'He's more interested in the mating dances of chromosomes than the reactions of real people their genes create,' Mabel said viciously. 'If I dress up like this and he actually notices, he just says, "Oh? Are we going out tonight?"'

'That's not exactly the reaction I would have,' I said, more to make conversation than because I really meant it. That was my first mistake.

Velvet said: 'What *would* your reaction be, Tony, if you came home at the end of a day and found a girl dressed the way Mabel's dressed waiting for you?'

'Well,' I said truthfully, smiling at Mabel, 'I guess the first thing would be that I'd hope we *weren't* going out tonight!' That was my second mistake.

'Exactly!' Velvet said. She swallowed a mouthful of vodka. 'I don't know if you ever have this feeling,' she said to me, 'but – perhaps it's because I *am* at heart a voyeur – I think so often, looking at folks the way one does at social gatherings: I wonder what he or she would look like, standing or sitting there, if only one could imagine away, as it were, all their clothes and see them quite naked.' She laughed. 'The nude persona isn't always what you'd expect from the image you're presented with when people are dressed, is it?'

She looked at me inquiringly, clearly expecting an answer.

'Well,' I said awkwardly, 'I suppose not. But, yes, I have had that kind of thought from time to time. Especially if the gathering's a boring one. You get some surprises, too, if it ever happens that . . . well, you know.'

'Sometimes, though, the surprises are pleasant,' Velvet said, still looking at me. 'But, for me at any rate, the thought tends to come principally when I'm looking at people who are especially impressive – or especially dumb. What do you think?'

I found myself in a bit of a spot here. I thought I knew

what was coming. It didn't take an Einstein to read the steps. Verification seemed to be provided by the fact that . . . well, it seemed incredible, but Mabel was already breathing rather fast.

'Of course, I'm in no position to tell you what to do . . .' Velvet began. And I thought, Oh, yes? Because that was precisely the position she *was* in. Not only because I had gate-crashed her private scene but because she was the boss's wife – and a pro or a con from such a lady customarily meant that an employee either kept or lost his job, according to whether she handed out the bouquets or put in the poison when his name came up.

It was Mabel's turn to leave a sentence unfinished. She killed the rest of her drink in a single gulp and rose to refill the glass. 'If it was feasible in some way to bring a touch of joy both to Velvet and to me,' she began without taking her eyes from mine. 'But, God, I wouldn't want . . .'

'I can think of a way,' I said lightly. 'And you wouldn't be.'

I knew, at that stage, that the situation must be handled decisively, the bull taken by the horns and no hesitation allowed to intrude. This was no time for sensitivity: the delicate approach would seem – and be – insincere; the scene could so easily degenerate into awkwardness and bathos. Above all, the atmosphere must remain jokey: a pretence of sudden uncontrollable desire would ridicule both myself and my editor.

I pulled the lightweight tee-shirt I was wearing over my head. 'Allow me,' I said to Velvet, 'to bring a third dimension to your collection of imaginary nudes!'

I kicked off my sandals and unbuckled the waist of my white jeans.

Thank God for hot weather and few clothes. Another

rule of life obeyed here: a man without trousers whose upper half is still clothed invariably looks ridiculous, a totally un-sexy figure of fun, particularly if he still wears shoes and socks. When stripping before a lady, men, *always* leave the pants until last.

With what I hoped was a single lithe movement, I stepped out of the jeans.

Unfortunately, a heel caught in the narrow exit from one leg and I lost balance, stumbled and fell. I ended up on my back in front of Velvet, crotch fully exposed, one leg in the air flying the jeans like a flag at half-mast.

She uttered a shout of laughter. Mabel too was giggling, though perhaps with a touch of embarrassment, and I – the original stout party collapsed – was naturally obliged to join in. I did say jokey, didn't I?

'Well, baby, you sure got something useful in there!' Velvet said, leaning down to peer between my splayed legs. My cock, which the foregoing conversation had already persuaded to stiffen and lengthen, lay heavily across the base of my belly. 'With a little persuasion' – she prodded the shaft with a pointing finger – 'I reckon that could be just what the doctor ordered. Mabel's doctor, anyway.'

The moment she touched me, the cock sprang to attention, quivering at its longest and hardest a couple of inches above my flesh.

In fact my undignified tumble was no bad thing; it got us over the initial hump – three people not previously intimate had been theorizing; now, willy-nilly, they were into the practical; like it or not, the scene had started. And my cock, certainly, judging from the tightness at my loins, was raring to go!

I didn't get up. That might have put the clock back to

zero. Thankful at least there was visible evidence that could be interpreted as desire, I remained on my back supported on one elbow, my cock, darkly suffused and stiff as a pole, throbbing between my thighs. I held out my free hand. 'Come on down,' I said to Mabel. 'There's no water . . . yet . . . but the weather's fine!' I rolled over into a bar of sunlight and held the shaft vertical with one hand.

She licked her lips, then held out her own hand and allowed me to pull her down. The carpet, warm in the sun, was soft as a dream.

Now that the cameras were rolling, as it were, Mabel threw Bostonian decorum out the window. She lay on her back, spread her legs and drew up her knees. The silk stockings gleamed in the bright light. Above the sleek fit of the corselet, lacy cups thrust up her breasts. The high heels shone above the grey pile.

Bending her knees had drawn the lower edge of the suspender belt a little away from the flesh of her loins, exposing more pubic hair. I could see that she was wet: a pink crescent glistened in the centre of the dark bush. The heat emanating from her rivalled the sun's rays.

Reaching out one hand she seized my throbbing cock. 'I want to feel that in me,' she said harshly. 'Right inside. Right now.'

'With a body like yours,' I said, careful not to let her think it was the sexy gear that turned me on, 'that's no sweat, baby!' I turned over onto my hands and knees, leaving the shaft still firmly in her grasp.

On the chaise-longue, Velvet had drawn up her legs under her and settled back against a pile of cushions. A hand and forearm had vanished beneath the waistband of her harem pants. Beneath the flimsy material I saw movement at the crotch.

I crouched between Mabel's splayed legs, put a hand on either side of her corseted hips and lowered myself to the floor. I didn't really need the guiding hand to direct that part of me now so eager to penetrate, but it was clearly part of her private pleasure, so I waited until the distended glans nudged the warm wet folds of flesh and then flexed my hips and lunged.

In a single swift glide I was in up to the hilt, swallowed in the burning clasp of Mabel's tight but well-oiled cunt, her inner muscles clamped hotly around the stem of my thrusting staff.

She gave a choked cry, arching fiercely up against me as I withdrew and slammed it in again. I felt the sheer silk sheathing her ankles hard against my hipbones. We settled at once into that furious, almost ferocious, rhythm when both partners are seized by an urge to fuck that is virtually uncontrollable – two bodies driven by the demon lust in a reciprocating frenzy that knows no direction but onwards, no command that isn't faster . . . deeper . . . harder . . .

Mabel came almost at once. She must have been deeply frustrated sexually. Suddenly she was hissing like a snake. Or a boiling kettle about to blow its lid.

What she blew was her top.

The stiletto heels raked my calves; frantic fingers clenched on the flesh of my waist; the cheeks of her bottom smacked the floor as her pelvis rose and fell ungovernably and the spasms shuddering her belly forced inarticulate cries from her open mouth.

All I could do was hang in there, rigid, and hope that my cock wouldn't be snapped off like a carrot by these tempestuous exertions.

Christ, it was quite a performance! Eventually I rolled over onto my back and held her off me a little. Then she was all at once articulate again; 'More!' she gasped. 'I must have more. Do it to me again. Fuck me, screw me, make me come again and again!'

Velvet was off the chaise-longue, on her hands and knees on the floor. One hand and knees that is: the knuckles of the other hand were still hidden by the Turkish pants, the thin stuff rising and falling as they worked the flesh at the junction of her thighs. 'That's right, Tony,' she panted. 'Give it to her again; she can't get enough of it. Screw the ass off her!'

By now the penny had dropped right in and I thought I knew the score. This was a regular scene for them, perhaps one of many, and there was a scenario to be followed. 'All right, bitch,' I said to Mabel. 'Hands and knees for you too. Get down there and wait while I bull you like a cow brought to stud!'

Groaning deep within her chest, she obeyed. Velvet's eyes were very bright.

I sat back on my heels. I had begun to enjoy myself. 'I shall fuck you now until you come again,' I said. 'After that, at once, I shall sit back again like this and you will back up and lower your cunt onto my cock, screwing until I tell you to stop. Is that clear?'

Kneeling, she looked around over her shoulder to see my glistening cock spearing up from between my thighs. 'Yes,' she gasped. 'Oh, yes . . .!'

I plunged forward and stabbed it into her, pistoning in and out with all my force, hips splatting against her quivering bottom until she did come again. She was sobbing now. Her hair had come loose and hung over her face. Her breasts had been jerked out of the Merry Widow . . . and there was a rivulet of sweat trickling between her buttocks.

The harem pants were around Velvet's knees. She was kneeling up with both hands scrabbling at her inflamed cunt, wanking furiously as she swayed to and fro and the great breasts swung on her chest. Her mouth hung open and a thread of saliva had dropped to polish one nipple.

I slapped Mabel's bottom, hard, the marks of my fingers livid on the taut flesh. 'I said at once,' I grated. '*Now!*'

'Oh, no,' she pleaded tearfully. 'Not at once. Please . . .'

I slapped again, harder still. 'Now.'

Shaking, she shuffled back and impaled herself on my shaft. My pulses were racing and I could sense the blood hammering behind my eyes. 'Fuck me, bitch!' I shouted.

She obeyed, drenching my thighs with her juices as the savaged cunt squelched faster and faster up and down the quivering shaft jutting below my belly.

We were interrupted this time before either of us rose to a climax. 'Oh, Jesus,' Velvet gasped, 'I do so love to watch it plowing in and out! Chuck her on the couch so I can see it in close-up from below.' She was on her feet, pulling us apart, the soft flesh of her heated belly curved only inches from my face. The harem pants had been thrown under a coffee table.

I knew better than to switch, tempting though that voluptuous pelvis was, much as I would have liked to explore for myself the wet folds pouting from the damp blonde thatch below. A voyeur was a voyeur, just that: the actors on stage did not intrude into the auditorium.

Mabel's limp body jerked and heaved as we picked her up between us, belly muscles fluttering and slack lips trembling.

We lowered her to the chaise-longue. She lay on her back, parallel to the padded rail along the rear, her head among the cushions piled against the slope at one end.

Her buttocks rested on the open end of the couch, legs draped over the rounded upholstery to the floor.

Velvet picked up the girl's ankles and raised her legs, bending them at the knee and then forcing them back until the silk-shadowed knees almost touched the erect nipples where they showed above Mabel's displaced corselet.

Forget, for the moment anyway, about love and affection and tenderness, I thought to myself: the tableau in that penthouse, back-lit by the sunshine streaming through the windows, was a natural for a painter or photographer seeking models for a work entitled 'Unbridled Lust'!

A naked man, cock-stand at the ready, eyes wide with a salacious gleam, watching two women – the blonde, fully-fleshed with ripe curves and heavy breasts, bent equally naked over a prone brunette wearing the whore's uniform of high heels, black stockings and a corset, splaying her legs obscenely to expose gaping labia beneath a raised suspender belt! There was everything anyone needed to know about lewdness and the lascivious in the pose of that group and the expressions on the faces of the participants.

'Go on, Tony,' Velvet urged hoarsely. 'Stand at the end there and ram it into her! Kneel if you like – but screw that cunt so that I can watch it plunge in and out!'

My head was buzzing. I was breathing alcohol and hot flesh and women scent and the smell of heated elastic. I moved in and positioned myself in front of those shamelessly spread thighs. Velvet was face down on the carpet, her chin supported on one hand, the other arm tucked beneath her. With her eager face only inches from the edge of the chaise-longue, she could look up to enjoy the closest of close-ups as my bunched and hairy balls drove the thick wet shaft of my cock between the coral lips of Mabel's cunt, driving them in as I sank to the hilt, sucking them pinkly into view again as I withdrew, only to bury them amongst the dark hairs once more as I lunged again. 'Okay, give it to her,' Velvet ordered.

'No!' Mabel protested feebly from the far end of the chaise-longue. 'Oh, no – please: no more now!'

'Give it to her!'

What was I to do? I was only an employee, the hired help, after all. I gave it to her.

Chapter Ten

I rolled three sheets of paper and two carbons into the typewriter, swallowed the last half of a cup of coffee and started to tap. I wrote:

The lighting in the night-club was low. Julian Merrett glanced over the rim of his champagne glass at the flushed faces of his young wife and his new employee. The boy would make a satisfactory PA all right. He was presentable, quite good-looking, and smart – intelligent enough, too, to sense when to keep quiet. Merrett drained the glass. And if he knew Sherry, the young man's usefulness wouldn't end there!

The three-piece on the stage had swung into a smoochy version of Stars Fell On Alabama. *'Why don't you two take a turn around the dance floor?' Merrett said. 'You know I can't perform with this game leg, and it seems a shame to waste good music. No, no, please . . . I insist.'*

Stammering excuses, Martin rose, eased back Sheridan Merrett's chair, and led her out onto the floor. It was quite crowded; it always was for slows. But Martin was astonished by the warmth with which the voluptuous young blonde curled herself into his arms, making sure – he was certain of it – that he was aware of the taut, full tips of her breasts thrusting against his chest.

*Although she had said very little, Martin had felt all
evening that the glamorous Mrs Merrett had been eyeing
him, weighing him up, almost. He had tried to pay it no
mind, but there was no ignoring the way she was pushing
herself into him now. Christ, he had better be careful! He
couldn't let a deal like this be ruined by some stupidity on
his part. He had never come across this kind of difficulty
with a client's wife before, and he wasn't sure how to
react. He knew he had to please them both – but if he
pleased her too much, and Merrett was certainly watching
from the table, he could blow the whole thing. He tried to
pull back a little, but Sherry only huddled closer,
whispering warmly into his ear: 'Don't be scared, Martin.
I won't bite you!'*

*Pushing forward harder, spreading her legs slightly so
that the mound of her crotch ground against the top of his
thigh, she laid her cheek against his. Her thigh was
pressed tightly between his own legs as they swung into a
slow turn. She had contacted the soft bulge of his genitals,
pressing deliberately against it as her warm breath played
on his ear.*

*Try as he would, Martin was unable to suppress the
faint stirring of his cock at her overt move. She felt it of
course. 'Surprise, surprise!' she whispered.*

*He swallowed. 'W-we shouldn't really be d-dancing
this close, Mrs Merrett,' he said hoarsely. 'It doesn't look
. . . I mean Julian might feel—'*

*'Julian won't feel anything but the glass against his
lips,' she interrupted. 'He won't suspect a thing. You
know I was the one who suggested you as his new PA.
I've watched you pass the house every morning and I . . .
well, I just had to find a way, to work it so that we could
be together.'*

'B-but I'm a married man!' he stammered. 'And you're married too.'

'That always makes it so much more exciting,' she murmured. 'Don't you agree?'

The music stopped before he could reply, and the leader announced an intermission. Back at the table, Julian Merrett said: 'You two looked good out there. Sexiest couple on the floor!' He laughed wryly. 'Sometimes the loss of this bloody leg hurts more than others.'

'Your wife is an excellent dancer, Mr Merrett,' Martin said stiffly.

'Good body too, eh? Prettiest showgirl at the Lido in Paris, not so long ago either.'

Martin flushed again, not quite sure what to say. 'Don't mind Julian.' Sherry came to his rescue. 'He gets carried away when it's champagne time. He likes to think of himself as the 1970s Don Juan.' She laughed. 'You'd better watch that cute little wife of yours when she gets back from her Mum's!'

Martin winced inwardly at the mention of Jean in this context. Even though he had landed the job, she didn't have to become involved personally with these people, and the way things had gone in the last few minutes, he wasn't sure that he wanted her to. 'I think Mr Merrett looks as though he could handle himself pretty well so far as women are concerned,' he said diplomatically, forcing a smile.

A waiter stood by the table. 'Telephone for you, Mr Merrett. They said it was urgent.'

Julian pushed back his chair and stood up. 'Be right back,' he said before he limped away. 'No footie-footie under the table while I'm gone!'

'You'll have to excuse Julian,' Sherry apologized. 'I'm afraid he's—'

'I think he's fine,' Martin said. 'And of course I don't take him seriously when he's in this jokey mood.'

She stared at him for a moment, her eyes luminous in the low-key lighting. Then she smiled. 'You'd better be taking *me* seriously,' she said softly. 'I mean what I say, and I'm going to get you at the first possible opportunity.'

'Sherry, you've got to be joking!' he said in sudden panic. 'Suppose, just suppose something did happen and Julian found out. I'd be out in a second!'

'I can handle Julian, darling,' she smiled. 'What you have to do is handle me!'

Martin was thankful to see his new employer return and put an end to this wordplay. It was a dangerous game, and one that he knew he shouldn't be playing. A man with business ambitions had better stay away from it. Right away.

Merrett's face was grave. 'I've just heard from the factory in Toulouse,' he said. 'We've had a robbery and one of the night men's been shot. I have to get down there right away.'

Martin was on his feet. 'I'll come with you, sir. If I can be of any help?'

'No, no,' Merrett said. 'There's nothing you can do. I'm sorry to spoil your evening, kids, but there's no reason why you shouldn't stay here and enjoy the music. Have a good time. I'll drive out to the airport and take the Cessna to our field at Toulouse.' He paused. 'There's only one thing – I'm sorry, Martin, but I guess I'll have to ask you to call a cab and escort Sherry home for me.'

Martin was aghast. There was no protest he could possibly make. He sank back into his chair, stunned, the moment Merrett had left.

Sherry was smiling broadly. 'Someone up there is

> *answering my prayers!' she said.*
>
> *'But Mrs Merrett – Sherry – we* can't *do anything,'*
> *he pleaded. 'Not tonight. What if Julian came back*
> *unexpectedly?'*
>
> *'From Toulouse? Be your age, sweetie. He won't be*
> *back until tomorrow afternoon, and your wife's away.*
> *What better chance will we ever have?'*
>
> *'No,' Martin refused, suddenly obstinate. 'No way,*
> *and that's final. We can't do it and that's that. I could*
> *never face Julian or Jean again if we did.'*
>
> *'Just order us a couple of large brandies, darling,'*
> *Sherry said. 'And after that we can talk about the*
> *morality of it, okay?'*

I piled the three pages I'd written into my out tray and
wandered into the kitchen in search of whisky. Susan,
busy with a *blanquette de veau*, already had two poured
out. 'Three pages, darling, right?' she smiled. 'I always
know when it's time!'

I touched my glass to hers. I drank. 'The real time,' I
said, 'is when I finish the sixth page. That's my quota for
the day, that's when we move to the ottoman!'

The smile grew wider. She touched my face with her
hand. 'How does it go?'

I shrugged. 'Okay, I suppose. An introductory chapter
and then three pages with no sex: Edward will wear that,
but bloody Maddox may create. If he reads it.'

'Can I read it?'

'Sure,' I said. 'I'd like to know what you think.'

She put the pages back in the tray when she had
finished. 'The sex is implied,' she said. 'You know it's
going to come, inevitably. What you're doing here is
leading up to it, building the suspense. You can't have

nothing but sex. As someone said, the book becomes nothing but a *catalogue* of tits and bums and cocks and cunts.'

'My view,' I said. 'That's what I was trying to do here: the night-club scene is a carrot for the donkey reader. Is the *blanquette* for dinner?'

'If you're a good boy.'

'I have every intention,' I said, with what I hoped was a roguish smile, 'of being a thoroughly naughty boy. Long before dinner.'

'Then you shall have two helpings,' Susan said.

I sank a second whisky, rolled more paper and carbons into the machine, and settled down again at my desk. I wasn't telling Susan, of course – she was broad-minded yet there had to be limits – that this was art imitating life. The entire set-up, the divided loyalties – wife against temptress against job against boss – and the secret lives, was a direct result of what I had discovered about the Edward-Velvet situation. It had in fact suggested itself to me while I was still fucking Mabel under the lascivious gaze of Edward's wife.

I filled in a few lines getting Martin and Sherry into a cab, then readied myself for the stuff Frank Maddox would be expecting. I wrote:

The cab ride was a nightmare for Martin. The last two brandies had seriously weakened his determination to resist, as Sherry had known they would. And now, on the soft seats in back of the Mercedes, she was leaning against him with her head on his shoulder and one hand resting on his crotch. And despite all his reservations, there was a hardening bulge there provoked by the warmth and weight of her touch.

Christ, she was unzipping his fly!

And he dare not protest: he knew the Merretts were regular customers; there was no knowing how close the driver was to Julian, or what he might let slip next time Sherry's husband hired him.

Her hand had wormed its way inside his pants and teased him to full hardness. He sat in tortured silence as she stroked and fondled, relishing his discomfort as she whispered a steady stream of seductive remarks into his ear. There was already a wet patch at one side of the gaping fly, and he had difficulty shoving the rigid cock back inside as the taxi slowed outside the Merrett house. 'You could always leave it out,' Sherry murmured. 'It would save time later!'

Martin opened the door for her, darting a guilty look at his own darkened home further up the street as he paid the driver.

Inside the house, the wide living-room was all deep-buttoned leather and chrome, with indirect lighting suffusing everything in a warm glow. In one corner, a huge television was built into the wall above a complex hi-fi stereo chain. 'Now what shall we choose as a . . . nightcap?' Sherry inquired.

'I guess, well, hadn't we better stay with the brandy?' Martin said.

'I've a better idea. I shall feed you our party special. You may need an aphrodisiac later to stay in the race.' She slid open the doors of a cocktail cabinet and produced a dark green bottle without a label. Crossing to a bar at one side of a kitchen hatchway, she half filled two tumblers with a pearly, thick green liquid which rapidly turned milky when she added iced water to fill the glass.

'What's this? Pastis, Pernod?' Martin asked, catching a whiff of aniseed scent.

'Not exactly. This is the real stuff – absinthe. Have you ever had it before?'

He shook his head. 'I thought it was illegal, ever since World War II.'

'Everywhere except Nassau, in the Bahamas, and parts of Spain,' she agreed. 'Try it and see what you think.'

He took an experimental sip of the liquorice-tasting drink. It went down smoothly enough, cool without any noticeable kick. He swallowed a mouthful. 'It doesn't seem particularly strong,' he said.

'You have to wait: it comes up and hits you from behind,' Sherry told him. 'But it never deadens you or makes you sleepy like most liquor, just gives you a mellow lift.' She grinned, tapping the damp patch on his trousers. 'Great stimulant for JT here too!' she added.

She glanced at her gold wrist watch. 'It's late. I'm going to get in to something a little more comfortable. Why don't you watch television for five minutes while I'm away?' She pressed a switch beneath the big screen, smiled again, and left the room.

The screen glowed to life. Martin saw a bedroom set – a king-sized bed with a white fur rug, a dressing-table, framed landscapes on the walls and a half-open door leading to a bathroom. A blonde in a black cocktail dress walked into shot. She was stacked, a real bombshell with tapering legs, a snug waist and prominent breasts. It was only when she turned and advanced into close-up that he realized with a gasp of astonishment that it was Sherry!

'Don't be alarmed,' the image on the screen laughed. 'It's a closed-circuit hook-up. I'm in the room next door.

You can talk to me: I can hear you on the intercom. Meanwhile, wait there and watch until I call you.'

Martin drained his glass and moved across to the bar for a refill. It was odd how the bland, milky liquid appeared to be energizing him with a kind of courage: each sip was diminishing the fears he had been subject to ever since they left the night-club. A strength, a confidence that surprised him had instilled itself somewhere deep within him.

Turning back to the screen, he saw that Sherry was stepping out of the black dress. It was done with great subtlety – nothing overtly provocative, no veiled glances or sexy wiggles. She could have been alone in the house, getting ready for bed, sublimely unaware that she was being watched. He felt almost like a Peeping Tom, peering through a window from a hiding place among the bushes lining the driveway. The thought was obscurely exciting. His prick began to harden again.

Sherry bent over to pick up the dress, revealing the full, rounded globes of her buttocks, and the narrow nylon strip of her panties between firm thighs which tightened momentarily as she leaned forward. The flimsy garment, drawn into the vaginal cleft by the constricted position, somehow underlined the presence of the pouch of secret flesh it was designed to hide.

Martin, breathing a little fast, gulped down another mouthful of absinthe.

Sherry put the dress on a hanger and walked away to stow it in a closet. And this time – there was no doubt about it – the movement of every muscle was designed to provoke and tease. It was the lithe and supple showgirl coming to the fore, sexually suggestive with each tiny practised sway.

Watching her, he held his breath. There was no going back now. If she wanted it – needed him – this bad, was determined to go this far, there wasn't a hope in hell of him keeping the job if he didn't play along with her. All the way.

In any case, God damn it, it was as much Jean's fault as his. The entire situation would have been a non-starter if only she could have delayed her trip home by one day. She deserved his infidelity, he told himself, if that was the price to be paid for the job she should have been doing herself: occupying the wife with small talk while he chatted with his new boss!

Sherry was dressed now in nothing but bra, panties, suspender belt and stockings. The dark silk veneering her splendid legs gleamed sexily in the softly lit room, emphasizing the hard shine of the high-heeled shoes she wore. The bra was low-cut and lacy, the twin cups cradling her fleshy breasts as snugly as he hoped to do soon – oh, soon, please, soon!

'Martin!' the voice said suddenly out of the screen. 'Bring me my drink now. Turn right into the corridor, and it's the first door on the left.'

He had been lost in his own lascivious thoughts, so surprised by the summons that he almost knocked over his glass. He grabbed it just before it fell off the bar and drained it again.

'Martin?' she repeated, the voice imperious. 'Are you there?'

'Yes, yes,' he stammered, confused. 'Sorry. Coming right away.'

'Well, hurry: it's not polite to keep a girl waiting when she's cold because she's hardly any clothes on!'

Hastily, he poured himself another refill, freshened

Sherry's drink and left the room. His cock was so hard now that he had been obliged to ease the shaft out through the leg of his shorts to lessen the ache as it strained against his fly.

She already had the bedroom door open, wearing a short nylon négligée, the soft shifting of flesh beneath the sheer material revealing that she had removed the brassière while he fixed the drinks. The deep cleavage between her breasts was shadowed within the open vee at the neck of the robe. But he was glad to see that the stockings and high heels were still in place.

(I knew I wouldn't be able to keep thoughts of Mabel out of it, I mused with a wry smile as I tapped out those last few lines!)

It occurred to him suddenly that he would like to take her like that, with the hose and heels still on. What didn't occur to him was the change in his own attitude: he had thought automatically that he would take her – not that he might be taken by her, as he had at first feared. He was suffused with a power and a self-confidence sexually that he had never experienced before; he felt marvellous, as if finally he had found the true strength within himself that had remained latent all the time he had been married to Jean.

Jean, with her modest, schoolgirl concept of making love, he had never seen her dressed like that! In fact he had never seen any woman dressed that way, although he had noticed the provocative underclothes often enough in the window displays of lingerie stores. The furthest he had ever got with his wife was a playful attempt to pull her down on the bed while she was undressing . . . but she had always, in her most puritan manner, pushed him away and continued her preparations for the night in the bathroom. He had tried, as tactfully as he could, to explain, but it seemed almost as if Jean felt that sex was somehow not quite nice.

This Sherry Merrett though – God, she knew what sex was about; she knew the way to get a man horny . . . and keep him there!

She was sprawled on the bed, leaning back on her elbows, staring at the telltale bulge thrusting out his crotch. The shiny softness of the négligée had ridden up over her thighs to expose the silky down of her pubic mound at the base of a smooth white belly.

So the panties had gone too. One more hurdle he didn't have to jump; one more possible cause of awkwardness or clumsy behaviour removed!

'You want me, don't you?' she teased. 'I can see.' She raised her glass, smiling wickedly at him over the rim. 'So how does our party special grab you, man?'

Deliberately, he held her gaze for a moment, staring deep into her eyes. 'It makes me less inhibited, I will say that,' he replied, smiling in turn.

He leaned over to cup a hand beneath a swell of nylon where it was thrust out by the mound of one breast, relishing the soft, warm weight of the flesh against his palm.

'Mmmmm,' she intoned, shifting slightly on the white fur coverlet. 'Makes you braver too! At first, tonight, I didn't know if I was going to get you into bed at all.'

'That was about a thousand years ago,' Martin said.

He glanced openly at the thin, hair-fringed lips of her vagina, clearly visible between her slightly parted legs. Sherry's mouth twisted into a slow and lecherous smile and she shifted again, opening the thighs a little wider.

He could see that she was excited: the first small dewdrops of moisture were visible, glistening in the tight, narrow slit as she exposed herself shamelessly to his fascinated gaze. He took the glass from her hand and placed it with his own empty one on a night table. When he turned back to the bed, she had loosened the front of the robe to reveal the ample, swelling mounds of her breasts. The ripe red nipples, swollen and erect, gleamed up at him where she had moistened them with her own saliva. Her eyes, wide open, were dilated with urgent desire.

'God, but you're so beautiful!' Martin murmured, staring lustfully down at her semi-nakedness.

Abruptly, Sherry thrust herself forwards. Reaching out one hand, she jerked the zipper of his pants forcibly down and dragged out his throbbing cock.

Martin caught his breath, the air of the bedroom cool on his rigid, heated flesh. 'Oh, my!' the sexy blonde cooed. 'What a man we have here!'

The grip on his distended and aching staff tightened. Martin knew that this was the crunch moment, the instant that could spell glory . . . or disaster.

He leaned forward, took her head in both hands, and kissed her on the mouth.

She reached up, curled her arms around his back, and pulled him down on her. One of his legs fell tightly between her open thighs. Supple and soft, her voluptuous body melted into his embrace as inevitably as a magnet clamped to an iron bar. Her pliable lips gave under the harsh pressure of his teeth with a yielding, rubbery release, and he speared his tongue deep into her throat, relieved at last of the unbearable tension provoked by inactivity in *the face of her taunting and teasing seductiveness.*

Now he would give her what she was asking for; now he would show her whether or not he was bashful or timid; now was the time for his cock to make its point!

In the hot, wet cavern of his mouth, Sherry forced her sinewy tongue up against his own, randily exploring his palate, his gums, the inside of his cheeks. Her thigh ground against his crotch, massaging his cock to an even more painful hardness. Wetness seeping from the bulbous tip was already drenching the material of his pants and he felt as if the head was about to explode. He could sense a terrible urge for relief building deep in his testicles below.

Hot breath jetting from her nostrils played jerkily against his cheek. Her whole languorous length was quivering beneath him now. 'Let's get naked,' she panted hoarsely. 'You want to fuck me, don't you?'

'God, yes. I do, I do,' Martin whispered, excited even more by the lewd words framed by her lips.

'Then tell me.'

'I want to fuck you, darling Sherry.'

'How?' she groaned beneath him. 'Tell me how.'

'Deep and hard. I want to fuck you the way you've never been fucked before!'

'Oh, God,' she moaned, arching up to displace him from her body. 'Get your clothes off before I die.'

He pushed himself up from the bed and began desperately stripping garments off. A fleeting tinge of selfconsciousness manifested itself as he dropped his pants and shorts and stood over her prone figure with his penis standing out from his belly in naked erection. What if Jean could see him now, standing over their neighbour's wife in that state! He pushed the thought from his mind. The neighbour was his new boss, okay. But although

*everything had been agreed verbally, the contract had yet
to be signed. And if that signature depended on Sherry's
approval – well, for the moment Jean and fidelity had to
take a back seat!*

'Is your wife good in bed?' Sherry suddenly asked,
almost as though she had read his thoughts.

'She's not experienced enough,' he said easily, thrusting
the image away for a second time.

Sherry had squirmed out of the nylon robe. Now she
lay lustfully spread on the white fur, wearing only the
suspender belt, stockings and shoes, teasing him with a
lascivious smile as she fondled her own nipples. 'I'll teach
you a thing or two that you can take home to her,' she
murmured.

She reached out a hand to take hold of his cock,
urging him nearer the bed. 'I like it, I like it,' she said. 'I
know it's going to feel great inside me, ploughing deep
into my cunt. Oh, God, I want you to screw me with it!'

He lay down on the bed and dragged her over to him.
She crushed the full length of her body against his and
ground her pelvis tightly against him before twisting over
to pull him on top of her, opening her legs wide to let him
sink between them. His cock was jammed hard against
her thighs, pressed into the narrow, hair-lined slit of her
vagina. Sherry arched up, levering them both off the rug
while she reached under her buttocks with both hands,
pulling the lips of her cunt slowly apart to give his aching
staff better contact with the wet sensitive flesh as it lay
trapped between her thighs.

Martin forced his hands between her shoulders and the
rug, running them down the pliant curves of her back
and hips. He could feel the raised ridges of her spine move
almost imperceptibly against his touch as she undulated

her body against him in a slow, teasing rhythm. The tendons of her thighs were hard against the outside of his hips. For a moment he imagined them gripping his waist when the knees jerked up and he sunk his stiffened rod deep within her.

She was becoming wetter every second. 'Jesus, what you do to me!' she whispered, smashing her mouth against his lips again, writhing her belly close against him. Her nails scrabbled sharply across the skin of his back.

Martin pushed his hands further down beneath her, cupping the fullness of her buttocks so that he could pull her open crotch to him still more tightly.

Her backside began a frenzied rotation against his loins . . . and then suddenly, unexpectedly, her legs snaked out wide on either side of his body and her calves zeroed in to lock against he back of his thighs, smashing him harder still against her. 'Oh, Christ yes – fuck me now, darling! Fuck me now!' she cried.

He started to shift his weight, but she beat him to it. Her hands slid between their sweat-streaked bellies to circle his pulsating cock, guiding it between the inflamed lips of her lustfully moistened cunt.

Martin groaned above her as she moved the blood-engorged head up and down between her legs, parting the soft, silky hairs to graze her intimate flesh.

The pressure in his cock was no longer supportable; he couldn't hold back another second.

Lunging forward with a sudden cruel thrust, he slammed the whole hot, hard length deep into the hungry mouth of her pussy.

Sherry cried aloud as the warm, elastic-like sheath of her vagina slid wetly over his seething, sensitive shaft. His stiffened cock raced up her cunt to the full depth of

*her belly, tight at first, aching the entire length of his rigid
staff, and then easier as the ridged muscles of her inner
passage relaxed, accommodating themselves to the powerful
thrusts and withdrawals of the invading stem.*

*Sherry moaned ceaselessly beneath his pounding body,
opening and closing her legs around his hips as her loins
hinged up and down in ecstatic abandon. Her mouth
gaped wide; her head flailed wildly on the pillows.*

*'Your . . . f-f-fingers,' she croaked suddenly, the
gasped breath hissing hotly in his ear. 'In both . . . both
. . . places!'*

*Astonishingly – he never knew afterwards exactly how
it happened – some sixth sexual sense told Martin what
she was demanding. Sliding the flat of his hand between
their slapping bellies, he searched through the wet hairs of
her pubic mound for the trembling apex of Sherry's
distended cunt, homing in finally with two fingers on the
inflamed bud of her clitoris.*

*She yelped explosively with joy, screwing herself harder
still against his forceful penetration as he massaged the
ultra-sensitive button of flesh.*

*Now it was time to comply with the second part of her
command. With his free hand, he reached under and
between her buttocks as he continued sawing into her. He
stretched the crevice wide with forefinger and thumb,
exploring the rivulet of warm moisture seeping there with
the tip of his middle finger until her found the puckered
ring of her anus. Pushing against the lubricated flesh, he
felt the tight, elastic nether ring give way and sunk the
finger in up to the second knuckle.*

*Sherry gave a low scream and jack-knifed her legs up
high to scissor across his back, offering his ravishing cock
and hands the maximum opening of her upraised crotch.*

It was neither the easiest nor the most comfortable position for Martin to maintain, but the results were so electrifying that he determined to pursue it. Through the thin wall of muscle separating her two passages, now he could feel the rigid underside of his own penis sliding powerfully in and out. Massaging her throbbing clitoris, he sunk the marauding finger behind deeper, rotating it in the hot and fleshy depths as she screwed her backside back onto his hand.

The panting blonde, trebly skewered now, threshed up and down in a frenzy of excitement, every nerve ablaze under the lewd manipulations of her husband's new assistant, her grimacing mouth spewing out a stream of mumbled obscenities as she bucked and writhed.

Martin could feel his cock growing and expanding inside her until he feared it must burst from the exquisite pleasure building in his balls as they slapped against the bared buttocks quivering below. She was nearing her release now, he knew; she must be. But he had to hold it himself until afterwards. He began ramming it into her harder to bring her on, timing the strokes to jibe with the fingered intrusions stimulating her rectum and clitoris.

Her eyes rolled uncontrollably in her head. 'Oh, God!' she coughed suddenly. 'I'm going to come . . . I'm going to come. Oh, Jesus!'

Her ankles rose to lock over his shoulders. Her nostrils flared as she arched up onto his thrusting cock, locking herself to him with all the strength in her thighs while her loins jerked spasmodically against his belly.

For an interminable moment she held her breath . . . and then expelled it as violently as if she had been fisted in the stomach, collapsing limply on the white fur rug with a low, keening cry, motionless except for the heaving spasms agitating the quivering pussy still locked around his tortured prick.

Martin had never in his life seen anything like it. He had never felt anything like it either. It was all he could do to keep from continuing to screw. But he pushed deep into her and then lay still himself, allowing her time to recover and remember where and who she was.

What a night! And for him – the agonizing anticipation keeping him as stiff and hard as ever – for him the best was still to come . . .

In the Merretts' living-room, Julian sat in front of the closed-circuit television screen with a salacious smile on his lips. The telephone call in the night-club had been a set-up; there had been no robbery in Toulouse; he had crept back to the house minutes after the taxi had driven away.

He had watched – and heard – the entire bedroom scene with lustful glee.

God, that little wife of his could go! He chuckled to himself, imagining the expression on the face of the kid's wife when he played her the recording – including Martin's dismissal of her as inexperienced!

It wouldn't be long before he had them both hooked into the swappers' network he hosted.

Chapter Eleven

I rolled back the office chair on its castors, stood up from the machine, and stretched. Unseasonably, it was raining again. Through the speckled windows I could see shiny yellow and white oilskins all over the boats tied up in the harbour. No charter trips today, so the yachties might as well do some work holystoning the decks, polishing brass, refilling the bottles and that kind of thing.

'Is it because of the weather?' Susan asked, wandering in from the kitchen.

I yawned. 'Is what?'

'You said three more pages. You must have done seven or eight.'

'Nine actually. It was going well, so I thought I might as well finish the chapter.' I shuffled the sheets together, separated the carbons and patted the edges of the top copy to make a neat pile.

'Bravo for you, darling,' Susan said. 'Except it's too late to go down to Nini's for an *apéro* now. Unless you want carbonized *blanquette*, that is.'

'I'll take the *blanquette* the way it is now,' I said. 'It smells delicious. Do you have time to cast an eye over this?' I handed her the chapter.

'Yes, if you'll get out the glasses and lay the table.'

'Into each life,' I said, 'a little rain must fall.'

The *blanquette* was good. We were finishing off the bottle of Côtes du Rhône with a slice of Basque Étorqui when Susan said: 'What's all this with the high heels and garter belts? I didn't think the kinky stuff interested you.'

Prudently, perhaps, I hadn't told her about my lunchtime session with Velvet and Mabel. She was broadminded, okay. But there are always limits you don't expect. 'Boss's orders,' I lied. 'It's what the *readers* are interested in – or what Edward thinks they're interested in.'

'I see.' It sounded as if she didn't. 'I guess a twelve-page fuck is good enough value any way. It's a fine chapter, but where exactly is it leading?'

'The Merrett character,' I explained, 'is crazy to seduce Martin's prissy wife. She hasn't appeared yet, but she's stacked. He aims to play the outraged husband, take the video to her, and complain: 'Hey, your old man's been sleeping with my wife! It's a scandal. What are we going to do about it?'

'And what *are* they going to do about it?'

'It's scarcely credible, but she's going to be staggered, he's going to console her, make her drunk and – er – have his way with her. In this way they'll both be drawn into the neighbourhood wife-swapping orgies which are the subject of the book.'

'My, my. Tell me, though: how come this deathless chronicle happens to be titled *Teenage Victims*?'

I laughed. 'Edward thinks up the titles; Maddox specifies what's to go on the jacket illustration. It's up to us, the writers, to quarry out a story that fits. I guess some of the swinging couples will have to have adolescent kids. Maybe they'll be drawn in because they spy on the parents. Something like that.'

'Oh, wow!' Susan said. 'And do these kind of things really happen down here on the fabulous Côte d'Azur? Not amongst the movie people and the business tycoons, I mean, but to people like us?'

'Stick around,' I said.

We'd arranged to have a drink later with Jeff Adlam and Inge, the writer and his wife I'd met at Edward's party. Susan was a little late getting ready. When she finally appeared, she was wearing a white leather mini-skirt, black nylons and gold slippers with spike heels.

I gaped. 'You must be joking,' I said.

'If I am,' Susan said demurely, 'maybe the joke's on you!'

I stared at her.

'I thought it might help you, darling, in the practice of your art,' she explained. 'You're always on about life imitating art. And vice versa. I wondered what would happen if we did turn our own vice a little versa, and I dressed like one of the characters in Edward's books.'

I went on staring. The scarlet sweater she wore looked as if it had been sprayed on. The whole effect was like one of those Hollywood film stills where the photographer has retouched the picture to make the subject's breasts look bigger. Larger than life, shall we say?

I swallowed, feeling a little like Martin in the book I was writing. But I wasn't going to chicken out. If I had a petard, I guess I had to admit I was hoisted on it. 'Very well,' I said. 'I can always pretend you're a whore I picked up in a waterfront bar in Cannes.'

'That's the whole idea,' Susan said.

Jeff Adlam was an athletic American college-boy type with curly, tow-coloured hair and one of those moustaches wider than the mouth that droop a little at the ends. Inge

161

was blonde, petite, with very large blue eyes and finely chiselled features. He was wearing jeans, trainers and a checkered sweatshirt; Inge was dressed in a white silk blouse and a plain, pleated skirt that reached halfway down her calves. A tan raincoat was thrown over her shoulders.

It was still raining when we arrived at the boardwalk brasserie built out over the water. 'You may find it difficult to believe,' I said, 'but this is Susan.'

If Jeff was surprised by what he saw, he was either too well-mannered to react or too ignorant of European customs to know the difference between what was and what wasn't. Done, I mean. Inge simply raised a thinly-pencilled eyebrow, smiled, and said how nice.

In Edward's office, Jeff himself was regarded as quite a character. It was said, truthfully, that he could write a book in a long weekend. But what he wrote and what was published did not always perfectly coincide. He was in fact secretly known to the girls as First-draft Adlam – because the redhead named Mandy in Chapter One was likely to have become Millie the brunette in Chapter Three, and the lecherous butler, Mason, six-foot-two, was likely to have shrunk to five-foot-seven within fifty pages and changed his name to Frobisher . . . All of which was fun for everybody except the editors responsible for checking his copy.

He was a generous soul, just the same. The very first time I met him, at Edward's party, he drew me aside and confided: 'Piece of cake, all this rubbish. I've got it worked out, categorized, filed. Everything cross-indexed for venue and style of sex activity.'

'Well, bravo for you,' I began. 'That must be a great help—'

'Anything you want,' Jeff said, 'just let me know. Rape in the men's locker room at the country club, anal sex in the schoolroom, a threesome in the operating theatre, I've got them all. Just call me on the blower and you can have a photocopy the next day. Change the names and save yourself a lot of time.'

'Well, it's very kind of you,' I said. 'I might take you up on that.'

'My pleasure,' Jeff said.

That rainy evening in Golfe Juan, he suggested we might all drop in at a golf club party a friend of his was giving in Monte Carlo. 'I don't say they'll actually provide any action for *us*,' he confided, 'but there could be good background stuff for you and me and the next few books!'

'If Leggy Peggy Metford will be there,' I said, 'I wouldn't be surprised!'

The party was held at a very large villa whose grounds bordered the Mont Agel mountain golf course some way inland from the Principality. The place was immense. A gravelled driveway jammed on each side with expensive parked machinery – the cheapest car I saw was a top-of-the-range BMW – led to a turnaround itself circled by a white Doric colonnade separated from the house proper by a marble terrace. Flaring lights resembling Roman torches cast a wavering, rather romantic glow over this, but rain was still pelting down, bouncing high off the flooded stone, and chairs scattered across the wide space had been tilted forward against a dozen garden tables. All the activity was inside.

Armoured glass doors slid apart as we approached the entrance. The noise as one went in was deafening; a roaring crash of voices shouting, laughing, calling – singing, even, for somewhere in the distance a band was playing jazz. A fat man with a white suit and mirror shades greeted us with an outstretched hand and a huge cigar projecting from his mouth. Jeff might have introduced us, but although the two men's mouths moved, no sound was audible above the din. There must have been more than a hundred men and women crowded into the vast entrance hall alone.

We threaded our way to a long bar staffed by six waiters at the far end, past cocktail dresses and cowboy boots, hippies and high fashion, turtlenecks and tuxedos. So far as I could see, nobody even noticed Susan's outrageous attire – but that might have been because the crowd was so dense that nobody could get far enough away to view her as a whole.

Jeff took over. Clearly he had a flair, a formula for everything. He prised drinks out of the barmen in record time, reaching over gesticulating guests struggling for space. 'There's a drill at this kind of shindig,' he shouted.

'A what?'

'A drill, a routine, old lad. We separate, each go our own way. Case the whole joint and see what the form is. Then we meet up again here in, say' – glancing at his wrist watch – 'fifteen minutes. And whoever's sussed out the most interesting scene, we follow him or her back to it and join it.'

'Join it? You don't mean join *in*?' I asked.

'Not necessarily. Depends.'

'Depends on what?'

'Well, on the people, the atmosphere, the state – as they say – of the art. And on whether we're interested, of course. Might just be a watching brief. You have to remember yourself as an *artist*, a recorder of social customs. What we are doing here, old lad, is fieldwork. Research, if you want to be academic about it.' He grinned, draining his glass. 'Of course nobody may come up with anything worthy of our attention. In that case we furnish ourselves with fresh drinks and separate again.'

'Well,' I offered, 'they do say a good guest circulates.'

'Exactly.' Jeff waved a parting hand, snatched a full glass from a tray held by a passing waiter, and vanished into the crowd. I turned to have a word with Inge, but she had already gone.

'Okay, darling,' I said to Susan, patting her on a bottom only just covered by the leather mini-skirt, 'you're on your own!'

The villa was on two levels. Beyond the busy hallway there was a wide corridor and off this open doors showed a dining-room, a television den, a library-study and a billiard-room. All of them seemed to be fairly full of people. At the far end of the passage there was another open space: black and white checkerboard floor, a five-piece combo on a palm-fringed stand beating out a Dixieland version of *The Lady is a Tramp*, a knot of energetic dancers.

Behind the band, a double staircase, marble again, led in twin curves to a balustraded gallery and – I suppose – the sleeping quarters and suchlike. The party had spilled the less gregarious members of its extensive guest list here too. Couples, heads together and hands sometimes entwined, squatted on the stairs exchanging confidences; small groups, shrill with laughter, gossiped or recounted dubious stories with lowered voices; in the distance, one was aware of the opening and closing of doors. One collection of supercilious-looking men in evening dress stopped talking as I approached and turned to eye me coldly when I passed.

I didn't quite know what I was looking for. A gang-bang in the conservatory perhaps? Shamefaced gays emerging, literally, from a closet? Something in any case – judging from Jeff's manner – that verged on the libidinous. A quest, surely, which could more fruitfully be followed on the upper floor.

I wandered left and right through a network of passageways and landings, trying to look as though I was on the way somewhere specific. They were not entirely empty, though most of the guests I passed were couples. From behind some of the closed doors I heard subdued laughter, and in one case a muffled shout that could have been a man coming. But I could hardly turn the handles and peep in to check. There were open doors too, beyond one of which a bed was visible which had quite evidently been recently occupied – energetically too, by the state of the covers. I wondered which of the demure couples I passed had been in there. At the end of one long corridor two doors flanking an enormous flower arrangement were decorated with little black silhouettes, one with a skirt, the other with trousers, of the kind usually employed by hotels, restaurants and clubs to denote *Ladies* and *Gentlemen*. Odd, I thought, to have separate loos in a private house, but maybe it was a whim of the owner's. Or his wife, if he had one.

I was veering back towards the double staircase when I heard an unmistakable cooing murmur, followed by stifled feminine giggles from the far side of a partly open door which had previously been closed.

I glanced hastily around. For the moment the passageway was empty. I slipped through the opening after a swift glance inside. I was in an upstairs sitting-room furnished in the oriental style and packed with jars and *chinoiserie*. The voices were coming from a divan half hidden behind a silk screen painted with flying birds.

The women, there were two of them, were almost completely hidden by the padded back of the divan. I don't know if it was prurient curiosity or some kind of sixth sense that kept me standing there, just inside the door. Certainly there was no doubt that the murmurings I heard were of a sexual nature. In any case, I must have made some slight noise, because the head of one of them rose abruptly into view, staring at the door.

Leggy Peggy, who else!

Despite the low-key lighting, she recognized me at once. Grinning, she laid a finger against her lips and favoured me with a large wink. The head disappeared once more.

At once there was a renewed murmuring, not in Peggy's voice, and the softly, sensually uttered words: 'Yes. Oh, yes . . . that's so lovely! Do it again; do it just once more. There . . . and there . . . and – Oh, you darling!'

I was transfixed. My cock was already rigid.

Whoever it was that she was caressing so expertly, must have been lying almost flat beside her, because the voice was suddenly muffled and Peggy herself voiced a purr of pleasure. The lower half of two legs, elegantly tapered, slid into view over the open end of the divan. Crossed ankles separated and spread; the two voices crooned out a litany of lust.

I remained transfixed – and not just as an inadvertent voyeur.

The feet I could see were shod with gold, stiletto-heeled slippers.

And the second voice was quite definitely Susan's.

My head was in a whirl. Don't ask me what I felt: I

didn't know. I mean, it was all very well *writing* about this sort of thing, joking about it – or even watching it – when it concerned other people. But when one of the subjects was one's own particular girlfriend . . . what then?

Did I feel jealous? Angry? Rejected? Put down? Cheated? You tell me.

Certainly I experienced surprise and perhaps confusion. But I couldn't honestly say that I had the right to feel any *moral* indignation. Who was I to complain, when I wrote what I wrote – and for that matter did what I did when Susan was away? Knocked for a loop I might have been, but I have to confess that the overriding reactions I felt were curiosity . . . and excitement.

I wanted not just to hear but to see.

Peggy, smart old Peggy, must have been aware of this. Perhaps it was a situation with which she was all too familiar. At any rate her head bobbed momentarily back into view and she nodded almost imperceptibly towards a second screen, at right-angles to the first, which stood behind the head of the divan.

I took the hint. Without a second thought, I stole past the divan back and stationed myself behind this second screen. It was about seven feet high, divided into five hinged sections, and filled in with multicoloured strips of silk arranged horizontally. There was room between the strips, if the eye was close enough, to enjoy a birds-eye view of the whole divan, from behind Peggy's head, as it were.

My eye was so close that the lashes touched silk when I blinked. Blink is what I did too, as soon as I took in the full scene.

Peggy was half reclining against the sloping end of the divan, with her legs apart and one foot on the floor. Her button-through dress was open to the waist, exposing both bra-less breasts. Susan, wedged almost face-downwards between her and the divan back, was sucking one breast, which she held up with a cupped hand. The other hand was between Peggy's legs.

Peggy's hands were busy too. She had pulled the leather mini-skirt up over my girlfriend's hips and pushed a pair of black nylon briefs down to her knees. The long, skilled fingers of one hand were buried in the downy hair darkening Susan's loins; the second, which had dragged up the scarlet sweater to spill out one of Susan's luscious breasts, was buried between their clamped-together bodies. But I could guess what it was doing with that splendid handful of flesh.

I watched with a thudding heart and bated breath. Peggy, of course, was quite unaware that there was any connection between Susan and myself: she would, knowing me, simply assume that I was doing my customary voyeur number.

It was a remarkable sight anyway. It would have been a stimulating and sexy scene even if there hadn't been the extra thrill and piquancy of spying on the seduction of one's 'own' girlfriend!

The two female bodies, at first sight in repose and yet so intimately linked, were alive with a myriad of subtle movements, a complex stirring, quivering, discrete series of tiny spasms that pulsated with desire while leaving the couple as an entity apparently immobile.

Even the two hands cupped with masturbatory skill over vulva and crotch, teasing infinitely exquisite pleasure from the two pairs of loins, seemed scarcely to move.

A case, I thought, striving not to allow the quickening of my own breath to betray me, where the sum of the parts was greater than the whole.

A long way off, I could hear the murmur of the crowd and distant strains of music, but here in this upstairs sitting-room there was nothing but the contented humming groans of the two breathlessly excited young women and the occasional stealthy sucking sound as a finger sank into the wetness it had created.

My cock was hard against my leg, trapped there by the constriction of my shorts (which was probably just as well, because otherwise I might have been tempted to take it out and try a little manipulation myself). Most difficult of all was the stifling of a manic desire to rush out from behind the screen and join in!

But the scene was suddenly changing. Susan was kneeling up on the divan, staring out over Peggy's head, directly at the screen. For an instant my heart almost stopped . . . and then I realized the lighting was such that she couldn't possibly see me. I'm not sure that she could see anything: she wore that bemused look I knew so well that meant she was really high. 'God,' she mouthed in a low, vibrant voice, 'the things you do to me!'

Peggy's hand was still massaging her inflamed and glistening sexual lips. She pushed the sweater higher still, so that both Susan's taut but heavy breasts with their erect and reddened nipples were exposed. 'Bring those gorgeous things a little nearer,' she said throatily, 'and you'll learn some other things I can do to you . . . My Gard, that cute little skirt's the most *accessible* thing I ever saw!'

With a knee on either side of Peggy's spare body, Susan shuffled towards her – and me. She was the picture of a lecher's delight: big boobs bared, pale belly, dark damp hair, and the black-stockinged legs shamelessly spread.

I knew what was coming – apart from Susan herself, that is. Peggy prided herself on 'giving great head', as she put it. And now she was going to give.

Right enough, relinquishing her gaping crotch, Peggy put firm hands on Susan's hips and pulled her naked loins down until her damp thighs were on either side of her eager face. Then, lifting her head slightly, Peggy closed her mouth over her enticing cunt.

Susan uttered a slight yelp as the lips worked and the tongue penetrated. Peggy used her hands to rotate, very gently, my lady's hips, twisting, gyrating belly and pelvis so that the quivering cunt continually slid and changed position over and around her gobbling, sucking mouth.

Susan's eyes were glazed. Her mouth hung slackly open. I could see her heart beating wildly within her breast. Abruptly the upper half of her body pitched forward and she supported herself with two hands on the back of the divan. It was extraordinary: her face couldn't have been more than eighteen inches from mine.

I held my breath. But I don't think she could have seen me, even if the screen hadn't been there: she was already on her way up among the stars.

She threw back her head, shuddering all over, and sobbed out a low, keening cry as Peggy's practised lips and tongue sucked her into delirious release.

I glanced at my watch. They'd done pretty well in fifteen minutes! But I reckoned – regretfully – that it was time to get back to the others. I stole out of that room before Susan came back to earth.

Chapter Twelve

Inge and Jeff were already back at the bar, and Jeff, splendid guy that he was, already balanced four brimming glasses in his competent hands.

Susan joined us shortly afterwards. Apart from a slightly heightened colour, she showed no visible trace of her recent adventure. 'Any luck?' Jeff asked.

She shook her head.

'What?' I jested. 'No bedroom floor scattered with fucking couples? No sapphic ladies lustfully entwined?'

'Not really.' She flashed me a quick glance, then ducked her head to accept a glass from Jeff.

'With that outfit,' I pursued, 'I should have expected you at least to have been propositioned yourself – if only by a hairy golf pro.'

She shook her head again, gulping her drink rather fast.

Jeff and his wife also made negative reports. 'What about you?' he asked.

'Nothing to speak of,' I lied. 'Apart from couples snogging on the stairs, the only action was on the dance floor . . . Oh, and one thing I found a bit odd, on the upper floor.'

'Such as?'

'Well, separate toilets up there. I mean like Ladies and

173

Gents. Complete with the little black silhouettes to say which is which.'

'That's not odd at all!' Jess sounded excited. 'Indicative, though.'

'Indicative?'

'Sure. You must have realized who our host is?'

I shrugged. 'You probably introduced us, but I didn't catch any name.'

'The Greek shipowner,' he said. He mentioned the name. 'The third richest after Onassis and Niarchos. With the second biggest boat on the Med. And the worst reputation!'

'Of course.' No wonder the face had seemed familiar. Mister Swinger himself. I vaguely recalled gossip column stories hinting at dissolute parties among the heavily loaded, of all the whores from the fourth floor of the Martinez being shipped aboard the huge floating palace for dirty weekends.

'Our friend,' Jeff said, 'has multiple business interests. He has to entertain a lot of different folks – not all of whom are swappers and suchlike. The boat is reserved for the wilder stuff. Here in the villa it's sometimes the squares, sometimes the swingers.'

'And sometimes both?'

Jess nodded. 'Sometimes, when he's writing off a whole lot of different kinds of hospitality in one go, there's a choice. Like tonight, for instance.'

'How do you know?' I asked.

'Your little black ladies and gents, old lad. That'll be the signal for those in the know, the *cognoscenti*. The two doors you saw probably lead to guest suites . . . and that's where tonight's action will be – the one labelled Gents for gays and the kinky fraternity, Ladies for the dykes and heteros.'

'To me that smacks of discrimination,' I joked. 'I should have thought the last thing queer girls wanted would be to be lumped in with the straights. Ditto the gays with fetishists and SM types.'

'There are two reasons,' Jeff said. 'One: what silhouettes would you use, or could you find, for the other categories? Without tipping off the rest of the party, I mean. Two: there will certainly be more than one room in each suite, so there's a choice again. The suites probably communicate too. Also, by mixing things in this way, mine host may hope to entice people to cross over from one category to another. Stimulated by what they see around them, they might decide to have a go at something else.'

I forbore to look at Susan. 'Divided they fall,' I said. 'What happens if straight guests take the silhouettes for real, and go in hoping to take a leak?'

'There'll be a bathroom in each suite for sure. Let them take it. And if they should see anything that displeases them, well, the host can't help it if some drunken guests abuse his hospitality. But what he really hopes, of course, is that such people might themselves be tempted to join the club.'

'This sounds uncannily like the book I'm writing,' I said.

'Not to worry,' Jeff told me. 'I have a suspicion that tonight we may prospect a rich vein of sociological fieldwork which could well provide ample documentary material for at least a dozen such works.'

'You mean we're going upstairs to take a shufti?'

'I mean we're going upstairs,' Jeff said.

We chose the rooms behind the door with the female silhouette. Neither Jeff nor I wished to be propositioned by gentlemen, even rich ones, and none of us wanted to see rubber or leather-clad enthusiasts whipping each other (apart from which, I thought secretly to myself, there was always a risk that we might meet our employer). The two girls – Inge with her usual Nordic calm, Susan still slightly high on her recent experience – seemed game for any sexual re-education, even if it was only to watch.

The door was not locked, opening easily and silently as soon as the handle was turned. It was however heavily insulated at the edges with draft-reducing strips and padded all over its inner surface.

That acoustic isolation was efficient too. Because it was anything but silent within the suite. The noise, totally inaudible from the hallway outside, was raucous, a little drunken, tinged definitely with excitement. I could hear at least a dozen men and women chanting something in unison, with others shouting what sounded like encouragement, punctuated by bursts of laughter and guffaws.

Immediately inside the entrance, a short passageway led past a bathroom and kitchenette to a small lobby with two doors opening off it. One of these was ajar, and we could see that the room beyond was very dimly lit. We could hear too, in the pauses between the chanted cries, a subdued rustle and the unmistakable creak of springs very definitely of a sexual origin. The second door was wide open and the room inside brightly lit. It was from here that the noise was coming.

I exchanged glances with Jeff and we all sidled in.

It was, I suppose, the kind of scene one might have expected. The room was quite small, with easy chairs around the walls and two upholstered massage tables in the centre. The guests were crowded around these tables, some leaning forward, others upright and clapping in time to the chant, some even standing on chairs.

A woman lay on each of the tables, one blonde and one a redhead, and each had a skirt pulled up to her waist and a top either opened or pushed up to expose her naked breasts. Each was being energetically fucked by a totally naked man. And the chants and clapping were timed to coincide with their powerful strokes.

'The old game,' Jeff murmured in my ear. 'To see which guy can make his partner come first without shooting off himself while he's doing it. The twist here is that they've swapped: the redhead's man is shafting the blonde, and blondie's hubby is screwing Ginger!'

'How do you know?' I asked.

He grinned, favouring me with a large wink – the second that night. 'Inge and I get around,' he said.

The crowd, and the competitors, had obviously started at square one, presumably just as we came in. They were now into the thirties.

The blonde was fleshy, with heavy tits squashed against the man clamped to her. He was thinnish, not quite skinny, balding, with a great deal of black hair on his chest and arms. His hands were underneath the woman, grasping her padded buttocks to hold her pelvis close as he thudded into her. Her legs, half drawn-up, jerked forward a little each time his cock rammed home.

' . . . thirty-five, thirty-six, thirty-*seven*, thirty-eight,' the spectators chanted gleefully. 'Thirty-nine, *forty*, forty-one, forty-two . . .'

Blondie's husband, a sturdy man with a thatch of sandy hair, had adopted a different stance from that of his rival, perhaps to give himself better leverage. He was poised above the redhead, one arm on either side of her pointed breasts, supporting himself on his hands. Her hands were clenched on the cheeks of his bottom, drawing them apart each time he lunged. The only point of actual contact between their bodies was at hip level, when their loins splatted together. His long, thin cock, glistening and clearly iron-hard, was visible to all of us on each withdrawal, swallowed by her voracious cunt as he thrust in again and the hairy sac of his balls swung against her vaginal cleft.

' . . . fifty-two, fifty-three, fifty-four, fifty-*five* . . .'

Unlike the blonde, the redhead held her legs straight out, jerking them outwards and then in again each time the shaft speared up into her belly. Her tits too shook with every stroke, big nipples very much erect, as stiff and rubbery as a baby's thumbs.

'. . . sixty-seven, sixty-eight, sixty-*nine*, seventy . . .'

'Do they ever make treble figures?' I whispered to Jeff.

'Not often. It's a treble thrill for the chicks, see – being fucked by a stranger *and* being watched. Brings them on pretty quick, usually.'

Very conscious of an ache down below and the hardness of my cock against one leg, I stole a glance at our own chicks. Inge was watching intently, one eyebrow raised, a slight smile curving her elegant lips. Susan's eyes were wide, her lower lip glistening.

'. . . eighty-one, eighty-two, eighty-three . . .'

The redhead's lips were drawn back from her teeth as she strained up, arching her hips to meet the powerful thrusts of her partner. The blonde's head rolled wildly now from side to side; her tongue, polished with saliva, protruded from her mouth and the pale hair at her temples was darkened with sweat.

'Well, I guess there's safety in numbers,' I said. 'What's the prize for the lucky winner?'

'If he hasn't shot his load – and if he still has a cockstand hard enough to work – he gets to fuck whichever girl he fancies most from among the spectators.'

'Well, there's certainly material here for my Chapter Thirteen,' I said.

'I already used it in my Twelve,' Jeff said.

The tension around the twin tables had been mounting remorselessly. The atmosphere in the room was electric, taut as a bowstring the instant before the arrow flies. They were already into the low nineties, and whichever way it was going to go, it was evident that arrows were going to be shot pretty soon – either into the air or someplace a little warmer!

The redhead's calves had jacked up to clamp her stud's waist; one of the blonde's big tits was in her partner's mouth. All four of the bodies were glistening with their exertions, and the hoarse, gasping breaths of four pairs of lungs were punctuated now by the squelch and sucking slap of savaged genitals.

In each case the frequency of the strokes, and the rapidity with which they were delivered, was increasing. But the *rhythm* – as orgasms all around were perilously close – had become broken, almost sporadic. Each of the contestants was at the mercy of his or her singing nerves and spontaneous instincts rather than the conscious control of the mind.

Put it another way: they had reached a pitch of excitement where they no longer knew what they were doing.

The watchers too were feverish with excitement. 'Ninety-four, ninety-five,' they yelled. 'Come on, you know you can do it! Ninety-six, ninety-seven . . .'

The men were panting; the two skewered women groaned aloud.

'Ninety-eight, ninety— *Aaaaah!*'

The chanting broke off one stroke before the century, partly with disappointment, partly in approval.

The goal had been scored, the winning hit made. With a strangled cry that was almost a scream, the blonde convulsed, arching off the table with spasms so strong that her partner was almost thrown off. Drawing back her knees, she hugged them to her heavy breasts as she sobbed out the dwindling quivers of her titanic release.

The thin man squatted back on his heels, smiling proudly as he held his long, gleaming, still-stiff prick in one hand.

The guy with the redhead was only a second too late: withdrawing as quickly as he could, he was unable to hold himself in, and his hot, wet penis jerked uncontrollably, the veined and pulsing shaft spewing a fountain of white-hot sperm over the heaving belly and breasts of the girl beneath him. When the chorus of congratulations and shared excitement had died down, I heard him say. 'Sorry partner. I guess you were just too good – well, too sexy – for me!'

'Don't worry,' the redhead said. 'We must practice when our other halves are out of town!'

The thin man with the hairy chest stood up on the table. His smile was almost a smirk.

Over the applause, someone shouted. 'All right, Jack – you won the competition; now who's going to be your prize?'

Jack looked around the circle of eager faces. He was still holding that shaft as though it was a battering ram and he was seeking doors to force.

'Does the chosen 'prize' have to submit to a public fuck too?' I asked Jeff.

'Well, naturally,' he told me. 'If you come in here, you

have to accept whatever the crowd demands. Majority decisions, you know. That's the rule.'

Jack had made his choice. Looking over the heads of the nearest spectators, his lewd eye brightened. He pointed at Inge. 'You, darling,' he said. 'I'd like to give it to you.'

There was a fresh round of applause. Inge nodded. As if it was the most natural thing in the world – for all I knew, for her maybe it was – she stepped forward, unfastening the waistband of her long skirt. Unconcernedly, she stepped out of it and stripped off a pair of white lacy panties. She peeled dark grey nylon tights down to her knees, unbuttoned the white silk blouse and snapped open the clasp of her bra. 'How do you want me?' she asked.

I stole a glance at Jeff. His face was as expressionless as Inge's.

'Seeing as how this time it's quality rather than quantity,' Jack said, 'I think we'll have you on the table, on hands and knees, so I can take you from behind. That way, the boys and girls can have a real look at the working parts!'

Strange, isn't it, how one's reactions can take one by surprise? I hardly knew Inge; I certainly knew nothing of her private life. Yet somehow the thought of seeing her bulled like a cow, publicly allowing that exquisite, petite body to be humiliated, turned me right off.

I backed away, determined to transfer my attention to the other room. As I turned, I saw that Susan had already left.

She was leaning against the wall, just inside the second door.

The atmosphere in here couldn't have been more different. The lighting was very low indeed – a soft rosy

181

glow from a single bedside lamp. There were two naked women on the wide bed, and the silence positively vibrated with tenderness and intimacy. Half a dozen men and girls, unrecognizable in the gloom, sat around in easy chairs, quietly smoking or sipping drinks. The two women were locked in a tight embrace, their hands scarcely moving but their breathing fast.

'Marvellous!' Susan whispered.

'Well, I suppose it's always better second time around,' I murmured in spite of myself. 'Especially when you can see from outside!'

The brightness of her eyes shone in the semi-darkness as her head twisted my way. 'Bastard!' she hissed. 'You know, don't you? You spied on me!'

'I just happened to be passing,' I said.

'Well, I'm not ashamed of it,' Susan said. 'It was lovely.'

'You don't have to be ashamed,' I soothed. 'You just gave me Chapter One of my next book.'

Chapter Thirteen

The two women on the big bed in that second room were very different: one was blonde, the other brunette; the blonde was huge, a Brunnhilde Nordic goddess type; her partner small and dainty, with elegant, tapered limbs and small but perfect breasts. The goddess must have been over six feet tall, her lover what the rag trade calls a natural five-foot-two.

What they shared in common was a rapt concentration on what they were doing: each was so totally immersed in the other that nothing outside of that bed and their bodies existed. The rest of the room, the silent watchers, the wreaths of cigarette smoke curling through the subdued light, the rowdy crowd next door – these were the figments of someone else's imagination. Only their own hands and mouths existed in their private world.

They *were* lovers too. This was no chance coupling, no thrill-seeking embrace designed to stimulate the lubricity of others, nothing in the nature of a defiant gesture aimed at the conventions or something one did for a dare. Every movement and each tiny sound on that bed was heavy with tenderness and an intimacy so complete that it could only have been the result of long experience together.

Forget the porn business and the swinging scene for a

moment. Let's be brutal and risk being called sentimental or old fashioned: those two women loved one another.

How they came to be at that party, in that room, with those other people, I have no idea. Perhaps they already knew it, or discovered at the start of the party that it was there and installed themselves before anyone else came to the suite. Perhaps later they became so engrossed with each other that they neither noticed – nor cared – that they had an audience. It was even possible, I supposed, that their thinking might be precisely the reverse of this: that they welcomed an audience because the very fact that they could ignore it underlined the inviolability of their physical togetherness, the sealed compartment in which they loved.

Psychological considerations aside, this was a knockout spectacle!

Brunnhilde was vast in every way: her thighs were massive, her breasts voluminous and her waist muscular and thick. But her shape as a whole was delightful and perfectly feminine. Her flesh was firm, resilient, the skin glowing with good health, her prominent features relaxed in an expression of sensual contentment.

When I came in, she was lying back against the pillows with her legs spread and one knee raised. Her eyes were closed and she was cooing softly to herself behind the twin mounds of two great breasts cupped in her own big hands.

The source of the contentment was not hard to find. The petite brunette kelt beside her, with one knee hooked over the blonde's spread leg, her long, slim fingers gently stroking, from bottom to top, the outer lips of the cunt nestling in its pale, springy thatch of pubic hair. Even as we watched, the featherlike touch, teasing softly below the big woman's shivering belly, worked its special magic.

Her labia, visible as a pinkish, wavering slit gashing those hairy loins, began to open flower as sweetly as a rose in the sun. The creased outer folds separated under the brunette's beguiling caress, drawing apart to reveal the pouched pads of the inner pair, darker in colour and glistening now suddenly with moisture as her juices began to flow.

All at once smoothly sliding, the inquisitive fingers explored, investing each tiny crevice and every tremoring curve until the entire cunt with its darkly tunnelled centre was pouting outwards. At the upper limit of this indecently exposed vulva, distended and inflamed, the swollen stub of the clitoris appeared.

Over the very slight creak of the mattress, we heard the blonde catch her breath. Her big body shifted. Sly fingertips had tweaked the throbbing organ as half the hand plunged into the wet depths.

The brunette's dark head lowered and she whispered something into her partner's ear. The blonde uttered a deep groan and her hips heaved up to meet the invading, massaging hand, now quickening in its thrusts and probes to rape the nakedly exposed secret flesh.

Because, you see, one thing had at once been clear: despite the disparity in size and strength, instead of being the butch dyke one might have expected, Brunnhilde was the passive one and the petite and delicate brunette the one in the saddle with the reins in her hand. I don't mean it was an SM relationship, but it was she who made the decisions and took the initiative, Brunnhilde melting waxlike under the tormenting extravagance of her caress.

She looked almost fragile, this girl, but she was tough

and she was strong, birdlike in the precision of each lustful movement. Between them, her mouth and hands covered the whole of her partner's big body in a sensual tattoo. A bobbing of the head here . . . a sharp peck there . . . a light slap followed by a tickle . . . a nibble of this piece of flesh between sharp, even, very white teeth.

The blonde was rolling from side to side on the bed, writhing her hips each time her lover's marauding hand vanished completely inside the maw of her outsize cunt. Her own hands roved the tight planes of the brunette's slender form as she moaned out a scarcely intelligible litany of love and desire.

'Oh, you sweetheart! Again, again, again . . . God, why are you so good to me; why do I love it so? Please, honey, please: yes, yes, I like it . . . Oh, Lord, you wonderful, darling *you!*'

Leaning forward to whisper something scabrous between prolonged sucks at each big breast, the brunette was showing the whole furred length of her genital cleft between the tight little cheeks of her backside. And it was evident that not all the manipulations before I came in had been on her part: the cunt at the lower end of that enticing furrow gaped wide and wet; the blonde's huge hands must have been working there.

The smaller girl shuffled backwards on hands and knees, her lips and tongue tracing a lewd course across the wide, quaking belly, into the crease of one thigh, among the damply curling pubic hair, finally to lock on the glistening lips she had so expertly prepared.

The blonde squealed with delight as the dark head jerked up and down; the liquid lapping of a sucking mouth was audible over her quickened breath. And it was then – perhaps unable any longer to stand the agony of her ecstasy – that she gave a demonstration of her extraordinary strength. Raising the upper half of her body by the force of her belly muscles, she reached down towards the obscenely bobbing head, and past it to her lover's wide-splayed legs.

Seizing the brunette by the hips, she lifted her clear off the bed, holding her for an instant, facedown, at arm's length above her own prone body. Then, spinning her round through a hundred and eighty degrees, she lowered her again, still with the head between her legs . . . but this time with the damp thighs and hungry cunt over her own face.

A murmur of astonishment and admiration rose from the watchers as she wrapped powerful arms around the brunette's back and began herself to suck.

Jeff was standing beside me. 'Inge will be through at any minute,' he told me. 'I think maybe it's time we split . . . unless of course you two want to hang in here a little longer?'

I shook my head. The two on the bed, heaving and writhing in their shared joy, were in any case so tightly locked together that there was really nothing left to see. Not in a sexual sense; not unless you had a thing about arms and legs. 'Let's go,' I agreed.

In the brightly lit room next door, a fleshy woman of about forty lay on her back, naked, on one of the massage tables. Four men, fully dressed, stood around the table with their stiff cocks jutting from open flies. The woman was tossing off the two on either side with expert hands, tilting her head back over the table edge to suck the cock of a third, and being fucked between upraised knees by the last.

There was no chanting or clapping this time, but a

small group of the watchers sung a slightly updated version
of two old nursery rhymes:

> 'Fee, fi, fo, fum:
> 'There's pubic hair below that bum!
> > 'Be it brunette, blonde or red
> > 'I'll have that cunt within my bed!

> 'Eeny meeny, miny, mo:
> 'Tonight's the night for sex, you know:
> > 'Be you timid, scared or lewd,
> > 'You'll see your other half get screwed!'

'There you are, you see,' I said to Jeff. 'There it is in a
nutshell – the difference between the vulgar, the coarse,
and the real thing.'

'You can say that again,' Inge agreed, joining us in the
hallway. 'That bloody man with the thin cock went so far
up me that I was afraid he'd block my throat and I'd
choke!'

'What are you talking about?' Jeff asked me.

I told him about the giantess and her companion,
adding my psychological reading of the scene and what it
implied. Plus of course the contrast with the brightly lit
room.

'Bollocks,' Jeff said when I was through. 'You're nothing
but a bloody romantic!'

'What do you mean?'

'They're both married, your idyllic sapphic lovers,' he
said. 'Each to an eminent and highly placed guy in politics.
This is the only kind of place where they can have it off
without the risk of news hounds or *paparazzi* sussing
them out and splashing the story – which would not only

tip off the husbands to the affair but also ruin the gentlemen's careers.'

'What the hell,' I said. 'We're in the fiction business, aren't we? That won't stop them making a telling chapter in a future book!'

PART THREE

Stags at Bay!

Chapter Fourteen

Lafayette Briggs was a large, indolent, very laid-back black man who lived in Antibes and occupied himself in a desultory way with the chartering of boats which might otherwise find themselves all summer without a client.

Lafayette, who had a wife in Harlem – and probably children too – was originally from Kansas City, Missouri, and had gravitated to New York in the sixties as bass player and singer with one of the jazzy jump bands finding favour with the smaller record companies in that swinging epoch. He had come to the Coast, he told us, to escape his wife. In fact he was trying to contact Denver Hume, the best-selling author of ferociously violent crime novels set in Harlem, who had settled in Vence, a small town in the hills behind Nice. There was some question of an all-black film based on one of Hume's books, Lafayette allowed us to believe, and only he – an ex-schoolfriend and neighbour – was capable of persuading the writer to sign a contract.

The fact that Hume had left Vence two years previously and gone to live in Spain, deterred Lafayette not one bit. 'He be back' he drawled in his lazy way. 'Bound to be, sometime. Any case, I like it here . . . and *I* dare not go back. Man, she have the knives out for me by now!'

I happened to know, nevertheless, that Lafayette sent money to his wife every month without fail. And the lazy manner masked an extremely active business brain. He was, I think I told you, indirectly the contact who fixed my job with Edward.

And the secretary-girlfriend propositioned by Ronald Stokes-Alberry was Miriam.

I found this out quite by chance – because the one thing that seemed to me not to jibe with Lafayette's character – or the image he displayed to the world – was the fact that he was a car buff. And by that I don't mean just that he liked automobiles, was interested in how they worked and enjoyed driving them, I mean his enthusiasm was all-enveloping, voracious. It ranged from the latest mini town car to staid saloons dating from the vintage years, from runabouts to racers. And none of them seemed to satisfy him, for he never kept one for more than a few days, whether it was new or old, bought, borrowed, rented or, for all I knew, stolen.

This would have been odd for anyone, but it seemed especially bizarre for a black American. I've known a lot of jazzmen and I have black friends in the medical and legal professions, but not one of them has ever regarded a car as anything but a means of conveyance or, in the case of an actor, a status symbol. Lafayette on the other hand was wild. I saw him once crammed into the cockpit of a Healey Silverstone; he gave me a lift in an ancient Delage with a decked tail like the stern of a speedboat; he drove Renaults and Citroëns and Fords and Wolseleys of every model and era. But it was mainly the rare and exotic that appeared to tempt him. I saw him on a busy summer day manoeuvring an enormous pre-war 57hp Hispano-Suiza along a narrow gangway in Golfe Juan.

But it was not until that autumn – when I was on my seventh book for Edward – that I found the key to his behaviour in my hand. It was in Cannes. He was preparing to hand over the keys of a vast Delaunay-Belleville landaulette to the doorman at the Carlton Hotel . . . and sitting up beside him with a flushed face and very bright eyes was Miriam, the secretary from Expadink.

Of course! Remembering the girl's passionate thing about automotive sex, I caught on at once. Lafayette was simply pleasuring his lady's hunger for variety!

What devotion, I thought! I wondered if he had managed yet to lay her within the cramped confines of a Grand Prix Bugatti . . .

Lafayette was a big man, he must have weighed in at well over two hundred pounds, but he was muscular as well as tall. He dressed very casually, always, like many jazz musicians, with an old felt hat of the kind that used to be known as a pork-pie, the battered brim shielding his sleepy eyes. He was a local institution. I knew him well enough, though not, as you might say, intimately. That came after he unearthed the Isotta-Fraschini.

It was the largest motor car I'd ever seen. Italian. Mid thirties, I supposed. The letters IF crowned a colossal chromed radiator, behind which was an eight-foot bonnet and an open touring body with a separate windscreen for those in the rear seats. The car was yellow, with sweeping black mudguards, the front pair housing two immense spare wheels. Lafayette – nobody ever dreamed of shortening his name to Laffy or Fay or even Etso – Lafayette was wedging the thing into the yard below my pad when I came back from a shopping expedition. 'Good parking,' he said, setting fire to a cigar from the lighter in the teak dashboard. 'I need to see you.'

'You certainly like to shoot with two barrels!' I said. 'Aston-Martin, Austro-Daimler, Alfa-Romeo,

Napier-Railton . . . and now this!'

He grinned. 'Me, I make out good enough with one barrel,' he said. 'But the chicks like class, see.' He swept an arm towards the rear of the Isotta. 'Man, you could hold a Charleston competition in there, and still leave room for a five piece! As for the motor, there're seven and a half litres under that hood.'

'Where did you get it?' I asked. 'Why do you need to see me?'

'Friend in Italy,' he said. 'About a party. Kind of a floating ballroom.'

'I'm listening,' I said. 'Pour it on.'

It seemed that Lafayette had an 'interest' in a charter boat that slept twelve, not yet hired for the season but with a possible client teetering on the brink. If he could see a chic, rip-roaring jet-set *soirée* brawling aboard, he might think it a worthwhile bet . . . and sign. 'He wants to go to Madeira,' Lafayette said. 'And maybe Lagos. Six weeks minimum. At ten percent . . .' He shook his head.

I saw the point. 'What exactly did you have in mind?' I said.

'A stag,' he told me. 'With chicks.'

I frowned. 'Isn't that kind of a contradiction in terms?'

'Terms have to be agreed,' Lafayette said. 'But there ain't no contradictions.'

'It may be about a boat,' I said, 'but you've leaving me at sea. Fill me in, man! In English if possible.'

He grinned, rumbling out one of his infectious chuckles. 'The boat should sell itself,' he said. 'Provided he likes – and trusts – the parties selling. So we show the guy a good time, a whale of a fucking time. Good food, good music, glamour on tap, champagne and glorious, I mean glorious, gals. A ball!'

'Okay,' I said, 'but I don't see . . . ?'

'He be plunged into a wild party,' Lafayette explained. 'Party of the year, right? All around him good guys. Having good sex. Party like that, there be someone else's broad you want to lay. Maybe several. Obviously. Well, the wrinkle here is that he can have *any chick he fancies*. Any one.' Another chuckle. 'And no hard feelings . . . 'cept of course his own! He like us all right after that.'

'You're crazy,' I said.

'Crazy like a fox. I get results.' Leaning back against the resplendent yellow bodywork of the Isotta, Lafayette tipped his hat further forward over his eyes. He flicked ash from his cigar onto the cobbles. 'Now I explain you the stag part.'

'I was beginning to wonder,' I said.

'This kind of a deal,' Lafayette said, 'ain't no percentage if the talent is obviously bought. He could do that himself. Has to be that *he seduces other guys' gals*. On account of his manly charm. You dig?'

'Well, yeah. But . . . ?'

'Some folks' gals wouldn't be too happy wearing this scenario.'

'You surprise me,' I said.

'Especially as the punter's kind of a skinny little runt. But I know the type: he believe he's Casanova's great grandson, cannot understand the rebuffs.'

'So?'

Lafayette jabbed the cigar in my direction. 'So we got the perfect opportunity. This week. For the stag scene with chicks, I mean. Jeff's old lady's in Paris with her mummy and daddy. Your Susan's on a cruise. Van Eyck's a freelance anyway. Edward and Velvet have taken Miriam to Rome for some big deal conference with Maddox and

197

the distributors. I might even row in Roland. Author of romances is always a catch.'

'Thank you very much,' I said. 'And the girls?'

'Fourth floor of the Martinez,' he said. 'I got a contact he looks after some of the prettiest. We school five, six of the best to make like they're our personal property or even our old ladies.'

'I imagine that's where the terms come in?' I said.

'Maybe. I'm working on that. It's possible the thought of a millionaire mark could even that up. Any case, like I say, I got contacts. We see soon enough.'

'And who will be driving this ship on its . . . shall we say *maiden* cruise?'

'I have certain talents that way myself,' Lafayette said surprisingly.

I laughed. 'How far do we go?' I asked.

'About a mile and a half,' he said. 'We anchor on the seaward side of one of the islands off Cannes.'

The boat was an unusual design. It had originally been a torpedo recovery craft – a purpose-built naval auxiliary used to bring back tinfish without warheads fired on a range – the driving part of a torpedo being too expensive to leave floating about on the high seas.

Pinched from Germany as part of the war reparation in 1946, it had lain idle in Newhaven for almost twenty years because the superchargers alimenting its twin diesels were broken and the factory making them had been bombed out of existence. Then a Cornish fisherman and a motor racing mechanic had teamed up to find the £350 necessary to buy it, worked on it for a year to make the engines work without superchargers, and sailed it to the Med. Two years later they had fitted out the armoured hull as a luxury cruiser, painted the rakish craft white, and added a flying bridge with dual controls in a wheelhouse below.

It was a strange, but impressive, vessel, with a sharp, high destroyer prow and a very long stern section, low in the water because that was where the recovered torpedoes were stored. It was eighty-five feet long and could make, on a calm day, almost forty knots.

At that time, French law only permitted non-French owners to charter to other foreigners, so eventually the two owner-designers had sold the ship, at a fair profit, to an oil-prospecting company with interests off West Africa. It was now owned by a rich ship's chandler with a waterfront store in Cannes – and it was he who had entrusted Lafayette Briggs, after what conning expertise nobody knew, with the chartering business.

Proudly displaying his prize, Lafayette, with his cool, cool threads and heavy, lazy carriage, looked anything but a seafaring man. And the hat tipped far forward to hide his yellow eyes gave no actual indication of the clear-sighted, intrepid mariner who would risk all to bring his ship unscathed through the fiercest of storms!

He'd certainly done his homework on the craft's technicalities, and I was suitably impressed as he showed me around. But it was when, later, we arrived at the fourth floor of the Hotel Martinez in Cannes that I had to recognize the true expert on his home ground.

The arrival itself was symptomatic of what was to follow – smooth, swift, ultra-discreet and efficient. It was effected via a little-used door and passage penetrating the railway embankment running behind the hotel. This led to a yard at one side of the hotel's kitchen wing and thence, by way of the cold-store, the transfer of two hundred-franc bills to a room service waiter, and a service lift, to the right part of the building.

There were three of us: Lafayette, myself and Jeff Adlam. 'Since we going to have ourselves a ball, man,' Lafayette had explained, 'seems right we should choose our partners. I mean, shit, this ain't no honkie escort agency scam!'

The fourth floor smelled equally of suntan oil, very expensive perfume, rich materials and, indefinably, woman. It was five o'clock. Through the landing windows we could see the late sun sliding down towards the humped silhouettes of the Esterel massif on the far side of the packed marinas.

Most of the girls had already come in from the beach. It took a while to get out of the oil and into the sexy cocktail dresses in time to be coolly alluring in the foyer when the apéritif drinkers arrived.

The floor looked much like an upper floor in any of the big time hotels on the coast: the Majestic, the Carlton, the Negresco, La Reserve at Beaulieu, Monte Carlo's Hotel de Paris. The deep-pile carpet was perhaps a little bit more worn – all those panting punters hurrying to make the bedroom! The paintwork was a trifle less glossy, but there was the same hushed air of efficiency, the low voices behind closed doors, the unseen and anonymous presence of staff typical of any place where it costs.

We trod stealthily past the murmur of female voices, an occasional musical laugh. My mind was already feeding me disturbing images of lacy knickers drawn up over tanned thighs, of breasts hanging as bodies leaned forward to varnish toenails, of insidious deodorant perfumes squirted into hairless armpits. I wondered how many of the arms behind those doors were bent up behind backs to fasten the snaps of low-cut brassières. And whose fumbling hands would be paying an arm and a leg later to unsnap them!

Lafayette's goal was Room 412. It was discreetly situated. The white door with its panels picked out in gold closed off a short passage around a corner in the wide main landing. There were only two other doors leading off the passage, one on either side.

He tapped lightly three times, twice, and then three times again. That was one of the most noticeable things about Lafayette: despite his bulk, everything he did was feather-light. His feet seemed scarcely to touch the floor; when he lowered himself into a chair, there was never the slightest sense of weight descending; the chairs never even creaked! In the same way his knocks on the door, although clear and distinct, were barely audible.

The door swung open at once and he ushered us in.

Lafayette's contact, at least for this particular operation, was called Cindy. She was gorgeous. What else is there to say about her? She had green eyes and dark red hair. She had a 38-24-34 figure and long, tapered legs. Her voice was low and throaty and she came from Munich.

The package was wrapped, sarong-style, in a jade-green bath towel when she received us, but it did nothing to hide the contents.

'Well, lover man,' she said to Lafayette when the introductions had been made, 'what have you and your friends got to offer?'

'An evening afloat,' he said, 'awash with unbridled lust and fantasy. There will be food and drink as well.'

'Sounds about par for the course, this time of year,' Cindy smiled. Her English and French were both perfect. 'Explain.'

Lafayette explained. It was clear, however, that the

matter had been broached before, because there was no mention at all of money. 'You chicks don't have to pretend that we're married couples,' he told Cindy. 'But it's important to get across the idea that we're going steady. The mark has to believe that his manly charm is strong enough to drag a lady away from her loved one. You dig?'

'No problem,' Cindy said. 'So run me down the personnel. I mean like who screws who.'

'The three of us, baby,' Lafayette said, 'plus Randall Van Eyck and a very British Brit who writes ladies' romances.'

'And of course your mark?'

'Yeah, but there's no question of fixing him up with a blind date. Makes the whole thing look too much like a set-up. He got to think he makes it with *someone else's* lovey-dovey. Make him feel a big man, seven feet tall.'

'I get the picture,' Cindy said. 'So you'll be wanting . . . ?'

Lafayette grinned at Jeff and me. 'This one's mine,' he said, laying a dark arm across her beautifully tanned shoulders. And then, to Cindy: 'Yourself and three of the best, darling.'

'Give me a minute then,' she said, smiling. 'You can look at the book while I dress, then I'll try to give you a private view of the flesh you choose.' She unwound the towel and allowed it to fall to the floor, as unconcerned about her nakedness in front of strangers as a salesman handling stones in Cartier's. What the hell, it was the product: her body was the work of art responsible for her income. Her pubic hair was ginger too.

She opened a drawer in a bureau and took out a leather photograph album. 'Browse,' she advised, handing it to me. 'I'll be back in five.' She vanished into the steamy, perfumed interior of a bathroom.

The album contained nude studies of a dozen young women, full cabinet size. Each was smiling, provocative, and all of them were stunning.

When Cindy returned, she was wearing high-heeled, black patent court shoes, dark stockings and a black sequin sheath that hugged her thighs and exposed almost all of her above the nipples. No man with money to spend, I thought, would hesitate a single second before opening hostilities!

While she was away, I had looked up from the book and murmured to Lafayette: 'I don't want to butt in. But you said Cindy and *three* other girls. And there will be five of us . . . ?'

'We're on budget, man,' he told me. 'And this merchandise ain't exactly given away free with the cornflakes. No, but I found the cutest little French pastry cook for Number Five – and she'll do the whole number just for kicks.'

'Oh, boy!' said Jeff.

We'd made our choices. The girl Jeff had chosen, as it happened, was in the next room to Cindy's. On our way to her 'private view' she tapped on the left-hand door in the short passageway. I'd seen a naked photo of the girl who opened it, but nothing in two dimensions could do justice to the third.

You know the phrase 'in the flesh'? And you're familiar with the terms 'voluptuous' and 'sultry'? Well, underline all three. Twice if there's room.

I saw shoulder-length dark hair, slumbrous eyes (there I go again!) and a mouth as wide and generous and full-lipped as Sophia Loren's, if that's possible. That evening, I was convinced it was.

Her name was Marysa and she came from Budapest, Hungary.

Another husky voice, with a touch, perhaps, of the smouldering gypsy. The body was soft but firm, wrapped in a dark crimson confection of floating panels and creamy slopes. I can't be any more explicit: I was too busy staring at that mouth.

'Oh, boy!' Jeff said again.

Marysa joined us as Cindy led the way to a service lift and then down three floors to a kind of rotunda balcony overlooking the main foyer of the hotel. Here amongst potted palms behind the reception desk and porters' lodge, there were already at least a dozen beautiful girls lounging in leather armchairs, looking as though they were waiting for a late escort to show. Which of course they were – except that they didn't know yet who the escort was going to be.

The floor space was pretty crowded too, with white tuxedos showing among the expensive beach gear although it wasn't yet six o'clock, guests streaming toward the bars, arrivals and departures clustered around Reception and stacks of luggage beside the constantly revolving swing doors.

The two other good-timers we had chosen were already in place down there.

'There she is, just beside the newsstand,' Jeff exclaimed, pointing in the direction of the beauty we had selected for Randy. 'Perfect!' he said to Cindy. 'The guy's a mediaevalist, and she looks like one of those Pre-Raphaelite heroines painted by Millais or Holman-Hunt. He should be delighted.'

The girl, who was dressed in a floor-length evening gown in a flower print with long sleeves and a decorous neckline, looked anything but a whore. She was leaning back indolently, almost languidly, toying with a gold vanity bag and a long ebony cigarette-holder, her elegant, rather refined features set in an expression of faint distaste. This was the unapproachable, ladylike type many men were so eager to possess and despoil.

Her name, I knew, was Aurelia. But she was a case where the photo in fact revealed far more than the reality. Because above the slender, rather chaste nude body, the photographer had caught a wicked half smile and eyes slanted at the lens as lasciviously carnal as anything I had even seen.

My own choice, Gina, was a lean, almost stringy blonde with hard, prominent breasts above her narrow waist. Not my usual type, but then I had a buxom girl of my own. And frankly it was the cunt in her photo that had turned me on. It's difficult to describe but there was something about the thrustful projection of the mons, the pouting eagerness of the half-open labia beneath that sandy thatch, that told me without a shadow of a doubt that to be engulfed in and swallowed by that aperture would be no more than a preliminary to the wildest of muscularly contrived ecstasies.

Looking at her as she sat bolt upright in a tight white leather dress with black lacing at the sides, I could almost see those loins burning with lustful desire between her crossed thighs!

'Okay, guys?' Lafayette asked. 'Cindy has to go below now, before the carriage trade has picked up all the hopefuls.'

I nodded energetically. I stood by my choice. The others might be prettier but Gina looked by far the horniest. I learned later that she came from Blackpool. 'Swell,' I said.

Jeff was grinning all over his college-boy face. 'Just lead me to it. Boy, oh boy!' he enthused for the third time.

'Okay, then,' Lafayette said. 'My thanks, honey' – another squeeze of Cindy's shoulder – 'and we stroll out the entrance like paying guests! Just a little call to make, to order some – uh – delicacies, and the day will be over.'

The delicacies he had in mind were in Rue Hélène Vagliano, a short street near the railway station named after a Greek girl in the Resistance who was tortured and executed by the Nazis in 1944.

The shop was clearly extremely chic and enormously expensive. You could tell that by the very small number of exotic pastries on display beneath brilliant glass covers on the slanting, doylied shelves.

The young woman Lafayette had recruited stood behind the counter. She was alone in the shop. Her name was Violette – and she was just about the Frenchest thing I ever saw in my life.

She wore a crisp white blouse with a lace *jabot* at the neck, and a dark, full skirt printed with flowers. Low-heeled shoes accentuated rather than diminished the elegance of her calves and the creases on the long sleeves of her spotless blouse were razor-sharp.

Violette looked in fact as if she had just been unpacked from a couturier's gift box.

Add to this wavy chestnut hair caught at the nape with a black velvet bow and unemphatic but expertly applied make-up, and you get the picture.

The picture, yes, but not the whole story. You get the image but not the movement, the motivation, the breathing life behind it.

Because all this was in fact incidental. The thing you noticed most about Violette was this: there was a certain stillness about her, an economy of movement; the clothes she wore were amply cut, they scarcely touched her anywhere. Yet in some way one was instantly – in my case almost agonizingly – aware of the nubile, fleshy body beneath them. The very anonymity of the garments, their lack of explicit gender, emphasized – practically shouted – the existence of the nipples and buttocks and bush and belly they concealed.

There she was. A woman.

In that quiet side-street shop, the rustle of a turned-back cuff as she reached for the tongs to grip the pastries Lafayette selected, the whisper of silk when she moved her legs to walk to the till, were the sexiest things I'd heard in months.

Clearly Lafayette was similarly affected. He cleared his throat, raising a large hand to flick the brim of his absurd hat even further over his eyes. '. . . and three *millefeuilles*, two coffee éclairs, a couple japs and one of those whipped cream whorls,' he said. 'I guess that'll be all' – the big laugh rumbled out – 'for now, honey.'

Violette glanced at all three of us and then looked him straight in the eye – her own *were* violet too, I saw. 'We are always happy to accept advance orders, sir,' she said levelly.

Lafayette grinned. 'Me too, baby,' he said. 'See you Friday.'

The loveliest night of the week, I thought as we trooped out of the shop. Or was that supposed to be Saturday? A bell tinkled musically above the door. No, shit, the song was about the *loneliest* night of the week!

That certainly wasn't on the agenda for this Friday! My pulses were still tingling. Gina was going to be fine when we played couples, but I couldn't wait to get my lecherous hands among all that softness under Violette's blouse. When the party switched into the swap mode.

Jeff opened his mouth. 'Don't say it,' I warned, one hand on his arm. 'I'll do it for both of us. Oh, *boy!*'

Chapter Fifteen

To call Winstone McPhee 'a skinny little runt', as Lafayette
had done, was a little unfair. He was certainly shortish
and lean. But there was muscle on his thin legs and arms
and hair on his chest. His features, though, were not his
strong point. His face, almost cadaverous, was lantern-
jawed, thin-lipped and sunken-eyed. It was the sort of
sallow, ascetic fanatic's face that wore a five o'clock shadow
at four.

And fanatic the man definitely was. About sex – or,
more specifically, his own exploits and successes in that
line. Unfortunately, despite the fortune, the practical failed
regularly to live up to the theory. He had a wife, tucked
away somewhere on a huge estate in Connecticut, but on
the extra-marital plane he was rejected far more often
than accepted. There was something – a harsh self-
assertiveness, an overwhelming conceit, perhaps just
something physical – that seemed singularly effective at
turning off the beauties he fancied.

Thus Lafayette's plan, McPhee for the buttering-up of.

The guy was agreeable enough, just the same, allowing
for the usual rich man's fear that he was being taken for a
ride, with an occasional talent for the wry stateside one-
liner. I had at first imagined that he *was* American, but he
was in fact born in Australia and made his fortune there

pioneering supermarkets in out-of-the-way rural areas.

He turned up for the party in a white suit with braces, a stiff collar and a Highland Brigade club tie to which he was not entitled.

The other virtually unknown quantity, to me at any rate, was Ronald Stokes-Alberry. We'd met of course. As Brits in a region spattered with Anglo-this and Anglo-that clubs, friendship societies and what I called colony-groups it would have been difficult not to. But I hardly knew the man. I just hated him, jealously, for his success – undeserved, according to yours truly – with stuff that I chose to consider rubbish. He was a great favourite, though, with old ladies and languishing widows, on everybody's guest list all along the Coast.

I don't know how it had been put, but he'd jumped nevertheless at LaFayette's shipboard party invitation. Perhaps the word cunt had cropped up somewhere in the conversation.

Ronald was what all foreigners expect an Englishman to be: tall, upright, large of bottom and red of face, with sandy hair, a neat moustache and staring, very blue eyes. His language was neo-Wodehouse and his voice very loud.

In French, however, I regret to say, he was elegant, witty, fluent and virtually accentless. You can't have everything negative.

Stokes-Alberry also wore a white suit. Maybe he always did when he went out. It was less expensive but rather better cut that McPhee's. It came with a lizard-skin belt (the Friday cut-price market in Ventimiglia, just over the border), a plain peacock-blue tie from Gucci, a silk handkerchief of precisely the same colour flopping from the breast pocket, and white suede shoes.

The rest of us were rather more casually dressed, bearing in mind the ease with which clothes would need to be discarded later in the evening. We all wore open-necked shirts, pale-coloured jeans in one material or another, and kick-off sandals. No socks of course.

We met in a bar at the far end of the Croisette. There was less chance of Cindy and her girls being recognized, and the boat was berthed nearby at Port Canto.

McPhee was to meet us on board, when the party was supposed already to be under way. Lafayette and Cindy would go first, and lay out the drinks and prepared food which had already been delivered. The other couples would roll up at different intervals, just in case the Australian millionaire was suspicious enough to arrive early and keep secret watch to suss out exactly what kind of shindig he was heading for. To keep up the idea of guests from different parts of town, Gina and I were to be last of all – after McPhee himself – and be formally introduced all round, as though Lafayette and Cindy were the only folks we'd met before.

Seen together in that bar on the Croisette, I have to say that we must have looked a pretty stunning crowd. The girls were splendid – Cindy in a pleated white dress, Aurelia in what was practically a long-sleeved ball gown, Marysa wearing black velvet and the other two sporting bare-midriff beach pyjamas.

Violette looked marvellous. Her pyjamas were lime-green, and like the clothes she wore behind the counter, their ample, flowing lines did everything possible to suggest what they in fact concealed. Only the faintest of laugh lines fanning out from the corners of her eyes hinted that she might be nearer forty than thirty.

If she was aware that her fellow 'guests' were what

used to be known as ladies of easy virtue, nothing whatever
in her attitude showed it. Most shopkeepers in France
were pragmatic about the whores on their street anyway.
In one way or another, they were all *commerçants* after all.
The girl swinging her bunch of keys in a doorway or
standing at the corner had something to sell, and so did
they: the product was different but the *métier* was the
same; despite a certain difference of degree, it was all part
of the neighbourhood scene.

By the time Cindy and Lafayette took off, a real party
was already warming up. And I guess we, the escorts,
looked about right too. We were all tanned, Randy suave
and bearded, Ronald doing his Bertie Wooster number,
Jeff at his most clean-cut, vibrant with boyish charm.
Maybe those girls were onto a good thing anyway!

Gina was nice enough. A little reserved on the personal
side, more than the others perhaps inclined to regard the
evening just as a job. Sure, she'd play along – she admitted
that she did actually like fucking – but don't expect any
lasting or caring relationship. Whatever her contract was,
and I supposed Lafayette had conned his chandler into
stumping up the ante, she'd honour it as energetically as
she could. But small talk, for a start, wasn't written into
the clauses.

We were hidden in the rear of a huge old Boillot
sedanca-de-ville our host had stashed in the Port Canto
parking lot, invisible behind darkly tinted plate glass
windows. The boat – it was for some reason called *Offshore
II* – was already a blaze of light; music was audible from
the interior, and every now and then Cindy or Lafayette
would appear beneath the striped awning over the long,
low stern, laying tables or arranging chairs. Just a normal,
homely couple expecting friends.

Lafayette had been right too. Winstone McPhee did arrive a full half hour before the time the party was scheduled to start. Driving an unobtrusive Renault runabout, he parked between two palm trees some way from the boat, settling himself as low as he could in the driving seat to wait and watch.

We watched and waited too. Stokes-Alberry and Violette drove up in a white E-Type Jaguar – what else! – parked, and went aboard. Effusive greetings beneath the awning. The popping of champagne corks. Animated conversation.

A Mercedes taxi next, braking to a halt by the gangway. Aurelia and Randy drifted aboard. Very chic, straight off the social register. More greetings, kisses all round, laughter now amongst the music.

This seemed to decide the Australian. He slunk away from the Renault, made a wide circle among the other parked cars, and approached on foot, arriving at *Offshore II* just as Jeff and Marysa, resplendent in her black velvet, drove up.

Gina and I, following instructions, waited another ten minutes before we approached the gangway.

Laughs, hugs, introductions, explanations. Randy was an historian on a Sabbatical in Europe, I was a columnist and Jeff a novelist. Stokes-Alberry, damn him, was well enough known not to need explaining. Nothing was said about the girls: it was just assumed that each was 'with' or 'belonged to' her particular escort. Except, that is, for Violette. There was too much chance that McPhee might have been to the shop and noticed her. If he had been, he certainly would have! And it was after all the best in town. So she was awarded her rightful style and estate, as they say.

I won't go into details of the social bit. There was a lot

213

of talk and a quantity of food and drink was sunk in quite a short while. The Australian's greedy eyes flicked over Gina and away again (as she didn't smile as much as the others he probably assumed we were man and wife). They lingered lasciviously on the nubile figures of Marysa and Violette, and stared with frank, almost rude sexual curiosity at Cindy. The covert gaze he switched from time to time on Aurelia included something equivocal that I couldn't quite place. A mixture of admiration, envy and wariness perhaps. It was clear that he was less cocky, less at ease with her than with the others.

By the time Lafayette started the engines, cast off and steered *Offshore II* out across the bay, most of us had quite a buzz on. McPhee had become a little loud and self-congratulatory, explaining at length his business successes.

We had agreed no fixed plans for the serious part of the evening, but I noticed that Ronald and Violette were no longer with us when we were opposite the new casino and the boat turned through ninety degrees to head out to sea. Play it by ear was the name of the game.

Gina walked a little unsteadily down the ladder leading from the wheelhouse into the saloon. 'Let's fuck,' she said in a loud voice, taking hold of my arm.

McPhee's eyes glittered. 'You lovebirds want a little pri-va-cy,' Lafayette called down, 'you have to take Cabin Two. One is kind of occupied.'

'You – uh – got a kinda liberated crowd this neck of the woods,' I heard McPhee say to Randy as we moved into the narrow companionway that led to the cabins. There were in fact five – two double, two single, and the skipper's; if there ever were twelve people aboard, the others had to make do with bunks in the saloon. 'We like to call it radical,' Randy replied. 'Just because folks have shacked up together, that shouldn't deprive them of choice. I mean, you know, either of them.'

'Well, sure,' McPhee said warmly, looking at Aurelia.

The cabin was comfortable, with a wide bunk, fitted cupboards, drawers, etc., but it was pretty cramped. 'You want to strip, love?' Gina asked with her broad Lancashire accent.

'Whatever you like,' I said.

'Look, I'm being paid to do what *you* want,' she said. 'So choose.' I nodded. 'Okay, so we strip.'

'I start to get interested when it's right there inside me,' she explained a little more warmly. 'Long and hard and hungry.'

This was exactly what I had suspected – and hoped – so I hauled off my tee-shirt (even if I didn't belong to the Teamsters' Union, Mr Maddox!), stepped out of jeans and underpants, and kicked away the sandals as fast as I could. Even so, she was on the bunk well before me, the pyjamas pooled on the floor and the briefest bikini bottom, not much more than a G-string, still in one hand. She was wearing dark nylon stockings rolled down to the knee in the French fashion, and very high-heeled, white sling-back shoes.

That was fine with me: it emphasized the total nudity of her shaven mons and the big, thick nipples projecting from her small, tight breasts. She had no need, as I thought, of a bra, but there was enough there to grab hold of if in danger of drowning.

There *was* a danger of that, too, once one was engulfed, as I found out pretty soon.

My cock had, frankly, manifested itself a trifle hesitantly so far: things being perhaps a little contrived. But the taut lines of Gina's naked body, pale against dark covers, with the shod legs spread and the nipples finger-and-thumbed by her own hands, did the trick all right. Hard, and indeed hungry now, to use her term, I gazed at the smooth and, as it seemed, positively upthrust mound of Venus proud between her splayed thighs. Her cunt was a wound, unexpectedly dark amongst all that shaven, whitely gleaming flesh. The lips – for Gina, unusually, was a pouter as well as an ingester – the lips alternately closed to a vivid, creased gash and flowered open wide enough to reveal a definite opening and the unfathomable depths beyond.

It looked as though the phenomenon was natural, an instinctive, unconscious reaction in parallel with her breathing. But of course it was pure muscular control and she was doing it deliberately. Each time the fleshy folds opened, a small drop of moisture pearled the apex of the sexual slit . . . and as I watched this welled and spread, so that by the time the cunt had opened and closed a couple of times more, the entire distended whorl of those parted labia was glistening and wet.

This was just what I expected, what I had hoped for and what I wanted.

Gina smiled for the first time. It was a nice warm smile, full of complicity, and it reached as far as her eyes. 'Give it to me, lovey,' she invited in a voice that was suddenly crooning. 'Put it right in!' She reached for my stiffened tool.

I needed no further coaxing. Her cunt seemed to be smiling a welcome too. She wagged the cock-head against the opening as I lowered myself between her legs, stirring the folds. And then easily, smoothly, warmly and wetly I was in, sliding satinwise into the sucking, milking clasp of Gina's hot and quivering belly.

I can't really explain it, but this was the perfect entry: one minute there were two people on the wide bunk, naked but a little wary – at least on my side – and then suddenly there was this warmly intimate, this *friendly* and delightful, complex and simple organism, perfectly working and perfectly in tune, sharing a singular and delicious experience from a double point of view!

I mean, like, Christ, it felt wonderful in there!

Gina's hips weren't all that fleshy, okay, but the muscular power of that whole educated pelvis, thrusting and withdrawing in an easy but compelling rhythm, made up for that. It was extraordinary. With the arching and collapse of those loins to counter my own thrusts and withdrawals, the dilation and contraction of her ridged vaginal muscles inside and the forceful, sliding grasp of the labia outside, Gina seemed to be fucking, sucking and wanking me all at the same time.

The boat rose and fell to the advancing swell as we headed offshore, adding to the inexorable surge of our shared lust as we plunged and withdrew.

Our hips pounded together, the big nipples of her tight breasts swelled against my palms, her fingers clenched the flesh at the small of my back and her writhing ankles were hooked over my calves.

My tongue was engulfed in her throat and my cock – in a sweet paradise all of its own – was buried within the channel of her cunt.

Man, it was bliss! But once on the track in that direction, with every signal showing green, there's nothing to do but press on to the end of the line.

A sexologist studying orgasms, if he was plotting sensual excitement against time, would have discovered that our mutual graph, starting in the bottom left-hand corner, rose straight as a die to the top-right at an angle of precisely 45 degrees!

That was when we soared off the page in a great spasm of shared ecstasy.

Cindy, buttoning the white dress, was emerging from the galley as we emerged. Clearly, since Lafayette was engaged at the wheel, McPhee had banged in after her when she went in to clear up dishes or wash the glasses or something. This of course would all have been according to plan.

The Australian himself was nowhere to be seen. Probably still buttoning up his fly behind the icebox.

Marysa, half-smiling with those luscious lips, was looking quizzical. Cindy shrugged. 'He's got a big cock,' she told the Hungarian girl's raised eyebrows. 'End of story.'

Marysa nodded. 'Par for the course,' she said. And then, turning to Jeff: 'Be a darling and pitch a woo at Cindy, eh? Then I can try and get in my turn before he's sloshed enough to ruin this dress. Okay?'

Jeff grinned in his obliging way, put an arm around the redhead's white waist, and led her towards the stern. The lights of the Cannes waterfront rose dizzily into view, diamond bright as *Offshore II* breasted each incoming wave.

The powerful beat of the twin diesels increased. The craft shot ahead towards the dark bulk of the islands, leaving deep, foamed furrows etched into the dark water. Randall thumbed open a champagne bottle and poured a glass for Aurelia with some difficulty as the boat keeled over, to spray the frothing wine across the tilting deck.

Veering a little unsteadily from side to side as the swell increased, Marysa shot into the saloon as McPhee materialized at the entrance to the galley. 'Why, Monsieur McPhee,' she exclaimed in honeyed tones. 'Your glass she is empty! Let me at once put this aright . . .' Holding onto the brass companionway rail, she reached out into the night and tweaked the freshly opened bottle from Randy's grasp. She splashed champagne for herself and McPhee into two glasses standing on the saloon table. 'Whoo!' she gasped. 'Rough now. I think I must for a little while sit.'

Seconds later, the door of Cabin No. 3 closed and the party was reduced by two.

The rest of us opened another bottle, and then we drank some more.

There didn't seem much point in starting something energetic while McPhee was shut away: the whole point of the party was that he should be drawn into a wild scene, an orgy, and believe that he had luckily crashed it because of his powerful personality. At the same time, it was necessary that, when he finally emerged with Marysa, he should find himself surrounded by a swinging, ongoing session.

Lafayette, always the man of the moment, resolved the problem without even being asked. Leaning down through the hatchway that led to the wheelhouse, he called: 'Hey, guys – you wanna keep an eye so you got all systems go when our hero returns, right? But there no need to waste yourselves, or the gals, before. You dig?'

I walked to the foot of the companionway. 'Sure,' I said. 'We want to be hard at it, right and left, not lying there panting after we just made it with whoever.' I lowered my voice. 'Trouble is, there's no way of knowing where the mark's at. I mean like no tipoff. They went into a cabin, and—'

'Number Three,' Lafayette interrupted. 'Ron's in One with Violette, you just quit Two. But if you stand on the bunk in Four, there's a knot-hole just left of the Buffet repro. That give you all the view you want to organize your schedule.'

I laughed. 'Waal, good on yer, sport!' I said in the best Australian drawl I could manage.

Very quietly, I opened the door of the fourth cabin and eased myself inside. I didn't switch on the lighting. And, right enough, a thin shaft of brilliance lanced the gloom under the roof at one side of the picture.

Stealthily creeping onto the bunk, I put one eye to the hole.

Bingo!

In the suffused illumination distilled by a pink-shaded lamp, I saw Marysa spread-eagled on a narrow bunk, her black velvet dress pulled down to her waist and up to her hips, her marble-white thighs with the damp twists of pubic hair between them as clear as carved ivory against the dark bedcovers. There was a brassière on the floor and her large, soft breasts, sliding a little down the incline each side of her rib-cage, looked voluptuously fleshy in the subdued light.

Her hands were linked behind her dark head and she gazed dreamily at Winstone McPhee as he leaned forward to thrust apart the black stockings sheathing the lower part of her legs.

Cindy, in her dismissive way, had not exactly exaggerated. Nor had she done justice to her partner in the cramped confines of the galley. McPhee did, indeed, have a big cock. That in fact was an understatement: the thing was enormous. To tell you the truth, the more I looked at it, the more I became convinced that it might well be the biggest cock I had ever seen in my life.

Freed from the constriction of his white pants – along with the braces, they were twisted around his ankles – it speared massively up from his loins, ridged with knotted veins below the enpurpled head, the epitome of lustful maleness. Standing there bent over her, the man looked, I thought momentarily, almost as though he was literally weighed down by the great staff and the hairy, bullish testicle sac pouched below it.

Marysa propped herself up on her elbows and craned her head forward.

She opened her sultry wet lips and closed her mouth gently over the stiffened tip of that huge cock. McPhee tensed, his hands halfway to the thatched mound sheltering her labia. Her mouth, tightening as it greased down the shaft, wedged wide by the sheer bulk of that throbbing penis, sucked with lewd insistence until the wet head nudged the back of her throat and she could sink her head no further.

The muscles of the Australian's buttocks tightened, hollowed. For a moment he hung there, entirely motionless, a human questionmark, a freeze-frame in a blue movie. Then, clearly abandoning the idea of a straight fuck in favour of the delight already offered, he reached up to grab a rack above the bunk and allowed his body to sag forward, a hostage to her invading mouth.

Marysa withdrew her head, the lips tightening, tightening, massaging the distended skin over the hard muscular core of the huge prick, tongue flickering against the sensitive underside of the head, until only the extreme tip with the seeping moisture lubricating its slit remained between her teeth. Then she plunged firmly down at once with ballooning cheeks again engulfing almost all of the quivering staff in the hot depths of her throat.

A little regretfully, I stepped down from the bunk, left the cabin, and rejoined the conspirators beneath the awning and in the saloon. 'Ten minutes,' I announced. 'Maximum.'

In fact it was fourteen. Perhaps it took the man some time to extricate his weapon from the proffered scabbard.

By the time they appeared – Marysa smoothing down the rumpled velvet, McPhee looking, as Lafayette predicted, as if he felt ten feet tall – by this time, Jeff was sitting on the taffrail with one hand inside the unbuttoned front of Cindy's white dress and the other up her skirt. In the saloon, bent forward over the table, Gina was now being humped – there is no other word for it – by Randy. The pyjama top was around her waist and the pants pinioning her knees. Randy's not inconsiderable cock, jutting obscenely from his gaping fly, was plowing forcefully in and out of that pouting cunt. Light from the bracket lamps gleamed on his wet shaft as it pistoned into her from behind.

By then I had myself sequestered Aurelia on the white hide bench running around the cockpit. Delicately, she unzipped the front of my jeans. 'Nothing personal,' she murmured with a wicked glance from slitted eyes, 'but if I'm going to be screwed by that rather horrible little man, everything else tonight has to be manual.' The smile she gave me was as wicked as the salacious glance. 'I'll toss you off,' she said, 'maybe even with pleasure. You can grope if you want. But for the moment, that's it, Jack.'

'Be my guest,' I said.

Ladylike as always, Aurelia took a white rubber glove from her vanity bag, drew it on her left hand, and inserted hand and wrist within. I stiffened, in every way, feeling those cold rubbered fingers seek, find and then drag into the open air my tingling cock.

With her right hand, Aurelia manoeuvred a pack of cigarettes from her bag. Extracted one, fitted it into her long holder, and lit it with a gold Dupont lighter. Blowing a long plume of smoke into the ocean breeze, she began methodically to pump my overheated shaft to trembling awareness – always with a professional eye on McPhee to make sure he noticed, and avoid making me come until he had.

He was noticing all right. His eyes swivelled as fast as the fruit in a one-armed bandit from Gina and Randy, to Jeff and Cindy, to Aurelia and myself and then back to the loose screw in the saloon. He poured himself another glass of champagne, but it wasn't the wine that caused the glitter in those eyes.

Offshore II was riding the swell more quietly now: Lafayette had steered her into the lee of the nearest island; the wooded bulk of the other blotted out the lower stars in the night sky. The thump of the diesels quietened, ceased. We heard a rattle of chain as Lafayette dropped anchor a hundred yards off the second isle.

Marysa wandered across and sank to the deck, laying her head in the lap of Aurelia's full skirt as she idly watched that gloved and masturbating hand.

Stokes-Alberry and Violette appeared from their cabin. Above the ripple of sea water running past the stern, the stealthy squelch of that rubber-gloved hand milking my cock and an occasional creak of woodwork as the boat lifted to the swell, the author's fruity Wodehousian tones sounded a curiously discordant note. 'By Jove,' he cawed, 'what an absolutely stunning bash, old girl! I mean hats jolly well off to you, and all that. Another basinful of that,

I fancy, before the night's out!' And then, further aft, to me: 'Where's the darkie then?'

'If you mean Lafayette, he's in the wheelhouse. He's skippering the craft; in case you hadn't noticed, we just dropped anchor.'

'No offence, old man,' Stokes-Alberry said. 'No need to get shirty, either. We're pals: I call the fellow that to his face.'

'His black face, you mean?' I said as icily as I could. There was a lot of heat in my loins: the rubber glove, which hadn't stopped working during this exchange, was fast approaching the end of my tether.

Stokes-Alberry stared at me. 'What an odd fellow you are,' he said.

Offshore II swung slightly around with the tide, allowing the long chain of lights garlanding the coast between Cannes and the Esterel to slide into view. I came with a rush. Aurelia peeled off the glove and dropped it over the side (I wondered how many she carried). She took Marysa's hand, smiled at me, and led the sultry Hungarian up the ladder to the flying bridge. In the saloon, Randy switched on the radio, picked up a half-full bottle and minced out under the awning jigging some kind of complicated dance step.

Face it, we were all pretty high by now. If anyone had inhibitions, they had long ago been carried away by the tide.

Lafayette appeared and sat down in the saloon with Gina. He was drinking bourbon from a large stone mug, with one proprietorial eye on the pairing which had developed among his guests.

The most important one, the guy the party had been staged for, had crept up the ladder after the two girls.

Now he was lying almost flat along the rungs, with his head just above the level of the deck. Turning, he looked over his shoulder and beckoned furiously to the rest of us. Jeff, Cindy, Randy and myself moved a little uncertainly his way. McPhee beckoned again and then held a finger to his lips for silence. We stole aloft and gazed over his back.

There were in fact twin ladders, one on either side of the saloon. Lafayette emerged and climbed the second one, followed by Gina.

It was a stimulating sight that McPhee was inviting us to share.

Reflected radiance from below and the coloured riding lights provided the only illumination. In this red, green and golden gloom we could see that, behind the dodger and windshield, deep white-hide cushioning surrounded the bridge decking aft of the steersman's swivel chair and instrument panels.

Aurelia was lying back on this padded seating with the full skirt held up to shield her face, long white naked legs lewdly spread below the waist.

And hunched between the thighs, Marysa knelt with her face buried in the ladylike thatch so obscenely offered to her invading lips. The black dress had been rolled down to her waist, and the big breasts swung and bounced as her lush head sucked and bobbed. Aurelia had kicked off her shoes, and one bare foot was twisted inwards so that the toes could tease the wet cunt at the base of the kneeling girl's quivering belly.

As I said, Aurelia's face was hidden, but I could imagine the sly, lascivious smile twisting her lips, the malicious glint in her eye as her lover sucked and slaved.

There had been a low, keening murmur rising from

one or both of the women abandoning themselves there. This was now replaced by small cries and short, choking gasps. Aurelia dropped the long skirt to hide Marysa's submissive figure, shaking her head very slowly from side to side as her slender frame shook with a rigidly controlled release and her face turned from red to green to red.

Lafayette rumbled out the big laugh from the top of the other ladder. 'Now what gallant cocksman's going to ride in there and take advantage of the ground so beautifully prepared?' he cried.

The rest of us, sensing that a girl-girl relationship hadn't exactly been on his organizing chart, took our cue and held back. But Winston McPhee was in there like an arrow from a bow. He'd already had Marysa, but now was his chance to prove, at least to himself, that he could make, take and lay any snobbish, toffee-nosed Lady Muck that he wanted . . . without the trouble – and possible rebuff – involved in an initial advance! Don Juan McPhee, the Casa-fucking-nova of Cannes.

He dragged Aurelia off the cushioned bench, literally threw her to the deck, snatched the skirt back above her waist, and ripped open the top of the dress to expose her small, pointed tits.

Bundling out the big, thick cock with its huge, blood-engorged head, he wrenched apart her thighs, wrapped her legs around his waist and shafted into her with enough force to startle a smothered cry from her lips. That was what he wanted: in theory anyway this was really a rape. I thanked God on her part that Marysa had already lubricated the passage with her marauding tongue.

Maybe that had been Aurelia's plan all the time?

We left the Australian plunging in and out of her like a maniac, snorting and grunting with the effort. Aurelia's face was expressionless – perhaps with a hint of well-bred disdain, as ordered – but I was pretty sure one mischievous eye relayed a definite wink at Lafayette just before we went below.

The breeze was freshening; *Offshore II* rocked at anchor. The radio was playing a Rolling Stones number from years back. Ronald Stokes-Alberry, in the saloon, was still leering at Violette as he splashed champagne into two glasses. It was clear he was – either through drink or the joys of Cabin No 1 or a combination of both – what we used to call slightly the worse for wear. The blue eyes bulged, the moustache bristled, there was a touch of the slur to his affected voice.

I'm not saying the rest of us were much better, the males at any rate. It might have been the boat and the swell, but I thought old Randy was lurching a trifle; Jeff's mouth was open and his eyes unnaturally bright; and I found that the stars had a tendency to wheel around my head each time I got up or sat down. The girls, sensibly, had taken enough to anaesthetize them against the assaults of McPhee but not enough to dull the senses sufficiently to fall down (if you will excuse the expression) on the job.

In any case there was no need to keep on with the motley, as it were, while McPhee was out of sight and at work aloft. Frankly we were all glad of the respite: since the breeze now carried a slight chill, we crowded into the saloon and occupied ourselves with a real party, talking of this and that. From time to time, amidst the laughter and gossip, I fancied I could distinguish a faint thumping penetrate the ceiling from the deck of the bridge above, but I might have been mistaken.

There were signs of activity now from the island. Someone had lit a campfire among the trees, and the wind carried the strains of distant singing. Overhead, a late-night jetliner with lights flashing planed low on its approach to the main runway of Nice airport.

Eventually McPhee reappeared, and we resumed the cheek-to-cheek, hand-touching, sex-maniac poses the gathering had been designed to promote. 'But no sex this time,' Lafayette warned. 'Have to be breaks now and then if he don't suspect no setup. You dig?'

Aurelia remained on the bridge. I imagined she was getting her breath back.

It was not long, nevertheless, before McPhee abstracted himself from the general conversation and allowed his eyes to wander. The man's appetite – and stamina – despite a certain lack of finesse, were extraordinary.

This time his lecherous gaze vectored in on Violette. 'Hey, baby,' he ventured, 'it seems to me there's things we ought to be discussing. What say we borrow one of friend Lafayette's bottles and retire to a cabin to find out just what those things are?'

He veered towards the girl, who was sitting at the table next to Stokes-Alberry, and laid a hand on the lime-green sleeve of her filmy beach pyjamas. He was pulling her, unresisting, to her feet when Stokes-Alberry turned, glared, and placed a firm hand on her shoulder, thrusting her back down into her chair. 'Sorry and all that,' he said, 'but it's no go. Answer negative, what.'

The Australian glared in his turn. 'What the hell . . . ?' he began.

'She's not coming, is what,' Stokes-Alberry said.

'Look, sport,' McPhee gritted, his fingers still gripping Violette's arm, 'I was under the impression that I was the guest of Mister Lafayette Briggs. If I was mistaken and this is your boat – if you are in fact my host, please say so.'

228

'Just take your hands off her,' Stokes-Alberry said.

'Otherwise stow your bloody gab and don't try to tell me what to do.'

Stokes-Alberry pushed back his chair and rose to his feet. He looked down at McPhee's flushed face. 'I don't think you quite get the picture, old man,' he said.

'What the hell are you talking about?' McPhee growled.

'Private property. You must have heard the term. The lady's with me.'

'Don't give me that shit. This is a party, ain't it? We swing, don't we? Haven't you kept open your baby bloody blue eyes the last two fucking hours?'

'I don't wish to be unduly offensive, old man,' Stokes-Alberry said levelly. 'But at the risk of being repetitive – and bearing in mind that you may not be familiar with the way one behaves over here – I repeat: *the lady is with me*. Now be a good chap and push off, will you?'

'Come this way, darl,' McPhee said to Violette, freeing her arm. 'There's a cabin waiting and we have things to talk about.'

'I already told you twice,' Stokes-Alberry said loudly. 'This is the third and last time. Definitely. I'm saying hands-off: the answer is NO! So shut up and fuck off before I lose my temper.'

'No fucking, plummy-voiced, la-di-dah Pommie poof is gonna tell me . . .'

'Violette: you stay right here with me.'

'. . . what sheila I date and what I bleeding don't!'

At the far end of the saloon, Lafayette, seeing the whole point of his carefully orchestrated scenario put at risk by the drunken author, rose in turn from the bunk where he had been sprawled. He put his stone mug on the table.

229

Violette herself was hesitating, looking anxiously from one angry man to the other. She had been briefed, but she wasn't a professional like the others: she knew she was supposed to make herself agreeable to the Australian. But this scene hadn't been in the script, and she didn't know how to play it.

'You're coming into that cabin with me,' McPhee told her.

'Look,' Stokes-Alberry said, the words definitely slurring now, 'one doesn't wish to be in the position of pushing colonials around, even small and disagreeable ones, but there does come a time. I mean there are certain things one does and does not do. A fellow's girl, for instance.' He moved in a threatening way towards McPhee. Violette opened her mouth and closed it again.

Her problem was solved by Lafayette himself. Scowling, the big man seized the collar of Stokes-Alberry's immaculate jacket, bunching the cloth in his fist to lift the man clear off the deck. 'If you can't keep to the rules, man,' he hissed, 'stay out of the fuckin' game!' He strode out of the saloon, carried the struggling author to the rail, and dropped him over the side into the sea.

'Sorry about that,' he said coolly to McPhee. 'Some guys can take their drink, and there's always some who can't.'

'What about Ronald . . . ?' I began.

'He can swim,' Lafayette said. 'We're no more than a hundred yards offshore. He can dry off by that campfire and take the ferry back to the mainland in the morning.'

McPhee was shaking his head. 'How d'you like that?' he said. 'What about that stuffed shirt! No harm done in any case, Lafayette . . . but thanks for getting the guy off my back. I might have hurt him otherwise.' He turned back to Violette and held out his hand. 'Okay, darl – let's go, eh?'

'Take any cabin you want,' Lafayette said smoothly. 'Violette will be happy to show you the way.'

'My pleasure,' the girl said. Not altogether convincingly, I thought.

'I'll need a guide,' McPhee said, 'if I'm gonna take this ship cruisin'!'

'You figure on chartering then?' Lafayette said with elaborate nonchalance.

'If she can support parties like this?' the Australian said. 'You bet your life, sport!'

Chapter Sixteen

It was three days later that the phone rang at seven o'clock in the morning. 'For Chrissake,' I said blearily. I swung the feet out of bed and picked it off the hook. 'Hallo?'

'Hi!' Lafayette's cheerful voice said. 'You up and about?'

'I wasn't,' I said. 'But never mind.'

'Want you to come to a party.'

'Jesus!' I said. 'Not again? Don't know if the frame could stand it!'

'No, man. A real party; no swing setup. My way of saying thank-you to you guys. Just the four of us: you, me, Randy and Jeff. And four chicks, natch. I'm pickin' up the tab, girls included.'

'McPhee did decide to charter then?'

'Charter?' The big laugh rumbled in my ear. 'Man, he's *buyin'* the fuckin' ship! And ten percent of that . . .' He laughed again.

'Well, that's great,' I said. 'When?'

'Tomorrow night. The party, I mean. Which of the girls you want – all to yourself this time? And can you make it?'

'Love to,' I said. Susan wasn't due back for another two days.

'And the chick?'

233

I thought of whipped cream and delicacies and sticky fingers and an ample, nubile body. 'Violette,' I said.

'You're on,' he said. 'Seven o'clock at the Blue Peter.'

'I'll be there.'

This I was looking forward to. The excesses aboard *Offshore II* had in fact stopped short with daylight – and before I got around to the sexy pastry cook. I was therefore still pretty keyed-up on her behalf, aflame with the desire to explore those fleshy secrets concealed beneath her free-fall clothes.

Also, I reckoned, by choosing her, I was doing Lafayette something of a favour: the other girls all cost; quite a few hundred francs, I imagined, even for him. Maybe into four figures. Violette, on the other hand, according to the man himself, was in the game just for kicks.

And that was another plus. If she was an amateur, she could choose, say yes or no. Which meant, if she agreed to be my partner, that there must be at least a possible set of vibes connecting us.

Since I had had no disclaimer from Lafayette by six-thirty the following day, I decided that the omens for the evening were definitely rosy, and it was with a sense of virtue rewarded that I backed the Alfa out of the yard and headed west through the evening traffic. Well, not exactly virtue perhaps, but rewards came into it somewhere.

Weatherwise, the evening was super. It was still quite hot. A regatta criss-crossed the calm sea off the Cap d'Antibes. The beaches were crowded and the strollers beneath the palms along the Croisette looked tanned and glamorous.

So did the four girls drinking apéritifs with us at the Blue Peter.

Lafayette, predictably enough, was still with Cindy,

234

Randy and Jeff with Aurèlia and Marysa. My host held out a hand, palm upwards, as I threaded my way through the close-packed sidewalk tables. I slapped it lightly with four fingers. 'Fine idea, big guy,' I told him. 'My thanks for the kind thought.'

'My pleasure,' Lafayette said.

I looked at Violette. 'Mine too,' I said.

She smiled, patting a vacant chair beside her. 'Oh, boy!' I said to Jeff.

'You worked the shipboard scene into your current chapter yet?' he demanded, grinning.

'Halfway through,' I said. 'You?'

'I pre-empted it, wrote it out of my head, day before the party.'

'Bastard!'

'Yeah, but the reality was sharper than anything I could imagine. I had to fake up an insert, take in your Brit friend's unexpected bath.'

'That's my boy,' I said.

Lafayette's laugh was a murmur of distant thunder. 'You guys!' he said.

I sat down next to Violette. 'You're absolutely, stunningly, wonderfully, one hundred percent gorgeous,' I confided.

It was true too. She was wearing a longish, pleated, ivory-coloured skirt with a very dark silk top printed with overlapping flower shapes in gunmetal, pewter and bronze. The sleeves were long and full, the shawl collar set back to frame a neckline that was very narrow . . . but plunged almost all the way to the waist.

Narrow, yes – maybe two or three inches at its widest – but open just enough to hint, no more, at the tanned, satiny slopes thrusting out the material on either side.

I guess the other three girls looked pretty smashing too, but my imagination was too busy crawling through that narrow gap to register them.

We had dinner in a very small, very expensive restaurant in Rue Hélène Vagliano. It was called La Reine Pédauque and was only a few paces from Violette's shop. We drank a splendid Burgundy and an iced Moselle with the sea-urchin *mousse*, and Lafayette insisted on liqueurs all round before we went back to the hotel. They must have palmed off that converted torpedo-recovery ship for a fortune.

'You guys,' he said to Violette and me, 'are booked into a room on the fifth floor.' He laughed. 'Frau and Herr Jan Schmidt!'

It was a lovely night, bright with stars, the warm wind alive with murmured voices and subdued laughter as we walked by the sea. The traffic on the esplanade above slid past with scarcely a sound.

Violette hung onto my arm in that way women have, both hands clasped around the upper part, dragging down with just enough weight to suggest the cargo of breasts and buttocks and belly they carry. From time to time she rested her head momentarily on my shoulder. Her chestnut hair was up tonight, and starlight glinted on the heavy, silver, double-hoop earrings she wore.

There were people bathing off the Carlton beach, and further out the shadow of a windsurfer rode the chuckling wavelets.

Lafayette remained the perfect host. There was no question of scuttling straight up to bed once we made the hotel. Suspense was the keyword that night. Delay the thrill. Savour the wait, knowing what was at the end of it. Let elegance temper the restless hand and the lustful eye.

For us it was now coffee and champagne in the terrace bar.

The place was crowded but not too noisy. Cindy wore green, Aurelia flowing mauves and silver, Marysa black again. We laughed a lot, told jokes, bandied local gossip about. At one point, during a lull that seemed, the way they sometimes do, to affect the whole bar, Randall Van Eyck said suddenly: 'You know something? I think this is the most fantastic evening I had in my whole life.'

Smiling, Lafayette clapped him on the shoulder. 'That case, boy, you better take your lady straight upstairs before something happens you change your mind!'

It was before I took my own lady upstairs that something very odd had happened.

Minor point, but necessary from the point of view of the conventions, the hotel staff and all that.

I'd brought with me a small valise carrying shaving tackle and that kind of thing. Violette had slipped into it a zippered bag containing anything she might need, and we'd stashed the valise in the hotel cloakroom on the way from the Blue Peter to the restaurant.

As soon as we returned to the Martinez after dinner, I'd officially checked us in and taken this valise up to the room. It was on the fifth floor, number 516. 'Just around the corner, third door on the left, sir,' a chambermaid in a starched apron told me as I stepped out of the lift.

I was holding the key in one hand. Partly because I'm always confusing directions, probably because I was thinking too much about what was going to happen in that room later, I turned right instead of left at the third door.

It was ajar anyway. Thinking that a chambermaid might be turning back the covers, I pushed it open, dropping the valise on the baggage rack. Then – might as well take the opportunity and spring a leak while I'm here – I went into the bathroom.

There was a woman in there all right, but it wasn't a chambermaid.

A brunette, with a close cap of dark hair. Smooth, tanned arms and a bare back emerging from a scarlet strapless evening dress. She was standing, legs straddled, with her back to me.

The one really unusual thing about her was that she was holding up the long skirt of the dress with both hands and peeing into the lavatory bowl.

I must have made some slight sound, because she turned, frowning. A strong, almost handsome face with heavy, very dark straight eyebrows. 'Who the hell are you?' she demanded furiously.

She dropped the skirt, but not before I had seen the cock and balls beneath.

I murmured an excuse and backed out of there fast.

There had been no recognition in her eyes, but there was in mine. This was the person I'd known as Zita, the one I'd met in the beach *vestiaire* and stood up because I'd become involved with Edward's little fetishist scenario in Monte Carlo!

Well, what do you know! The glamorous Zita a transvestite!

The breast implants had been perfect, I recalled, remembering the *vestiaire*; the genitals convincingly bunch-and-thrust to resemble a mons beneath the bikini bottom. I wondered what the hell would have happened if I'd made the date. Would I have been groped in the Alfa? Or was he-she just a tease, inflaming a hetero desire for the hell of it?

I reckoned, despite the anguish I suffered at the time,

that Providence – and Edward – had dealt me the right escape card that night.

As the French say: *Ouf!*

I noticed the number on the door as I escaped again. Five-seventeen, of course. Had my subconscious registered it and urged me to go in there as a throwback to the horny state I'd been in that other night?

This, anyway – I thought as I unlocked the door to the right room – was another case of life surpassing art.

And certainly, as in the case of Edward, one that was definitely *not* going to figure in my next book for Expadink!

Perhaps it was because of this non-adventure, and the previous one, that I found the entry with Violette to Room 516, when finally we made it, the most normal and natural thing in the world.

Once the door closed, I took her in my arms as avidly as any kid with a successful college date or new groom with a first-night honeymoon bride. She was soft and scented and infinitely desirable. Her body, warm through the lightweight stuff I was wearing, seemed vibrant with allure. She was nice too, easy and companionable and trusting: despite the fact that this was an arranged date, a setup courtesy L Briggs, Esquire, there was going to be no awkwardness, no fumbling now that we had arrived at the crunch moment. Everything would happen as naturally, as inevitably as the tides flowing in and out below the open windows.

Violette *was* in fact a natural.

Cool fingers laced behind my neck as we stood together there, breathing a little fast. 'Randall was right,' she said. 'This *is* one of those evenings. There's something special about it, something very right.' For a moment she laid her forehead against my cheek. 'I do want you, you know. I've thought about it ever since you came into the shop – and I'm going to love every minute.'

That, I thought, was a pretty elegant thing to say in the circumstances.

We kissed.

'I rather like the undressing bit, when it's someone with style,' she said when we broke apart. 'But of course if you'd prefer to go to bed straight away, that'd be lovely too.'

'I want to discover you,' I said huskily. 'I want to find out what you hide so well – and so sexily – inch by inch, curve by fascinating curve!'

Violette gave a sudden, enchanting giggle. 'Oh, boy!' she said.

I knew then that we didn't even have to play it by ear: the night was going to play itself.

A bottle of champagne in an ice bucket stood with two flutes on a bedside table. On a card propped against the bucket, I read in Lafayette's spidery hand the words: 'Sleep well. Courtesy *Offshore II*.'

'What a charmer!' I said, springing the cork and pouring.

'He's lovely, isn't he?' Violette said. She raised her flute. 'To our host.'

'Himself,' I said.

We drank. After a while, when the flutes were empty, we drank some more. An occasional car or taxi swished along the Croisette, the headlamp beams sweeping bars of light across the ceiling above the windows. Small waves sighed gently onto the sandy beach below. Once, several hundred yards away, we heard an argument: two men and a shouting girl, the slam of a car door.

I was sitting in a comfortable tapestry-covered chair.

Violette sprawled on the deep-pile carpet, resting her head on my knee. One of her hands gently kneaded the flesh of my lower calf, inside the hem of my trousers. I was stroking, softly, the hollows dimpling the perfect flesh of her shoulders on either side of her neck. A few inches away, hidden by the dark flowers of her top, I knew the sloped swell of her breasts would be nestling.

The only illumination, apart from that reflected from the street below, was diffused by a single table lamp on the far side of the bed. Its subdued light emphasized the depthless shadow within the narrow chasm of Violette's neckline. I allowed two fingers to wander playfully in that direction.

And suddenly she reached up both hands, grabbed my wrists, and thrust both of my own hands deep inside the dark flowers to cup her breasts.

A quick thrill flamed through my loins as the secret weight of those hidden treasures pressed on my palms. Two nipples, surprisingly hard in the midst of that softly swelling warmth. My fingers drowned in flesh.

She gave a small sigh and tilted back her head. I leaned forward and down, and we kissed. The moment our tongues interlaced, my cock stiffened to total rigidity. She felt it at once and rolled her hand this way and that, manoeuvring the shaft inside my pants.

It was then that our lovemaking reached a different dimension; we were playing in a different key.

I don't remember exactly how we transferred ourselves to the bed: whatever the mechanics were, they operated so smoothly, with such a lack of clumsiness, that we simply didn't notice. What was important was that now each of us had the whole of the other available.

I knew what Violette meant about 'the undressing bit':

it meant that we delayed still longer, for another few achingly thrilling moments, what we had in fact been putting off ever since seven o'clock – the final, actual, physical contact which we had known from the start would come at the end.

Basically it was the same technique, mentally, that Violette favoured in the way she dressed: suspense, titillation, suggestion rather than exposure was half the fun. It was back to the old Victorian concept that a half-dressed woman is visually more erotic than a naked one.

And of course it's why I have taken more than twenty paragraphs to bring you to the point where flesh touched flesh.

We were sprawled, fully dressed, on the bed, with pillows banked up behind us. She had pulled the shirt out of the waistband of my pants and, with an arm around my waist, was caressing the bare flesh in the small of my back. But the other hand, the one gently exploring the hard outline of my cock, was still on the *outside* of my trousers. She made, for the moment, no attempt to draw down the tab of the zip. Feeling, softly rolling, pressing, slowly trailing fingertips and nails around the long length of my erection, she was subtly stimulating me to the point at which caresses explode organically into action.

For the moment, however, I matched her restraint with a reserve of my own. The hand wedged beneath her followed the path her own hand had taken with me: I fondled the slight bulge of flesh above the skirt waistband where I had pulled away that flowered top; the fingers reaching up beneath the pleated skirt in front traversed a cool band of flesh above the dark stocking top but stroked only the outside of the elasticized panties tightly enclosing her mons and genital area.

I could sense nevertheless the springiness of the pubic hair beneath, the flowering of the labia as the pad of my middle finger traced their outline.

That pad registered wetness permeating the warmth at the same time as the hand on my outlined erection felt the sexy moisture drenching the material covering its head.

My mouth was nibbling at the strip of flesh showing between the edges of Violette's flowered top. I could taste the saltiness of skin against my tongue, the heart beating fast below my cheek. As this double wetness made its mark, I raised my head and we kissed again. This time the hot saliva flowed as we clasped our lips together, probing teeth and gums and the caverned recesses within the cheeks.

I moved my position, withdrawing my arm, and abruptly she jerked the top free, allowing one naked breast to spill into my hand. That soft and glorious weight at once sent electric thrills racing to my loins, and my cock jerked, quivering, under her touch.

My other hand savagely pulled aside the elastic at her crotch and my questing fingers at once homed in on the warmly sliding, streaming folds of her excited cunt. My zip jerked down; an invading hand wormed its way in, grabbed the cock, and pulled it out into the open. My hips jerked as the cool night air played on the inflamed shaft.

We were both panting now. She milked my staff to an agonizing ache, her lubricated hand skimming, piston-fast, the distended column. My roving fingers were lost in the sweet scald of her slippery lips.

I thrust away and kicked off trousers and underpants while she pulled my shirt over my head. Then she plucked the whole flower garden and I unbuckled her skirt.

'Oh, lover,' she said. 'Oh, yes!'

We knelt, face to face, naked on the bed.

My arms encircled her waist. The tip of my stiffened cock grazed the wet hairs furring her cunt. The hot nipples of her breasts marked the weight of them, lying against my chest. Her two cupped hands cradled my flaming balls.

I had imagined Violette's body. It was as I had imagined it – only better. I cannot think of the right word to describe it; as an entity, I mean. Buxom is far too jolly, too reminiscent of strapping wenches with healthy red cheeks and large bottoms. Nubile, for me at any rate, carries a hint of slackness, a lack of the taut quality typical of sex. The word sexy itself doesn't do it justice.

It was pliant and yet firm, resilient but malleable, more than slender yet without the slightest touch of flabbiness or fat. While gloriously soft, it retained its outline and shape perfectly in any position.

I can't think of a word, but by God that body was bliss!

Before long – don't ask me the manoeuvres: that night was a long, delicious dream – I was lying flat on my back and she was straddling my chest with her knees in my armpits. I had been holding my arms straight out in front of me, taking the weight of those breasts. Her head was thrown back; her hair, loosened, was tumbling about her bare shoulders; her eyes were closed. With the pink tip of her tongue, she was moistening her own lips.

Her breasts *were* big. They were extraordinarily soft, yet firm enough to retain their outline even when she was on her back. I was reluctant to let them go, but the position we had arrived at suggested an even more lustful coupling . . . one that might still permit me at least a blind touch of the breasts. Possibly one she had jockeyed herself into this stance especially to provoke.

I dropped my hands, to place the palms against her hips.

Violette's hips, like the rest of the lady, were worth an evening's investigation on their own. Softly padded, they implied an enthralling pelvic thrust. With that fine proportion of flesh over bone, they complemented the gentle bulge, with its tiny lateral creases, of the belly slung between them. And the skin covering them, satin to the touch, was feather-light under my manipulations despite the real heaviness of the frame underneath.

Flexing my arms, I drew the hips slowly, tenderly, towards me. I felt the roughness of her vaginal furrow, hot and damp already from the fervour of our mutual stimulation, grate against the hardness of my chest.

I slid my hands beneath her cool thighs, lifting her very slightly above me. I continued the pressure, drawing her heated pelvis nearer, nearer to the eager goal of my face. At the last moment she helped me, hinged off the mattress enough to negotiate my shoulders with her knees and pose the base of her belly immediately above me.

My hands clasped the hips once more and drew the lovely weight of her down again. Cool thighs imprisoned my cheeks. Dark hairs brushed my open lips. The spread thighs tightened, slid . . . and there, engulfed in the musky womanly warmth, my speared tongue rose to touch the interfolded, scented cleft of Violette's hungry cunt.

I craned my head. My tongue lapped, licking, probing in search of the entrance to the vaginal tunnel I had longed for so long.

She settled further still. And then, as my arms rose once more to close over the breasts hanging above me, I was there. My lips fastened on hot, wet, quivering flesh;

my tongue tunnelled into the secret, nutty darkness of the love canal piercing that night's darling's gorgeous belly.

For a small eternity we remained there, locked in a physical bliss. Then, uttering a deep groan of pleasure, Violette reached behind her with both hands, leaning slightly back as I sucked, to sanctify my own genitals with her magic touch. Nerves throughout the entire lower part of me fluttered. My prone body writhed against the mattress as she skimmed and slid; the breath jetting through my nose while my mouth slavered away was harsh and quick. My reactions almost unseated her, probably would have done if she hadn't tightened the vice-grip of her thighs.

Then, very slowly, she began tilting sideways, towards the centre of the bed, leaning away with my head still deliciously imprisoned. Involuntarily, automatically, I moved to help her, rolling out from under with my breasted hands now gripping her rib cage for leverage and support.

In a moment our relative positions were reversed. Violette lay on her back with her knees drawn up and spread; I was face down with my head gripped and my eager mouth still locked to her cunt.

I savoured her offered body, lips caressing, the tip of my tongue nudging a stiffened and bud-like clitoris, penetrating the hot, dark, liquid depths of the interior.

Her hips began to jerk spasmodically, and she conjured me somehow into the position she herself had been occupying a short time before – sitting astride her chest with the glistening head of my cock only inches from her mouth.

Now it was my hands which reached back to dabble with her juiced labia, drawing them apart, fingering the smooth interiors, venturing within the heated mouth beyond.

I tightened my knees, squashing her breasts together over my balls while her hands stole round to my buttocks, stealthily drawing me closer, closer.

I gasped aloud as the tight elastic sheath of her mouth closed firmly over the tip of my cock, licking the underside, sucking and then pushing. Sucking again. I couldn't resist it; I just couldn't, even at that moment of heightened passion. 'Oh, *boy!*' I breathed.

Once again she knew exactly how long to persist, precisely when to change a position, however enticing it was. My loins were on fire as we rocked there together, united in that tingling, shared thrill for which there is no substitute – and from which it is impossible to withdraw.

Yet withdraw, for just the right amount of time, she did.

Suddenly there was cool air again on my heated shaft. Below its quivering head, wet lips smiled. 'I think we're ready now,' she said softly. 'I think it would be right.' And then, in a strangled, all at once urgent voice: *'So . . . love me soldier! Do!'*

I did. Don't know just how I got there: it happened, the way it sometimes magically does. There I was.

My tool was gripped and guided; she spread her legs; I knew soft sliding, a graze of hair against the supersensitive staff, and then, with flexed hips, I was wonderfully, wetly, warmly in!

We settled at once into the right rhythm, hips thrusting, bellies clamped, mouths working as our encircled arms laced us together on that delirious bed.

At one point, I freed my mouth, raised my head as I pumped and withdrew, and looked down into her eyes.

'You are quite fantastic,' I said.

Violette smiled again. 'I know,' she said. 'Wait until we come together though!'

We did of course. It had to happen: it was written. Now, I thought when the hammering of my heart had quietened a little, now I *really* know what ecstasy means.

Later still, when I was stumbling behind the hotel to the car park, I ran into a solitary figure going my way. It was Randall Van Eyck. Grinning, he shook his head: 'That girl!' he said. 'That wicked, wicked Aurelia! What a night. Oh, wow!'

'I know,' I told him.

Maybe I was wearing a touch of the fat cat look myself, because he glanced at me sharply and asked: 'You too? The next chapter?'

I shook my head. A train shrieked along the embankment above us. Somewhere along the Croisette a car alarm warbled. 'I haven't the talent,' I said. 'I couldn't do it justice.'

Chapter Seventeen

The call was at seven in the evening this time. But it was still Lafayette.

'Miriam be back from Italy tomorrow with your boss,' he said. 'So tonight my last chance to make it with Cindy, at least for the moment.'

'Well, fine,' I said. 'Have yourself a ball.'

'Yeah.' He coughed. 'Only thing is . . . well, Cindy, she like to *see* things. You know. Like a black man and a white chick and some mirrors. The colours, the patterns, they excite her. You dig?'

'Sure. Plenty of folks like to watch themselves. I already have it in Chapter Nineteen. And so?'

'So . . . well . . . Thing is, Cindy also like to *be* watched in that sit-u-ation. She like you too, man. Taken quite a shine.'

'Well, that's nice, Lafayette. But—'

'She wonder . . . if you free tonight, maybe you care to take a late dinner with us, stay around after in a little private room? If you want, natch.'

I thought of the green eyes and dark red hair, the 38-24-34 figure and the long, tapered legs. And then – we were friends; I could say this kind of thing to him: 'You want me to black up?'

He laughed. 'Naw. Just borrow some of that leather gear of Edward's! That do.'

'Am I being asked as a third party – or just a plain ol' voyeur?'

'That depend on Cindy,' Lafayette said.

Cindy, as usual, was ravishing. The dark red hair shone like burnished copper. Her lemon-yellow tussore dress hugged waist and hips, flared out wide over tanned legs and only just – regretfully, I fancied – prevented the thirty-eight-inch bosom from spilling out over the lowest neckline I'd ever seen. She wore a choker of faceted white stones and white glacé kid shoes with very high stiletto heels.

We met in a very discreet hotel-restaurant in a grove of pine trees near the observatory, high on a wooded hill behind Cannes. It was a place, Lafayette told me, where cabinet ministers, movie stars and the like could safely bring girlfriends – or boyfriends for that matter – with whom they were not publicly associated. The discretion was such that every single entry in the visitors' book was Smith, Jones or Robinson, or the Continental equivalent. With a wry twitch of the lips and a sidelong glance in my direction, Lafayette signed us in as 'Mr Brown and guests'.

We were shown not to a room but a suite: a dining room, a dressing room, a bedroom-lounge and a palatial bathroom, complete with jacuzzi and every other water sports device invented by sanitary engineers. The lounge, as promised, was equipped with enormous rose-tinted mirrors on each wall. There was another, the biggest, set into the ceiling above the twelve-foot-wide bed.

After an approving look around, Cindy laid a hand on Lafayette's sleeve. 'Do you come here often?' she said sweetly. Her English was perfect, the slight touch of German accent rendering the husky voice even more seductive.

He grinned, white teeth brilliant in the dark face. 'Has to be a first time, baby, for everythin' and everybody,' he said.

The servants, all male, who wheeled in the trolleys bearing our admirable dinner were courteous but self-effacing. We would not be disturbed again, rule of the house, until the following morning. Unless, of course, we rang. 'Ain't no hidden cameras neither,' Lafayette chuckled. 'Amount they put aside for the police pay off makes for *real* privacy, man!'

There had been certain reservations in my mind concerning the after-dinner scenario. I'd been given no cues so far; the conversation had been totally anodyne: about the boat, about McPhee, about Stokes-Alberry and our friends in the porn business. After all, apart from the *Offshore II* romp, I'd no shared sexual experiences with Lafayette. I'd never even seen him in swimming trunks. I didn't know what I might be expected to do; more importantly, I was afraid of making some gauche or clumsy move, of going too far too soon, or not far enough. Scared, in fact, of being thought un-hip, of making a fool of myself.

I needn't have worried.

Lafayette carried on his rôle of perfect host, the man who made everything easy. The evening developed in exactly the opposite way to my session with the lovely Violette. We'd finished the champagne and were halfway through the brandy when Lafayette pushed back his chair and said in the most normal possible way: 'Hey, what say we strip off now, babe, and have us some fun?'

And then, to me: 'You ready to serve, squire?'

'Sure,' I said.

'That's what we're here for – thank goodness,' Cindy

said. She got to her feet and went into the bathroom.

'You make yourself real comfortable right here,' Lafayette said to me, indicating a low, extremely deep, plush chair opposite one corner of the bed. He poured brandy into a balloon and handed it to me. 'Could be something develops. Maybe not. Like I say, that depend on her.'

The situation was so far away from my normal routine that I didn't find it in the least odd. There was no room for surprise or self-questioning in a completely new world. I sat down meekly, fully dressed, and sipped.

Cindy came out of the bathroom on a cloud of Balenciaga Quadrille. She was wearing the white choker, the white stilettoes, and nothing else. Lafayette went in there and closed the door.

Cindy sat unconcernedly on the edge of the bed. Her fingernails, toenails – and, for God's sake, her nipples! – were varnished a deep bronze that toned superbly with her hair. And bush, I was happy to see: there might be embellishment here, but there was nothing false.

'This is very kind of you: I certainly appreciate it,' she said in the kind of voice you would use to thank a friend for helping with the baggage. 'I mean, you know, one can't just ask anyone, can one?'

I cleared my throat. 'No,' I said. 'I guess not. I . . . that is, well it's very . . . hospitable . . . of you to ask me. I'm sure that I shall be . . . I mean, shit, I'm going to have myself a . . .' I broke off, agonizingly aware that I was in fact about, by invitation, to watch this gorgeous, big-breasted German pin-up being fucked by a very large American who happened to be black. 'Oh, dear,' I said.

Cindy smiled kindly, sensing my embarrassment. 'The main thing, darling, is that I *like* you,' she said. 'I have this audience thing, you see – Lafayette will have told you – which is probably a reaction against having to be so damned secretive and *undercover* most of the time. But it has to be among friends.'

'No good for you,' I ventured, drawn willy-nilly into the conversation, 'if it was for a blue movie or like an act for a private theatre audience?'

'God, no!' Cindy said.

Lafayette emerged from the bathroom. His body was naked, but now he wore that ridiculous shallow hat, tipped forward as usual over his yellow eyes.

She gave a little shriek of laughter and collapsed backwards on the bed. 'Oh, *you!*' she gurgled. 'Oh, man! Come here at once to Mama's arms!'

It's a thing I often noticed among black friends stateside, particularly jazz musicians, that they seem to feel, in any place, at any time, performing or not, naked if they're *not* wearing a hat of some kind. Whoever saw a photo of Johnny Hodges or Lester Young or Coleman Hawkins or Pete Brown with a bare head?

On this occasion, anyway, Lafayette had as usual got it just right. The absurd hat, balanced above his nudity, struck exactly the right jokey note to transport what might have been an awkward beginning into the realm of loving giggles among old friends.

He was nevertheless a pretty splendid sight. He was a big guy, as I have said, and heavy. But it was all solid – muscle and sinew and hard flesh with plenty of tonus. Despite the lazy, indolent pose he affected, the boneless, loping gait he'd perfected, his ebony frame positively glowed with good health. This was a man who, presumably in private, clearly took a great deal of care to keep in shape.

There was very little hair on his body, none to hide the satin sheen of his chest. Even in the pubic region – and of course I looked there – the covering was sparse.

He caught my glance and laughed. 'You thinkin' about the Race and its big dicks, am I right?' he accused.

'No, no, not at all,' I said hurriedly. 'It was just that, naturally—'

'You take a looksee, why not? I tell you something. I got a the-ory,' Lafayette said impressively, 'about all that. Based on my own ex-am-in-ations.' He subsided onto the bed, took Cindy's bronze-nailed hand, and placed it on what looked to me indeed to be a very large cock.

'A well-hung black man,' Lafayette said, 'he have a big dick, okay? Your honkie dick be smaller. But when the honkie get horny, *his* dick, his dick it get longer, fatter, bigger as it get hard. A black guy get just as hard – *but the enlargement of the organ is proportionately much less*. Ain't near so much difference between the before and after with a black guy. This my explanation of the big-dicked black myth. You dig?'

'Well, thank you very much for telling me,' I said. 'That's a need-to-know deal.'

'Any time,' Lafayette said.

Cindy's hand had begun to move. A teasing, fondling, press-and-relax, marginally up and down motion of her wrapped fingers provoked an immediate reaction. And provided, incidentally, at least a personal proof of Lafayette's thesis. For although the shining, satined cock-head at once emerged, there didn't appear to be any appreciable lengthening of the thick shaft. It had certainly become rock-hard, though: when the voluptuous red-head temporarily withdrew her hand to change position, what had been a flaccid weight now speared forcefully

254

towards the mirrored ceiling more upright than the famous tower at Pisa.

I glanced that way, looking up at the inverted reflection of these two splendidly equipped people so intimately sprawled on the huge bed. And it was then that I realized – and admired – the subtlety with which that glass and the others had been installed.

The mirrors on either side of the bed, for instance, were not set squarely face to face, one immediately opposite the other, but very slightly angled, tilted through no more than half a degree. In this way the occupants of the bed were spared the hallucinatory vision of an interminable multiplication of their own reflected images, dwindling away to infinity on either side. Instead of being part of an endless series, they remained the central accent, the nucleus, with unexpected exposures and exciting fragments of themselves revealed wherever they looked.

The full glory of this arrangement was only apparent to me personally a little later. For the moment I was happy to revel in the sight of two aesthetically pleasing, two beautiful people carnally coupled. Reflections, after all, are for the benefit of those creating them. Why bother when you can objectively see the real thing, in three exciting dimensions?

They *were* beautiful together, too, each in his and her own way a perfect specimen.

The bedspread was white. Cindy's body, breasts and pelvis included, was exquisitely tanned all over, that almost orange tint so many Germans seem to acquire in the South – and which harmonized in this case so well with the auburn hair and bronze varnish. Lafayette's powerful frame was in places so dark that the skin distilled a sheen that was virtually blue. Pink, of course, suffused his palms, the soles of his feet and his inner lips. And the coarser skin of nipples, areola and scrotum was a purple black. But it wasn't just the matched symphony of colour that was so arresting. Naturally, the shapes took precedence: the variation of shades and tones was a bonus.

While I had been enjoying the spectacle in general, the couple themselves had moved definitely into the particular. Sprawled back now, each supported on an elbow, they were more or less face to face. And in each case an arm and a hand had crossed the divide to invade the space of the other – Lafayette's dark fingers deftly parting the tawny hairs of the red-head's pubic triangle, Cindy's pale arm laid over his wrist so that her fingers, still firmly wrapped around the shaft of his cock, could milk the distended outer skin expertly over the stiff inner core.

Lafayette's hand clenched and stroked; a middle finger vanished into the suddenly moist slit pinkly visible among the pubic hair. Cindy's hips jerked and she stifled a gasp; the milking hand accelerated a little, tightening its grasp. Lafayette grunted. He had been staring into the German girl's eyes; now he bent his head to kiss her, shifting his body so that he was leaning her way. Muscles trembled and twitched as the two hands, the pale and the dark, continued to work.

For them, for the moment, I no longer existed.

Then abruptly I saw a green eye glance sideways. Cindy couldn't resist the mirror. Looking the way she looked, I saw a different view of the lewdly splayed forms, an angled close-up of those masturbating fingers. I wished I *had* a camera!

Moments later I was in no position to wish anything at all: I was so enthralled by the visual scene in front of me that everything else went clean out of my head.

With very little apparent movement, hardly any appreciable shifting of flesh masses, Cindy and Lafayette were locked together, making love – fucking seems too crude a word to describe the near poetic rhythm, the fluid and pliant interlacing of limbs and bodies coupled on that bed.

And excitingly reflected from a score of different angles above and on every side.

The beauty – I use the word deliberately – the beauty of the scene was largely due to the colour difference. This was no tangled knot of arms and legs in jerking intimacy. The variations in skin tones rendered each part of either body clear, distinct and sharply defined in contrast to the flesh tint against which it pressed. A superb breast squashed beneath the weight of Lafayette's sombre chest; pale legs criss-crossed over his darkly labouring hips; the ebony shaft of his gleaming cock was occasionally glimpsed partly withdrawing from the sucking coral of the red-head's invaded labia – all these things contributed to the piquancy of the lustful tableau enacted before my eyes.

And this central theme was echoed with minute variations wherever I looked. Lafayette's big hands clenched on Cindy's buttocks in the mirror on the far side of the bed. The tightly bunched globes of his own thrusting backside were between her lewdly spread thighs. Gobbling mouths above the white covers could be seen on the right. Splatting hips and squirming bellies just behind me. Even, unexpectedly, a profiled angle of my own head, craned forward with an eager stare! We were slap in the middle of the biggest multiple orgy in the world . . . with only two participants and a single voyeur.

It was clear that, for Cindy, as I had been told, the reflections were all. Her eyes roved constantly, up, down and around; she changed position for purely visual reasons, not because they arose as a natural progression in their lovemaking routine. She was quite likely, at what could have been a critically ecstatic moment, to drag herself out from under Lafayette and kneel up in front of him, offering him with one bronze-nailed hand a luscious breast to suck. She could virtually spring from beneath him, push him onto his back, and position herself over his face so that, by looking over her shoulder, she could watch his tongue lap the gaping lips of her pussy in one of the rear-view mirrors. Once she straddled his chest, leaning forward over his hips to jerk him off manually so that she could see the reflection of the hot white drops spattering her belly below the black hands grabbing her tits.

Lafayette himself goodnaturedly permitted his body to be manipulated this way and that like a lay model in an artist's studio. Unperturbed at the manic changes in position and tension and even rôles, he remained always in the same state of sexual excitement, with the same stout erection – even after Cindy had manually brought him off. His stamina was – dare I say? – outstanding. I wondered once if by chance he had ever worked as a stud for a blue movie producer!

Cindy herself was so breathless with excitement that it was impossible to say whether she was enjoying what was virtually a continuous orgasm – or whether she never actually came at all, taking her pleasure entirely from the visuals.

All this of course was smashing for me. I revelled in every fucking minute, savouring each thrust, every gasp, the working hands, each sucking slurp of either mouth and the mirrored heaves of backsides and bellies from a dozen different points of view.

My own rôle, so far at any rate, was purely passive. I was entirely content to keep my mouth shut and watch: after all, this was no studied, mechanical performance put on by professionals for tired businessmen at some expensive 'live show' club; this was real people, enjoying real sex, each in his or her own way having a real ball. The grunts and gasps and small cries I heard were involuntary, instinctive, not rehearsed as part of a prepared script; the expressions of joy crooning out from between close-clamped lurches of flesh were stimulated rather than simulated.

So far as Lafayette was concerned, for the moment I no longer existed: I wasn't party to the scene mounted for Cindy's pleasure, so I wasn't there. With the girl herself it was rather different. The fact that I *was* there, an audience, watching her watch herself, was *part of* the scene. And this made, only in the most superficial way, for a kind of complicity between us. I was not involved, but at least I was present and, I hoped, correct.

This relationship, if relationship it was, confined itself on her part to an occasional smile flashed my way, a quizzically raised eyebrow directed at me from one of the mirrors in the middle of some contorted pose, as if to say: 'How about *this* for a position, eh?'

Naturally this made me feel good. I was accepted. It also made me, if you must know, horny as hell.

They also serve, I thought, who only wait and stand!

It was soon after this that Cindy pulled unaccountably away from a bullish rear entry by Lafayette and complained: 'Darling, I don't feel safe.'

'How's that again, babe?' He looked bewildered.

'They do say there's safety in numbers, don't they?' she explained demurely.

'Oh, wow, shit honey. Of course!' He turned to me. 'Your cue. Man, you're on!'

I rose to my feet like a rocketing pheasant, ripping off jacket and necktie. I was bent over, doing the shoes, when Cindy said, 'That's enough. No more.'

'Contrast black 'n' white, dick 'n' pussy, noodity 'n' threads – that what turn this chick on,' Lafayette told me. I approached the bed the way I was.

'Sit here by me,' Cindy said, 'and show me what you've got.'

What I had was already threatening to burst through the fly of my trousers. She was of course aware of this and drew down the zip very slowly, licking her lips as she regarded – in the mirror at the foot of the bed – the blood-gorged tip and then the distended shaft appear in her hand beyond Lafayette's carelessly sprawled dark thigh.

I was pretty enthralled myself, to tell you the truth, at the sudden revelation of my own stiff cock, obscenely withdrawn from my trousered loins, anachronistically exposed among all these planes and curves and glistening genitalia so shamelessly abandoned on the bed . . . and repeated with unending variation in all the mirrored surfaces enclosing us.

The loins were clothed but the lust flaming through them when Cindy took me in her mouth was naked all right. The whole of my nervous system raced to my glans as those practised lips closed over the cock-head and then slid lasciviously, tightly down the shaft. I hoped the erection was sufficiently upstanding for her to raise her head enough to see herself in at least one of the mirrors. It certainly felt that way. And it must have been because a moment later I was flat on my back with the tawny furrow of her vaginal cleft immediately above my face. The fingers drawing apart the wet lips of her pussy to make way for my exploring tongue, I saw, were neither mine nor hers.

Later I fucked her – this time it's the right word – kneeling up with hands clenched on her buttocks to clamp her pelvis against my hips while Lafayette's thick cock, hardened as teak, pistoned in between her slaving lips.

I shafted her from behind while she gave him head. We stood up and turned her upside down so that she could suck him off while I lapped her pussy with her long legs draped over my shoulders. At one time she had two cocks in her mouth and four hands busy about her breasts and vagina. The nude and the rude, we did just about everything one conventionally attired and two naked enthusiasts can do on a bed. And the orchestra of lecherous trios surrounding us, hemming us in on every side, obediently mimicked – although from a variety of different angles – our every lustful move.

An hour later, craving if not increased variety at least an extra element of spice in her love life, Cindy undressed me and we ran through the whole gamut again in triple nudity.

Let's face it – indeed we had no alternative! – our multiple activity provided a pretty splendid and comprehensive spectacle. For us and all the other siblings in the cast.

About three times as adventurous, at a rough count, as anything in the *Kama-Sutra*.

The really fascinating aspect, for me, was that the evening furnished a double as well as a treble thrill. In the opening phase, despite the mirrors and the fact that I was reflected in them, my rôle was totally objective: I was a spectator, isolated on the other side of the footlights, as it were. Subsequently, *following an identical scenario*, I was involved, a participant, so that my view was now one hundred percent *sub*jective.

It was almost as if, having watched a matinée of, say, *The Merry Wives Of Windsor*, one found oneself on stage during the evening performance cast as one of the wives!

With the added refinement that, in this very particular theatre, the actors and the audience – thanks to those mirrors – were one and the same!

The complexity of this wheels-within-wheels concept, as in the case of the Chinese boxes or the Russian dolls, lies in the identification of the precise spot at which the unending series starts. Or finishes. Were we really watching the reflections – or were the reflections watching us?

Hallucinatory, eh? If you keep at it long enough. At which point objective and subjective become indistinguishable and there is only *feeling*.

This dreamlike, surreal quality marking the whole night played such havoc with my memory later – with the *chronology* of my memory – that I find it impossible to describe in any detail the exact sequence of what we did or precisely how we managed to do it.

For me the only fixed point, the one incident that doesn't get lost among the phantom images activating the walls and ceiling, relates to a pause imposing itself just after the three of us had collapsed in the wake of a tremendous triple orgasm.

It was three-fifteen in the morning. Dozens of naked participants lay exhausted in every corner of the universe. And then Lafayette, still astonishingly wearing that hat, levered himself upright, wrapped a towel around his middle, and rang for room service, demanding refreshment.

A waiter appeared so quickly that he could almost have been stationed outside the door. Perhaps he was: I wouldn't blame him, specially if there was an outsize keyhole.

Lafayette, accompanied by a regiment of his identically-hatted reflections, went to the door. 'The Taittinger vintage,' he ordered grandly, 'not the house champagne.'

'*Jawöhl, Herr Braun,*' the waiter said.

PART FOUR

The Field – And How To Play It

Chapter Eighteen

I won a fifty-dollar bet with a friend once because I happened to mention in passing a Californian singer named H-Bomb Ferguson. 'Bullshit,' said the friend. 'There *can't* be a singer with a name like that. There's no such person.'

I swore there was. I even said I had a record with the guy's name on the label. 'Fifty bucks says you're mistaken,' my friend challenged.

I took the bet. I was onto a good thing: I *knew* I had that record.

Next time I saw him, I took along the disc. And there it was: *H-Bomb Ferguson (Blues Shouter)*. On the Esquire label. Not only that. He was accompanied by Jack The Bear Parker and his Rhythm-and-Blues Band!

I don't think the combination figures too often in the charts today, but, hell, fifty dollars was fifty dollars in the sixties.

One of the explosive gentleman's songs was entitled *Love in the Mornin'*. And the lyrics, attributed on the label to H-B Ferguson, included the blues couplet:

> *Some folks like to love in the mornin';*
> *Some like to love in Lovers' Lane.*
> *But I like to love in the evenin'*
> *When it's pourin' down rain!*

I was reminded of this wholesome sentiment some three months after my night with Lafayette Briggs – another ex-jazzman, incidentally – and Cindy, the good-time redhead from Munich. There was a log fire burning in my stone fireplace. The lowering autumn sky had darkened to blot out the early stars half an hour ago. The tinkle of wire stays and the creak of wood from the boats moored below was drowned by the swash of waves creaming into the marina. And above our heads, rafters and tiles drummed beneath the heaviest downpour of rain since the previous spring.

Susan and I had piled up cushions in front of the blaze and sat on the floor with our backs leaning against the ottoman. She was wearing dark red mules with black lace panties and a heavy, loose-knit sweater with nothing under it. Very sexy – shades of Violette again! – because I *knew* what was hidden there, and exactly how it looked and felt.

I was barefoot in denims and an orange sweatshirt. One long-fingered, red-nailed hand lay carelessly on my upper thigh, the thumb occasionally moving to check that the elongated outline pushing out the crotch of my jeans was what Susan thought it was. If she needed extra proof, there was a spreading patch of moisture darkening the blue material.

Lying there totally relaxed, listening to Glenn Gould attacking Bach, I was idly reflecting on how right Mr Ferguson was. What better than to lie here, warm, well-fed, relaxed, intimate, safe from the raging elements – and knowing that a night of fleshly delights lay ahead!

And thinking of the blues shouter and his dollar-winning name, I wondered, on just such an evening as this, what exactly did his girlfriend, or his buddies for that matter, *call* him? H-Bomb as a Christian name – an *un*-Christian name, I supposed – didn't exactly cry out for affectionate diminutives. Nor were the syllables suitable for shortening into a meaningful nickname. So how would the dialogue run?

'Whaddya know, Aitch, we need more logs! Hey, Bombie, pass over the rye, willya? Meet my friend Ferg. You got a extra dose that weed, H.B.?'

'Lover,' Susan said. 'Why don't you splash a little malt in to refresh these empty glasses?'

As usual, the woman gets it right!

I splashed. We drank.

Outside, the wind veered, blowing a scatter of heavy raindrops against the window. The thrumming on the roof grew louder. Guttering and stackpipes gurgled on every side.

I went into the kitchen to fasten a shutter that was banging. Through the streaming glass I could see the masthead light of some craft surging into the harbour against the dark sky.

When I came back, Susan was reclining a little lower among the cushions. Her legs, stretched out towards the fire, were slightly parted. She smiled up at me sleepily. 'Comfortable,' she said. 'Probably warmer to stay here than to slog over the far side of the room and get into bed.'

I nodded. 'And even more room to do whatever it might occur to us to do in bed,' I said. 'Also I look forward immensely to the play of light and shade, the effect of firelight on what Edward would call your swelling mounds of flesh.'

'Understood,' she said, spreading the legs a little wider. 'The moment the malt has evaporated.' A pause. 'Talking of Edward . . . there's something wrong, isn't there? Or at any rate something not quite right. You've been preoccupied for several days. Expadink doesn't seem quite the magic word it once did. Do you want to tell me?'

'Sure,' I said, sinking down beside her. 'But only as background music to the feature film.' I put down my glass and stole a hand beneath the hem of her sweater. I felt warm flesh, satin skin, the vibrant, pulsing evidence of the life powering the infinite complexity of organs, and glands and muscles and nerve fibres, combining to create the glorious creature beside me.

The hand smoothed higher. Rough wool sliding past my knuckles, and then the heavy curve, the sensual, erotic weight of the flesh sculpting one breast. I spread fingers and thumb, cradling that warmth and weight. 'Nice,' Susan said drowsily. One of her own hands was back at my crotch. I could feel fingers searching for the tag of my zipper. 'So about Edward?'

'It's not really Edward,' I said. 'He's as preoccupied as I am. It's bloody Maddox. Maddox and his megalomania.'

'What do you mean?'

The zip was down. The familiar fingers swept aside Y-fronts and wrapped around my cock. It was still just as hard and just as long. Somehow or other, my free hand had inserted itself inside a loose lace leg of the black panties. My fingertips grazed springy hair, touched moistly folded inner flesh. 'Although he's the boss,' I said, 'Edward's never given figures; he's never told which books sell or how many they sell; he's no idea of the profit involved.'

Susan squirmed her loins against my fingers. 'But that's extraordinary.'

'It is. But there's worse. The money sent here for Edward to dispense has started to slow down: he has to keep cabling or phoning to ask for funds.'

'But why? *Don't* the books sell any more?'

'We think they do. But Maddox has got it into his idiot head that he wants to make porno movies as well. We think he's using the profits from the books to finance those, paring down Expadink's cash flow to balance the books.'

'That's crazy,' Susan said. 'Are you sure?'

'All the signs point that way. We're being asked to do two books a month now, instead of one – for the same money.'

'*Two?* Each month? But you *can't*: it's not possible. It's as much as you can do to make one.'

'It's not as bad as it sounds. They don't have to be original books. The score now is, they give us a book published maybe a couple of years ago, and we give it a new title, change the names of the characters, but otherwise copy it practically word for word from the previous version. The way we do with the sex scenes anyway. It's easier than the old system from the creative point of view, obviously. It just takes longer.' I moved my hand fractionally between the coolness of her thighs. 'Twice as long,' Susan said. 'For the same money. But don't the readers *notice*?'

'Apparently not. They've already been doing it for two months with some of the writers. They haven't received a single complaint.'

'Perhaps the people who buy the books can't read,' she said tartly. 'And are you telling me that you're going to accept this . . . this *unprofessional* behaviour?'

'What can I do?' I said. 'I've nothing else in view. And besides, we need the money.'

'Maybe you could make it as a paid stud at that café on

the Croisette where all the widows and lonely old ladies go,' Susan said. 'If what you're doing to me at this moment is any indication, you should be a wow!'

'I'll think about it,' I said. I could feel the beating of her heart against the heel of the hand cupping her breast.

There was no point waiting any longer; nothing here was going to change the mind of Maddox. I quit the thighs for the moment and pushed the loose sweater up beyond both her naked breasts. The firelight sculpted these magnificent swells and hollows out of the gloom. With lips and teeth and tongue, I paid them the tribute they deserved.

'What are these bloody films like anyway?' Susan said, shifting again.

'Diabolical, according to Jeff. They showed one at a fringe cinema during the Cannes Festival. It was just a joke, Jeff said. Hopelessly amateur. Not sexy. Too bad even to be funny. In any case you can't be nearly as detailed with images today as you can with text. Without being prosecuted, that is. No close-ups therefore of genital contact; not even simulated sex if it's nude. So, as Jeff says, the idea's a dog from the start. Just the same, it costs to make a feature-length movie, even a bad one, which accounts for Edward's cash-flow difficulties.'

'If they're not using professional studs and whores then,' Susan said, 'who are the actors and actresses the audience see not fucking?' She drained her glass.

'Friends of Maddox and his Danish associates,' I told her. 'Rich guys and dolls, using fake names and doing it for kicks. Can you imagine!' And then, in an artificial, affected voice, '"My *dear*, it's simply *priceless!* Sven and Bjorn are playing the part of beach boys in a *sex* film! And Ingrid – you'll never guess – Ingrid is to be the madam of a *bawdy-house!*" Shrieks of girlish laughter.'

'With respects to your profession, I prefer real life to imagination,' Susan said, placing the empty glass carefully on the stone hearth. She settled further back still among the cushions, raising her arms above her head so that the sweater lifted clear of the breasts I had been fondling.

I kissed them both again and then removed the black lace panties. She uttered a small, contented sigh and raised her knees so that the thighs were spread.

I was bent double, prone among the cushions, with my head buried between those uptilted thighs and my unzipped loins within reach of her roving hands. And mouth. It is only when lips, tongue and teeth are actually in contact with them that the full complexity of the female cunt's distended whorls and fleshy prominences and juicy, sliding ridges becomes apparent. I lost myself, that rainy night, in the fullest ever exploration of the hotly sucking, wet and sometimes gristly embrace of the opening nestling amidst her auburn pubic thatch.

At the same time, things were being done to my own genitals that sent the blood rushing there and set every nerve in my body a-tingle.

Very gently the scrotum, bunched tight now with desire, was withdrawn from the clinging grasp of my Y-fronts, through the open fly into the warm firelight. The sensitive glands inside were eased within the fleshy sac, the dark skin itself smoothed, pulled tighter still until the clasped cock too was withdrawn. My balls, and the super-stiffened rod rising above them were nakedly exposed in the dancing light, obscenely bare projecting from sweatshirt and plundered jeans.

Susan drew the testicles further away from my body, so that the skin above them stretched tighter yet around my

273

swollen and quivering staff, so bursting now with lust that this outer sheath could scarcely be moved over the pulsating inner core.

Light as the touch of butterfly wings, the pads of her fingers skimmed up and down the veined hardness of my cock. Just occasionally, I was aware of the upper part of her body shifting and I felt hot breath on the underside of the head as the tip of her tongue flicked out once, twice, maybe three times to send fresh thrills rippling through me.

My own mouth was busy helping my hands explore. Tonguing the smoothly sliding cavity of Susan's cunt, I prised apart the burning labia, holding them open so that the oiled hollows channelling the inner lips could be mapped, the streaming, subtle ridges scaled, the lips closed over her fleshy, throbbing clitoris and finally the dark and salty depths of the secret inner passage penetrated.

I am always fascinated by the clitoris. The image assembled by the touch of lips, tongue and fingers is so different from that transmitted to the eyes when you actually *see* it. One knows of course that the organ itself is shielded by a tiny hood or prepuce, withdrawn when the bud is in erection rather like a miniature cock. But when it comes to extension, width, texture and sensitivity, no two are alike. Add this to the cunt as a whole, with all its lubricated variations of feel and form, and I am convinced that every woman in the world is totally individual in this one respect. The whorls of the female sex organ would provide a safer, more precise indication, at least among women, of exactly who a person was than any whorls transmitted to paper via the pressure of digital surfaces on an inked pad.

Maybe female burglars, terrorists, blackmailers, con-

persons and hold-up specialists should be identified by
their cunts rather than fingerprints or genetic data? Think
of the queues, though, formed by guys wishing to enlist in
the police!

Somehow, my jeans and underpants were around my
knees. Still sucking, I was nevertheless half on my side
and half on my back. Susan had slid a forearm, wrist and
hand beneath my buttocks and between my thighs to
grasp my balls from underneath and behind. She was
pulling the hairy sac hard down and backwards so that my
stiff cock stood away from my body with a rigidity as total
as an aluminium mast on one of the yachts tossing on the
water of the harbour below.

It was seeping now from the distended slit in the pulled-
back head, and she smeared this lubricating flow over the
head and around the shaft until the whole cock gleamed
and glistened in the rosy light. Unable to slide the tightened
skin over the core in the usual pumping clasp, she
smoothed the aching, agonized surface from tip to root
with a featherlight fingertip massage that made the entire
pelvis tremble. I felt as if all of my innards, every nerve
and muscle and fibre, were streaming into my loins to
force themselves out through the spearing nozzle of my
imprisoned penis. My hips twitched. My pulse rate
doubled. I groaned with desire as I renewed my gobbling
assault on the hot, wet cunt against my mouth.

'*Niiiice!*' Susan murmured, the highest award, the most
extreme appreciation she could bestow.

Locked like that, we continued our shared delight.
Then her mouth closed over the head of my cock.

It was the sudden warm pressure, the enclosure of my
most sensitive area in that moist and gently drawing
suction, that galvanized me into an even more active

expression of my lustful desire for Susan. My hands snaked upwards to cradle those large, taut breasts, grazing the pliant nipples to instant erection against my palms. I took even more of her into my mouth, penetrating to the full stretch of my eager tongue. My hips writhed under the delirious tension induced by her masturbating grasp.

At the same time, the pelvis of the alluring young woman reacting with such pleasing intensity to my oral caresses jerked rhythmically among the cushions, flexed into instinctive response by the ministrations of my bobbing head.

Why was this sexual game, on this particular night, so wildly exciting? Partly, I think, because it was in such contrast to our normal plunge-straight-in routine. Partly of course because it *wasn't* routine. But also because the very atmosphere of that stormy night – rain on the roof, the fire glowing, the boats outside heaving against the wet wind – was itself an invitation to a close and intimate complicity as unfamiliar as the unseasonal weather.

Whatever the reason, my voluptuous, pneumatic partner and I seemed equally thrilled by each successive move.

When finally I freed my tortured genitals and levered myself away from her shuddering thighs, I sank down onto her – and into the welcoming swallow of her cunt – with a movement as simple and easy and natural as drawing a curtain in the morning to let in the sunlight.

We fell at once into the eternal, inexorable rhythm, arms clasped, belly to heaving belly, thigh against thigh and the pistoning cock engulfed in the hungry hot suck of a lustfully aroused pussy.

We rode the same wave all the way to the top . . . and after it broke, leaving the two of us, still locked together, beached among the emotional shallows, we lay quietly at ease, listening to the wind and rain and watching the log blaze dwindle and fade to a friendly glow.

When at last Susan spoke, she said sleepily: 'Well, that was *lovely*. And the beginning was quite a change.'

'Yes,' I agreed, with passing thoughts for Frances and Peggy and Helen. And Miriam and Mabel. And of course Violette. '*Quite* a change, darling!'

Chapter Nineteen

It was to be the party to end all parties, Edward said. It was also a farewell and thank-you party, a sorry-it-had-to-end-this-way party, a nice-to-have-known-you party and a way of exhausting every penny that remained in the Expadink bank account. Most of all, it was a way of showing Maddox what he had missed, that life was infinitely more thrilling than his bloody books.

'Will Maddox be there?' I asked Edward.

'God, no. But I'm having the whole damned show video-taped. It'll be sent to him by special messenger, the day after we've gone. Just to show the bastard.'

'Christ!' I said. 'Who *will* be there then?'

'Strictly in-house. With partners if required. Those of us who work here, plus Miriam's boyfriend, Jeff's wife, your girl if you like.'

'Thanks,' I said. 'But she's on another cruise right now. I'd be happy, as they say, to play the field.'

'The big laugh,' Edward said nastily, 'if you can call this in-house, is that Maddox's own two daughters will be here!'

'His *daughters!* Shit, I'd no idea . . . I mean, how does this square with—'

'He thinks they don't know what Daddy's business is. In fact they're way ahead. In the Paris fast set they're

279

known as ravers.' Edward grinned. 'Angel, nineteen, and Annette, twenty-one. Wait until you see, boy. *Wow!*'

We were in the St Tropez penthouse. I had been summoned there officially to be informed that Expadink was to be wound up. Definitely. As of now. End, quite literally, of story.

Maddox's tacky soft-porn films, which could be sold to African, Oriental and some Eastern European countries on their advance publicity – that is to say without actually being seen by the buyers – were nevertheless costing more money to produce than the company could afford. Unless they cut down on the books.

The 'literary' side of the business was therefore to return stateside, where hacks – out of work students and the like – would slave away changing names and titles so that all the works already in the catalogue could be painlessly reissued as new and original. The premises were to be relinquished, probably with rent owing; the office equipment, much of it not yet paid for, would be repossessed. From the end of the week, Edward and his staff, repatriated if they were American, would be jobless.

Needless to say, Edward himself was very, very angry, even if the decision wasn't altogether a surprise. The brutal and cynical way in which it was communicated nevertheless was. Especially as it was left to Edward to break the unwelcome news to some twenty-five writers all over Europe that their contracts, with a foreign company which had ceased to exist, were unenforceable. If they were in the middle of a book, forget it; if they were owed for one already delivered, tough shit, Jack. Try suing a wound-up company with no cash in the kitty.

'There were two accounts,' Edward told me. 'One for paying the writers, the other for office expenses and things like that. From the first one, before Maddox closed it, I was able to square up you and Jeff and a couple writers in Rome and Paris. From the second, I'd already drawn every franc before the axe fell. It's not a lot, but's enough to pay off Miriam and Sonia . . . and stage the party of the century for all you guys who care to come.'

I grinned – if a trifle wryly. There were still bills to pay. 'I'll be there,' I said. 'Even if it's to fuck the shit out of Maddox's daughters!'

'That's my boy,' Edward said. 'Don't be vindictive though; their father's a sonofabitch but they're no part of the scam. They're nice kids, even if a little wild.' His turn to smile. 'The party's free: anyone wants to switch and swing, okay. Those who prefer to stay intimate, nobody's gonna trouble them.'

'Which is to say?'

Edward laughed. 'Which is to say you don't have to fuck Angel and Annette unless they turn you on!'

'The rain-check's wearing a little thin,' I said.

The day, or rather night, of Edward's spendthrift farewell party was as dark and stormy as the night I'd spent on the cushions in front of the fire with Susan. The song says Spring was a little late that year; for us, Winter was a trifle early.

Palms around the ritzy apartment block bent double before the wind. The outside pool had overflowed and the parking lot was several inches deep in running water. Even when I'd splashed as far as the porch, the driving rain bounced knee-high off the flagstones. I left a muddy trail all the way to the lifts.

Edward, or more probably Velvet, had done us all proud. Every penny had been spent as a two-finger gesture to Maddox. The evening was divided into two parts: our hosts had hired the most expensive restaurant in Cannes to provide a waiter-served banquet of hot crayfish and cold sea bass, of quails and ptarmigan and the eggs of gulls, of an entire cold fillet enrobed with flaky pastry. With enough liquor to rival the downpour outside. There was even a *sauté* of wild boar with chestnut sauce if you felt that way. The second part was to be entirely improvised.

The guest list was more or less as advertized. Edgar, Mabel's astro-physicist husband, had already returned to the United States because he'd heard of a possible opening in Silicon Valley, California. The rest of the Expadink crowd were there, along with Jeff, his enigmatic wife, Lafayette, and a couple I'd never seen before. And of course the Maddox girls.

As Edward had said, these could indeed be described, individually and as a pair, as a wow. Angel, the younger, was tall and svelte, with very bright make-up and waist-length, pale blonde hair cut off horizontally just above the swell of her buttocks. Annette was shorter, verging on the plump, with prominent breasts and backside. While Angel's hair fell down her back straight as a waterfall, Annette's dark curls clung close to her head. Brown eyes, very wide, were her best point. And these, smart girl, were exquisitely made-up, leaving the rest of her face virtually untouched.

'And if you think,' Edward said to me, following my appreciative glances, 'that I've asked them with some idea of getting my own back on Maddox by having the apples of his eye seduced, violated, debauched or whatever, think again. Those two kids, separately and together, are as horny as the rest of us put together!'

'I can't wait,' I said. 'You mind if I take notes and hawk

the results around a few publishers I know?'

He punched me playfully on the shoulder. 'Have yourself a ball,' he said.

The couple I'd never seen before were something of a mystery. They were both dressed in very simple, dark, rather formal clothes. He was about forty, well-built, handsome in a macho sort of way; she was blonde, busty and petite. They ate together, drank together and didn't mingle. If spoken to, they answered politely, non-committally, always in French. Who could they be? The bank manager and his wife? Owners of the two apartments? Suppliers of some kind? Surely there would be no need, at this stage, to butter up such people!

I asked Lafayette, Jeff, Randy, Mabel. None of them knew.

Finally I cornered Mrs Edward. She smiled her sexy smile. 'You know how it is at kids' birthday parties,' she said in a low voice, covertly eyeing the soberly dressed couple. 'After the coke and the animal crackers and the jellies have been consumed and most of the balloons burst, the parents call in a conjurer, a vent act, a puppeteer or some kind of magician to keep the little bastards quiet until the grown ups arrive to take them home, okay?'

I nodded, still puzzled. 'And so?'

'This is a grown up party,' Velvet said. 'They're our equivalent, those two.'

'They're magicians?'

'In a way. Let's just say that Edward thought it might be an idea to kick off – once the food's been cleared away and the drink left handy – with some kind of a . . . well, let's say F and F are a cabaret specialty.'

'F and F?'

'François and Françoise,' Velvet said. But she wouldn't say any more.

It was about eleven when the waiters began carting away the remains of the banquet, everything neatly stacked in special boxes, the leftovers in plastic bags, glasses and crockery in polystyrene containers and the whole lot loaded onto trolleys to be taken downstairs in the lifts and packed into a truck.

Some time before this, I'd happened to notice that Lafayette and Miriam were no longer with us. They returned as the first trolley was being rolled towards the elevator bank. Lafayette looked, I thought, rather pleased with himself.

Miriam grinned at me, hitching a wide flowered skirt up towards her black silk shirt. 'The back of a pastry cook's delivery van!' she murmured as she passed. 'How about that for a first?'

'Bravo!' I said to Lafayette.

The 'cabaret act' was spectacular, if only in the sense that the performers appeared totally unaware of the existence of their audience. Edward and Velvet didn't even clear the room or push back chairs or ask the guests to sit down or at least pay attention.

Suddenly, once the hired help had gone, this sober-suited couple, without so much as a glance at the rest of us, began to undress one another.

We were standing around, drinking and talking, a little flushed by now with the good living, when François put down his glass on an occasional table, unconcernedly removed his dark jacket, and hung it over the back of a chair. This could simply have been because the room was a little too warm. But then he unknotted his tie, folded it neatly, and put it in one of the jacket pockets. He fingered open the top two buttons of his shirt. His handsome face was completely expressionless. At the same time Françoise unbuttoned the jacket of her own black suit.

It was after she had taken it off that there was a sudden lull in the conversation. With an expression as neutral as her partner's, she unbuckled the belt at the waist of her skirt, allowed the skirt to drop to her feet, and stepped out of it. She folded the skirt and hung it in turn over the back of another chair.

It wasn't the fact that there was anything remotely suggestive or obscene about these actions; it was precisely because they were so commonplace, so everyday, that they were effective. No point, no gesture as it were, was being made here. It wasn't simply that the couple ignored the rest of us, either. We simply weren't there.

This made the scene exceptionally powerful in that we were at once, all of us, in the position of voyeurs, peeping-toms, spying through keyholes not at artists following a scenario but at private individuals intimately engaged and unaware that they were observed. It was in fact quite fascinating.

Françoise was now dressed in medium-heeled black court shoes, dark stockings tightly drawn up and attached to a suspender belt, simple, close-fitting white panties and a deep-cup white brassière edged with a minimum of lace.

Again, it was the non-overtly sexy nature of this ensemble that rendered it so 'private' and the scene so intimate that we felt we ought not to be watching it. I saw at once why the couple had refused to mix during the early part of the evening: the more we had got to know them, the less effective this voyeur effect would have been.

Françoise had undone two more buttons and pulled

her partner's shirt over his head. He was wearing a white string-vest underneath it. His body was muscular without being exaggerated, the flesh firm and healthy.

She unbuckled his belt and pushed his trousers, rather slowly, down to his ankles. As she knelt to lift his feet out of them and remove his shoes, we could see that he was wearing black Y-front briefs. The slip appeared to be well-filled but there was no sign of an erection.

Françoise rose to her feet and turned her back to him. She pushed up the back of her blonde hair with both hands so that he could unfasten the brassière strap on the nape of her neck, and then unsnapped the lower part of the garment herself. She shrugged out of the bra, allowed it to slide down her arms, and hung it over her skirt. Good breasts, C-cups I thought, firm and well-shaped. The nipples were erect.

The room was now completely silent – although I was aware of heavy breathing here and there. I fancied some of it might have been mine. Lafayette sat in an upright chair, his yellow eyes agleam. Miriam was on his lap, squirming her hips slightly. No prizes for guessing why.

Sonia was watching open-mouthed. Randy, Jeff and the others were equally riveted. Edward was nowhere to be seen, but Velvet had an arm around Mabel's shoulders, with the fingers of that hand draped over the flowered silk slope sheathing one slender breast. I stole a glance at the Maddox girls. They were the only ones with no surprise showing on their faces, but there was no doubt whatever about the rapt attention in their pose as they stood with linked arms – or the wet glisten on their lower lips.

François was kneeling now, his head level with the blonde's hips. He unsnapped the suspender clips, rolled down the stockings, and dragged – with a sudden swift jerk that almost shocked us all – the tight, unglamorous panties down to her feet. A smooth curve of belly and a thatch of pale pubic hair sprang into view. She kicked off stockings and shoes and stood before us naked.

There was now a general exhalation of breath all around. We knew what must be coming, but we didn't know how or when. I didn't notice anyone complaining.

François moved closer. He stretched lithely to his feet, facing her. They kissed, as any couple might, tenderly, affectionately but without passion, before retiring to bed – a peck, a slight clinging of the lips.

Until she was close enough for her mons to touch the slight bulge at the crotch of his Y-fronts.

At that instant, a lot of things happened at once. The lips so chastely kissing abruptly clasped, clung, worked. Cheeks hollowed as the tongues interlaced. His strong hands snaked around to the fleshy pads at the top of her hips, cramming her pelvis against him . . . although not before we had seen the sudden hard thrust straining against the black briefs.

Her two hands circled him as they stood locked together, one sliding subtly into the crack between his hairy buttocks, the other, nearer, inserting itself between them at crotch height. Slowly, she raised and lowered that hand so that the knuckles grazed the hardness at his loins.

His response was electric. Arching his hips, he drew back far enough for her to slam down the Y-fronts and drag out his cock and balls.

His cock was a pretty serviceable weapon, thickish, fairly long, and clearly rock hard – but without the exaggeration that would have made it like a strip-cartoon fantasy or the subject of a dirty story. The balls matched. They were neat, bunched, very male but not too bullish.

Everything in fact continued to impose the impression that we were watching a very ordinary couple: Mr and Mrs Everyman at play. That was the genius of their act – that and the fact that it took place without any warning in a room full of fully dressed partygoers. It wouldn't have worked half as well on a stage; it would have missed out on the particularly lewd and lascivious quality that voyeurism has.

Once we were hooked on that aspect, however, François exploded into action.

With the cock speared out in front of him, he seized his partner and threw her face down against the cushioned slope at one end of a chaise-longue. Kneeling up behind her, he prised her thighs apart, spread the cheeks of her bottom and drove that cock into her from behind with a force that flattened her against the upholstery. For the first time, from either of them, we heard something vocal: an involuntary '*Aaaah!*' forced from her lungs by the power of his penetration.

For several minutes, he fucked savagely into her, squashing her tits, splatting against the cheeks of her bared backside. Then he changed the rhythm – and the scenario – turning her upside down and around so that her back was against the slope of the chaise-longue and her legs were draped over the carved wooden rail at the top.

In this position, he shoved the rigid cock into her mouth, leaning over her inclined body so that he could splay apart the lips of her cunt and tongue her clitoris in full view of the assembled party. After that, he opened the French windows and carried her outside into the roof garden in the rain.

The behaviour of the said party during this was, I must

say, fascinating! Nobody, I think, failed to be turned on in one way or another. But the ways varied from the overt to the covert, from the secret to the actively salacious.

Lafayette, unconcerned as the naked couple, sat with a huge smile on his face, one hand and wrist hidden beneath the flared and flowered summer skirt that Miriam wore. She was now half on his knee, half perched on the arm of the chair. One of her own hands was concealed too, But I was pretty sure it was inside the loosened waistband of his trousers.

Velvet, standing directly behind Mabel, now had both arms around my editor's waist and was nibbling the lobe of her left ear. From time to time, very discreetly, she arched her hips slightly forward to thrust against Mable's tightly-jeaned backside.

Sonia, still open-mouthed, had sunk into a chair. She seemed unaware that she had a hand clasped over each of her neat little breasts. Jeff's wife was behind her, one red-nailed hand resting lightly on the shoulder of the jade green dress that the girl wore. I didn't imagine that the hand would remain there for long.

My fellow writer himself had an around each of the Maddox girls.

And out on that terrace, lewdly coupled on the wet flagstones between the potted palms, François and Françoise were giving a nape-prickling exhibition of unbridled lust in the driving rain.

She had been lying on her back with her legs splayed, while he humped her in the missionary position, half supporting himself on his elbows so that his clawed hands could massage and mash her streaming breasts. Now, suddenly, he rose to his knees, rigid cock gleaming, and seized her by the hips. He spun her roughly around so that she was on all fours. Then, wrenching apart the cheeks of her arse, her drove fiercely into her from behind once more.

The rain beat ceaselessly down on them as they fucked, flowing between the blonde's clenched buttocks to wash over their pistoned genitals, glistening in the lamplight reflected from the apartment. Her hair hung over her face in rats' tails, her breasts hung jerking from her chest, splashing water from the twin points of her nipples. François's expression was tense, teeth bared as he slammed into her with rain dripping from his chin and cascading over his hunched shoulders. Between them, in that torrential downpour, they presented a picture of naked lust that was almost animal in its rutting ferocity.

Without altering his rhythmic assault, François reached a hand into a terrazzo *jardinière* planted with drenched petunias and geraniums and scooped out a fistful of wet earth which he plastered over his partner's heaving back. The mud oozed sluggishly over her skin, dripping down rib cage and waist to smear her belly and breasts. He slapped on another handful, leaning forward across her back to squirm his body against her muddied flesh . . . and abruptly, unexpectedly, he came.

With a great cry, he jerked backwards away from her and knelt there with his stiffened cock spewing out spouts of pale semen into the rain. At the same time Françoise whirled around, wrapped her arms around his tensed haunches and took the still spurting shaft into her greedy mouth.

I found myself standing next to Randall Van Eyck. 'My God!' he said. And then, glancing around the hushed room, 'Lafayette's busy, bloody Jeff has two birds, four more are split into pairs, Edward's vanished and here's you and me standing alone like spare beds with nobody to sleep in them! Shit, I reckon it's time I started to cut in here with kind of an excuse-me dance, right?'

'Be my guest,' I said. I was getting to like the phrase.

It was only a little later, but there had been a number, as the old song says, of changes made.

Mabel and Velvet had retired to another room. Edward was still absent, although I thought I had seen a black-clad figure in gleaming leather through a half-open door at some point during the cabaret scene. The performers themselves had gone, re-entering the apartment by another door, showering, then returning to dress and leave as inconspicuously as they arrived. I assumed they had been paid in advance.

In the big living-room, Randy, as good as his word, had cut in on Jeff and spirited away the elder Maddox girl to a low divan scattered with cushions which lay behind a table still loaded with bottles of champagne and brandy. Jeff had his hands too full to protest: Angel Maddox had unbuttoned her white silk shirt and bared her breasts to his touch as she stood on tiptoe to kiss him on the mouth while she groped his straining crotch.

Jeff's wife, Inge, failing to score with Sonia, had wandered across to sit on the unoccupied arm of the chair in which Lafayette and Miriam were sexually engaged. 'Is this a private club?' she asked the Canadian secretary. 'Or can anyone join in?'

Sonia herself now stood by me. She was wearing very high-heeled shoes. The green dress, tightly belted at the waist, was gashed by a neckline plunging enough to reveal the lace edges of the uplift bra pushing her breasts into the familiar pin-up cones. This time, though, I was a little too high to remember that the sex-bomb gear was all an act . . . and why. I took the come-on scenario at face value and snaked an arm around her waist. 'So you see,' I said, nodding towards the rainswept roof garden, 'that the stuff we write isn't altogether fantasy dreamed up in our horny heads?'

'Mmmm,' she said, and I thought she turned slightly so that one breast nudged the hand on the far side of her waist. 'Could we go into one of the other rooms half a mo? There's still a question or so I'd fair like to ask ye?'

'At once,' I said. But the room I chose was if anything more active than the one we left. Edward, wearing a black leather suit, sat roped into an upright chair while Velvet, sprawled in an easy chair with her legs hooked over the arms, lifted her long black skirt so that Mabel, on her knees in front of the chair, had access to her naked loins. The tableau – Mabel's head bobbing between his wife's nude thighs – was not displeasing to Edward. At least if one judged by the rigidity of the staff thrusting through the gaping fly of the black pants.

'Och, my guidness me!' Sonia breathed, the Scottish accent suddenly strong.

'This, actually,' I said hastily, 'is part of another kind of book.'

'But do they really—? I mean does he not—?'

'Folks find their pleasure in many ways,' old schoolmaster me said craftily. 'They're not always . . . forthcoming, shall we say . . . about it. This is kind of Book Three material. Maybe we had better leave them to it and—'

'Wait.' She laid a hand on my arm. She was obviously fascinated, her gaze switching from the lewdly coupled women in the chair to her leather-clad employer with his erect and blood-engorged penis.

Edward obviously knew we were standing in the doorway, though his blue eyes remained fixed on his wife and Mabel. Clearly he didn't mind the audience, or the door would presumably have been locked. Velvet's eyes were closed and her face wore a dreamy, ecstatic expression. I don't think she did know. And Mabel, licking and tonguing and sucking, couldn't have seen anyway.

'Back to the school dormie,' Sonia whispered, still staring at the two women. 'I certainly know about that. But the other part . . . ?' She shook her head.

'I'll explain,' I murmured. 'But I think it would help if you – er – read Book One first!'

I led her away. Hell, looking the way she did, she was going to lose it one day anyway. Better me than some drunken oaf with a boat. Okay, I was smashed too . . . but so was she, or she wouldn't be so interested, would she? I found an empty guest room and we went in.

I'm not quite sure about the first steps, but pretty soon she was trembling in my arms, the whole pinup-girl length of her pressed hard against me, belly heavy, tits thrusting, as the warm lips timidly searched for, found, clenched around and finally savaged my mouth.

It was when we were on the bed – and I'm damned if I can recall in detail exactly how we got naked – that she breathed excitedly into my ear: 'Now show me . . . explain . . . tell me what to do!'

'There's no need,' I said. 'Just relax. Feel. Go with it and enjoy.'

I'm not so sure about the relaxation, but Sonia certainly felt and enjoyed! Once the fuse was ignited, she was a ball of fire, that kid.

For a start, she was so structurally perfect, so precisely

what the doctor ordered when it came to the arrangement and proportions of limbs and breasts and belly, so lovely to look at, that to be with her at all made me more than ordinarily horny. And this of course endowed me, at once, with the biggest and stiffest hard-on I'd worn for months. My cock visibly swelled and tightened, hardened even more if that was possible, the instant she touched it. The pressure of the blood distending the stretched skin reached back into my loins with an urgency that fired my lust to an exceptional degree.

At the same time I was well aware that, even if adventures at school had made her 'technically no vairgin', this was nevertheless a first-time for my gorgeous partner – an initiation, if you like, into the field of actual fucking. I had therefore an obligation, a responsibility, not to rush things, to make it an experience as pleasurable as possible for her as well as for myself. Above all not to trample on any dreams, to avoid in any way disillusioning her or shooting down in flames any romantic ideas she might have on the coming of love.

To put it more crudely, more personally, I wanted to make sure she remembered the experience – and me – with joy.

If Sonia herself was at all conscious of any such reservations, it certainly never showed. The first touch of her fingertips on my quivering shaft sent a thrill shivering through her that I could feel along the entire length of my body. As my own hands sculpted the splendid curves and hollows of her hips and waist, her excitement expressed itself in subdued squeals of pleasure and small, half stifled inhalations of breath caught and then slowly exhaled in sighs of contentment. These were followed by a dreamy humming noise from the back of her throat once my caresses reached the lower part of her rib cage and advanced to the tautly swelling slopes of flesh above.

Her breasts were a photographer's dream, full, resilient, perfectly shaped and subtly uplifted by muscular tonus. When my hands reached the erectile nipples, the breath imploded with a sudden gasp, and Sonia's fingers tightened around my cock, starting for the first time a tender exploration of its stiffened length.

It was only then that I allowed one hand to wander slowly below her waist.

She tensed, and I was aware of a slight, spontaneous jerk of her hips.

But I left the hand stroking for a while the gentle curve of her belly. Hell, unless you're one of those oafs who clamps a heavy hand over a woman's cunt, forces in two fingers and expects an orgasm, unless you're the type using a female body purely for what the medics used to call penile gratification – regarding the vagina as nothing more than an alternative vehicle for masturbation – unless you're one of those types there has to be a time and a place, as they say. Good sex, after all, is something *shared* by two persons, not a thing *done* by one to another.

Minute tremors fluttered through every muscle in Sonia's frame by the time my hand actually came anywhere near her cunt. I approached via the crease at the top of the thigh which defines the limit of the pubic triangle, drawing the back of one finger slowly, very slowly down the palpitating groove in her flesh. Even at the genital level, I smoothed only the very tips of the springy hairs thatching that entrancing furrow, allowing the caress to be transmitted to her skin by the roots of the hair. Kept up long enough, with a near-hypnotic rhythm and no change in the delicate pressure, this outermost stroking of the genital region – with the first three fingers rather than the cupped hand – can itself produce a state of intense excitement.

When at last the whole hand is lowered to cradle the whole outer part of the cunt – sometimes it will *be* grasped and clamped firmly there – then the subtler arts of the seducer emerge. Or perhaps enter is a better word.

The little crease, the wrinkled crescent of the outer labia, has been touched and the first instinctive arch of the hips experienced. The hand is clasped snugly there, centred on that fold of flesh.

There are four fingers and a thumb on that hand, each capable of independent movement. So with the little finger and thumb, those outer labia are spread open and held apart while the first and third fingers probe, caress and explore the inner lips and the fascinating hollows or runnels between them. The middle finger, until now virtually inactive, stretches out to press lightly down – even if only by the mass of its own weight – until suddenly, entrancingly, the juices flow, the whole opening is wet, warm and smoothly sliding . . . and that finger is free to bend back, doubled at the knuckle, and touch the irregular, stiffened bud of the clitoris. Or permit itself to sink, to be swallowed almost, by the hot suck of excited inner flesh. Or to venture further – once due respect has been paid to the clitoris – thrusting abruptly deep into the dark depths of the secret channel into which soon, oh achingly soon, the iron-hard cock is to be plunged.

It was at about this stage of the operation that Sonia moaned in my ear: 'Och, God, dear man, how is it ye know so well how to dae this if ye're no' a woman yairsel?'

I'd had this said to me before, principally by Susan, but I was flattered just the same. 'It's no problem,' I whispered.

'A little imagination perhaps. I just think to myself, if I was a woman . . . built that way . . . and if I had these shapes, what would I like to be done to me there. And I do it.'

I went on stroking and probing and smoothing, as softly as I could, and she opened to me like a flower. Her whole cunt was streaming, the delicious body squirming in ecstasy as my fingers massaged her sex alive.

I've noticed that most women masturbating, when they get really worked up, favour either a circular movement, rotating the erect clitoris, or a hard side to side alternation, really mashing the fleshy bud against the pubic bone. This can get quite violent, the entire body galvanized into erratic convulsions as speed and pressure increase. I was using both techniques on Sonia now, and she was raving, rolling this way and that on the bed, hands working at my throbbing cock, the blonde hair, which had been fanned out on the pillow, fiercely whipping left and right. At last she muttered huskily: 'God, I want it in there. I want to know it all. Man, dear, put it *in!*'

I kissed her on the mouth. 'Don't rush it,' I whispered, still scrabbling, harder now, at her cunt. 'Just let our senses and bodies take over. Go with it . . . and suddenly you'll find it's happened; we're already there.'

'I think you're wonderrrful!' she crooned, thrusting against my invading finger. Her hot, sexy little hips reacted like an instrument to a musician's hands. It was a pretty good scene, too, although I say it myself. And we did all at once find ourselves 'there', locked together without ever realizing exactly how we got there. It happens like that sometimes when a fuck really works. But I'm not in the habit of deflowering first-timers – it is after all something of a private experience for them – so I don't propose to go into any further detail here.

I found Lafayette and Miriam in a box-room at the end of a passage – Sonia had gone to fetch more drinks – and I must say the scene there was something else! The room was full of ancient steamer trunks, hampers full of old clothes, broken furniture, a rocking horse and valises half packed with stuff Edward and Velvet were taking back to the United States. In one corner, beneath a shuttered window, stood a wide, heavily upholstered, leather car seat which had once clearly graced the front of a sizeable saloon. The leather, slightly greyed with use, had originally been a pale oyster colour; it was still supple and rich with its luxury smell.

Lafayette Briggs, completely naked now, knelt on the seat, the muscles on his ebony back and hips rippling as he – to use an Americanism – fucked Miriam in the mouth. She was upside-down against the seat back, her inverted head between his powerful thighs, her legs draped over the padded top. The head-rest had been removed and my black friend's own head was bobbing up and down where it would have been, his tongue raking the exposed slit of Miriam's cunt, plowing between the reddish hairs to penetrate the wet flesh quivering there.

It was a scene I had both imagined and witnessed before – one, indeed, in which I myself had taken part, although on a smaller, less expensive seat. What was different about this one was the fact that Annette Maddox was astride the rocking horse, wearing nothing but long black stockings and stiletto-heeled shoes.

A pink dildo, strapped to the horse's saddle, was inserted between her thighs, and her wide brown, exquisitely made-up eyes glistened as she rocked the wooden animal violently in time with the movements of the pair obscenely coupled on the car seat.

From time to time she called out equestrian cries of encouragement – the horse creaking, the glistening phallus plowing in and out of her inflamed cunt, Lafayette's great tool lost in Miriam's hollowed cheeks and sucking mouth as her 'Tally-hos' and 'Giddy-ups' echoed through the cluttered room.

It was when Annette abruptly folded forward, dropping the reins to clutch her own bouncing breasts as she came, that the couple on the car seat changed position. Now it was Lafayette who lay his broad shoulders on the seat and draped his legs over the back. Miriam positioned herself with a knee on either side of his head and lowered her wet cunt to his eager lips as she leaned forward against his upside-down belly and took his cock in her mouth. At the same time, grinning mischievously, Annette swung herself over and re-seated herself facing the horse's tail, the dildo now buried between the cheeks of her plump backside. She began rocking the horse.

The car seat was placed with its back half turned towards the door where I stood in astonished admiration, my own cock already hardening again. As Miriam opened her lips to take in Lafayette's blue-black, shining staff, her eyes met mine. 'Whose car?' I blurted out.

She released the shaft momentarily. 'Owners of the apartment. They had it resprayed and the inside refitted with white hide.'

'And the make?'

Her eyes shone. 'A Rolls-Royce,' she cried. 'Fucked on the front seat of a Roller: my dream come true!'

To get back to the living-room and Sonia's drinks, I had

to pass through the room where the pinioned Edward was being forced to watch his wife's seduction by his senior editor.

He didn't seem to be having too bad a time of it.

Mabel stood on his thighs, facing him, her heels grinding the leather into his flesh. She had forced back his head with both hands. The tight jeans were bunched below her knees. And her naked loins, thrust lewdly forward, brought her genitals in contact with his mouth. Behind her, the skirt still hitched around her hips, Velvet straddled his roped legs, riding up and down on his stiffened cock as her hands snaked up to fondle the pink-tipped swell of Mabel's slender breasts.

I think they're called erogenous zones, those parts of the body particularly sensitive to touch and the caress. The bits that make you horny. Whatever, between the three people on that chair, since Velvet's lips were nuzzling the base of Mabel's nude spine, there seemed only one such zone unoccupied as I entered the room, and that was the editor's mouth.

I dragged across another upright chair, stood on the seat, and pulled Mabel's head down so that she could bend forward from the waist and close her mouth over the tip of the cock now spearing hard from my loins. She groaned as the thick shaft forced its way between her moist lips and into the hotly sucking cavern beyond.

For a while there was no sound but the rain beating against the shutters, heavy breathing all around, a faint keening moan from Edward, the stealthy squelch of wet flesh and a subdued creak of leather and rope. Then Sonia shouldered open the door and walked into the room carrying two glasses of champagne.

She stopped dead, staring at the heaving, groaning

quartet grouped in quivering, lascivious motion around Edward's chair, and then exclaimed: 'Och, away! I'd best be gaeing back in there and fetch another three drinks forbye!'

'In there' was occupied – very neatly occupied, I have to say – by Randy, Jeff, Inge and the young Angel Maddox, the other quartet between them forming the remainder of the Expadink party.

They were in fact more symmetrically arranged, and perhaps even more energetically occupied, than either of the groups I had just left.

The nucleus of the action (thoughts of Susan and the ottoman!) centred on a divan which had been moved into the centre of the room, within easy reach of the drinks buffet but not near enough for it to risk the bruising of a threshing leg or the contusion of a hastily raised head.

Basically this was the scene. Angel, the youngest but probably the most promiscuous and adventurous of the four, was being attended to at every point of her personal compass. She had obviously been straddling Randy's hips, for he lay naked on the divan with his cock deeply embedded in her girlish cunt, arching up his hips to meet her rider's thrusts. But now she was bent forward, still impaled, so that her backside was raised enough for Jeff, kneeling between Randy's spread legs behind, to penetrate her anus with equally deep plunges.

Inge for her part, bare as the others, knelt against the head of the long divan so that Randy's head, tipped backward over the edge, was in a position to wedge itself between her thighs and allow him to tongue her wet pussy. The two girls were thus in a position to lean forward and kiss one another lingeringly on the lips.

Not a single hand, of the eight involved, was not gainfully

employed. One of Jeff's, widespread, kept Angel's buttocks splayed as he plowed manfully in and out of her violated asshole; with the other, arm wrapped around her hips, he held open the lips of her cunt to ease the passage while she rode up and down Randy's tool. Angel herself needed one hand and arm to support herself. With the other she reached behind and underneath to seize my co-writer's balls.

Both Inge's hands were at the full stretch of her arms, one to fondle Angel's swinging breasts, the other to mash the girl's clitoris against the hard, oiled shaft of the cock skewering her belly. Randy, writhing and jerking on the padded surface of the divan, seemed to have hands everywhere. The one that wasn't skirmishing among Inge's breasts – or Angel's – was usually endeavouring to masturbate the lengthened clitoris emerging from the cunt he was sucking.

For an instant I paused, seeking a possible opening. There were only three available: the backsides of Inge, Jeff and Randy. The last was out of the running anyway because its owner was lying face upwards. As for Jeff . . . well . . . that is to say I was kneeling behind Inge almost as a matter of course.

Her pale body was extraordinarily supple, almost acrobatic in its ability to twist and writhe. Perhaps this was a result of the demands made on her by Jeff in the privacy of their home! In any case, without in the least inconveniencing Randy, whose gobbling mouth was still clamped to her pussy, she was able to spread her thighs, tilt her backside rearwards and up while still kissing Angel, and allow me what the airline companies call immediate access.

I wasn't the first passenger that night. I knew at once

from the easy, sliding, lubricated graze of the puckered anus against the tip of my cock that someone had already ravished that tight little opening, distending the contracted muscles to force in his heavy, stiffened penis. Inge rotated and canted her loins against my thighs as I pulled her buttocks apart and then held my hard shaft against the moving, heated moisture of her hairy cleft. I flexed my hips and pushed, circling her belly with a free hand to pull her back against me.

She thrust outwards with her sphincter muscles, welcoming the intruding staff. The head was in, vice-gripped by hot flesh. I shoved harder. The scalding ring of her clenched anus slid down the throbbing length of my cock as her lower body spread, opening to receive me.

I was in, buried to the hilt, the spearhead of my lust clasped within the pulsating heat of her inner flesh. All around my bursting prick as it lay clamped there I was thrillingly aware of the pounding of blood, the contractions of muscles and the flutter of nerves firing the slender, alien body I was violating. I could even feel on the sensitive underside of my cock the tremor of Randall's lapping tongue through the thin wall of flesh separating Inge's cunt from her rectum.

She uttered a choked gasp as I started to pump in and out of her, heaving back against each inward lunge before I withdrew for the next, still eating the wet lips of the doubly skewered Angel somewhere above.

My own mouth, I realized suddenly, was free!

At the rear end of the complex, easily pistoning, live tableau on that divan, much of it obscured by the silky curtain of blonde hair hanging on either side of Angel's head, my upper half rose behind Inge's labouring back like a hitching post with no rider to attach to it.

This wasn't for long. A bare and slender leg stepped over the area where my loins and Inge's backside slaved together, and I was aware of a tender belly and soft pubic hair in front of my face.

Sonia, having supplied Edward and his ladies, was now back in the room, once again the bearer of two glasses of champagne.

She was standing with a foot on either side of my kneeling thighs, leaning back against Inge's inclined spine, moving a little as the blonde bucked against my thrusts. Her cunt was inches from my mouth. Naturally I bent forward to pay it the respect it deserved with my lips and tongue.

It was then that Sonia, swaying back and forth with Inge's exertions, found a new use for vintage champagne.

She was holding the two glasses high up, one each side at shoulder level. Now, as my tongue bored into the hot recess of her sweet little cunt, a secretive, mysterious smile twisted her young lips, and she held one glass against each swelling, uptilted breast. Very slowly she tipped the glasses, so that champagne spilled over the slope of each breast, flowed down to the nipple . . . and splashed from there to the curve of her belly.

The sparkling wine cascaded from here to the crease of each thigh, among the tufts of pubic hair, over the lips of her gaping cunt . . . and into my guzzling mouth.

Delicious!

But I don't know whether it was the extra drink, the intoxicating effect of the fountain supplying it . . . or maybe just the result of the evening as a whole: whatever, the fact remains that from then on my recollection of the party is . . . well . . . indistinct.

I remember Velvet and Mabel bringing in Edward, still

leathered up but no longer pinioned. I remember the group on the divan disengaging itself, and Edward roaring: 'Come on now – this is a team. We've always worked as a team, all for one and one for all! It was a fucking good team and now it's a good fucking team. So even if it's the last time, I want to have every single fucker here take away a fond memory of every other . . . of every single other . . .' He stopped. There were actually tears running down his cheeks. I think he might have been drunk. 'For Chrissake, boys and girls,' he shouted, 'let's get in there and pitch!'

He dropped into an armchair, grabbed Inge, and pulled her down onto his upthrust cock. 'This *has* to beat anything that was ever in those lousy books!' he said.

I remember a seething mass of arms and legs and cocks and cunt. I can recall hot flesh and wet flesh and hard flesh shining. I have vivid memories of cool thighs gripping my head, of hard breathing and probing tongues. I think I may have fucked Velvet, the boss's wife; I know that, at some time, I sucked off Mabel again. For the most part, though, as in the best societies, the individual was lost in the demands of the group. It was as if the growing pile of obscenely splayed and lewdly coupled bodies with all their groping arms and jerking legs, as if all that lustfully throbbing secret flesh had for that one night coalesced into a single sentient, sensual being whose sole thought was sex.

And this was symbolized for me by the most vivid remaining image of all: a big cock – it might have been my own – surrounded by many hands, spearing towards the ceiling and jetting forth a shower of white sperm to spatter in shining spurts the breasts and bellies and bums surrounding it.

I think that was before Miriam and Lafayette rejoined us, but it may have been after.

In any case, curiously, it was about that time that the orgy, without any planning at all, happened to split apart again into couples – not necessarily those arriving together – and resolved into a series of separate, almost *private*, for God's sake, intimacies as banal as any weekend wife-swappers or swingers party: Lafayette with Angel, Jeff with her sister, Randy with Inge, Velvet and Mabel, and Edward unusually with Miriam. Maybe he'd used his sign-off pay to buy a new Jag.

It was about this time too that I realized that I was the sole guest to have arrived at the party, and who would leave it . . . alone.

'Come on, baby,' I said to Sonia, who was kind of hovering on the outskirts, wondering what to do. 'It's almost four o'clock. What say we slope quietly out and I'll run you home?' I smiled, a little wearily. 'You don't have to ask would I care to come in for a cup of coffee either!'

Sonia grinned back. 'I'm no' a sophisticate like them,' she said, nodding at the entwined couples, 'but I got a hot line of grapefruit juice in the freezer!'

EPILOGUE

Between the Lines!

Chapter Twenty

Thanks to the remainder of the Maddox money, that party was the final gasp of – shall we say corporate? – activity traceable on the Côte d'Azur to Export Advisers Incorporated (Cable address: Expadink).

The staff has scattered to Boston, LA, Paris, Galashiels, you name it. The writers are doing what writers do: waiting for cheques that can be rushed at once to the bank. Lafayette is in Torremolinos, probably still looking for his Harlem writer friend. Susan has a permanent job now, looking after the comfort of guests aboard a luxury yacht owned by an Australian millionaire businessman named McPhee.

In St Tropez, the oxidized nameplate has been unscrewed from the lobby of the expensive apartment block, leaving a pale, empty rectangle on the marble wall. The penthouse has been sold to a Dutch bulb-grower. The office equipment has been repossessed, leaving the suppliers in Nice and Marseilles to lick their financial wounds. The last I heard from anyone connected with the Maddox empire was a postcard from Miriam mailed in Canada. The message said simply: *You haven't lived until you have experienced a Massey-Ferguson tractor on a thousand-acre cornfield.*

My own life remains relatively quiet. I live with my wife

Violette in a pleasant duplex apartment above the exclusive pastry cook's shop she runs on the Croisette in Cannes. Apart from the film and TV festivals, when it becomes too noisy to work, this is a good place, looking out over the sea, to write.

Edward was on the ball about one thing, though, when he warned me at the very beginning: Don't regard this as a *job*; look on it as a way of buying time in which you can settle down and write the book you really want to write.

That is exactly what I did.

He wasn't to realise, however, that it was to be he himself who gave me the *idea* for that book. It's about a thriller writer living in the south of France who's unexpectedly asked if he would care to try his hand at hard-core pornography.

Thank you for reading it.

More Erotic Fiction from Headline Delta

Lust and Lady Saxon

LESLEY ASQUITH

Pretty Diana Saxon is devoted to her student husband, Harry, and she'd do anything to make their impoverished life in Oxford a little easier. Her sumptuously curved figure and shameless nature make her an ideal nude model for the local camera club – where she soon learns there's more than one way to make a bit on the side . . .

Elegant Lady Saxon is the most sought-after diplomat's wife in Rome and Bangkok. Success has followed Harry since his student days – not least because of the very special support lent by his wife. And now the glamorous Diana is a prized guest at the wealthiest tables – and in the most bedrooms afterwards . . .

From poverty to nobility, sex siren Diana Saxon never fails to make the most of her abundant talent for sensual pleasure!

FICTION / EROTICA 0 7472 4762 5

Headline Delta Erotic Survey

In order to provide the kind of books you like to read – and to qualify for a free erotic novel of the Editor's choice – we would appreciate it if you would complete the following survey and send your answers, together with any further comments, to:

> Headline Book Publishing
> FREEPOST (WD 4984)
> London
> NW1 0YR

1. Are you male or female?
2. Age? Under 20 / 20 to 30 / 30 to 40 / 40 to 50 / 50 to 60 / 60 to 70 / over
3. At what age did you leave full-time education?
4. Where do you live? (Main geographical area)
5. Are you a regular erotic book buyer / a regular book buyer in general / both?
6. How much approximately do you spend a year on erotic books / on books in general?
7. How did you come by this book?
7a. If you bought it, did you purchase from: a national bookchain / a high street store / a newsagent / a motorway station / an airport / a railway station / other . . .
8. Do you find erotic books easy / hard to come by?
8a. Do you find Headline Delta erotic books easy / hard to come by?
9. Which are the best / worst erotic books you have ever read?
9a. Which are the best / worst Headline Delta erotic books you have ever read?
10. Within the erotic genre there are many periods, subjects and literary styles. Which of the following do you prefer:
10a. (period) historical / Victorian / C20th / contemporary / future?
10b. (subject) nuns / whores & whorehouses / Continental frolics / s&m / vampires / modern realism / escapist fantasy / science fiction?

10c. (styles) hardboiled / humorous / hardcore / ironic / romantic / realistic?

10d. Are there any other ingredients that particularly appeal to you?

11. We try to create a cover appearance that is suitable for each title. Do you consider them to be successful?

12. Would you prefer them to be less explicit / more explicit?

13. We would be interested to hear of your other reading habits. What other types of books do you read?

14. Who are your favourite authors?

15. Which newspapers do you read?

16. Which magazines?

17 Do you have any other comments or suggestions to make?

If you would like to receive a free erotic novel of the Editor's choice (available only to UK residents), together with an up-to-date listing of Headline Delta titles, please supply your name and address. Please allow 28 days for delivery.

Name ....

Address ....

....

....